A SHIFTER VENGEANCE NOVEL

NEVER AGAIN

SILAS REAMES

ISBN 13 Paperback: 978-1-961057-06-7
ISBN 13 Ebook: 978-1-961057-02-9

Published by: Night Loch Publishers LLC

NIGHT LOCH
PUBLISHERS
nightlochpublishers.com

1

Let's Get This Party Started

I scowl up at the blue, cloudless sky. Even the temperature isn't cooperating with me today. In spite of the fact that it's January and prime time for dreary weather, Sacramento has insisted on a balmy temp well above freezing. I, meanwhile, am in the mood to stew and would prefer my surroundings to match.

The highlights of the last few months? Found the only other living intuitive Were, Nadia, and gained a family—or at least a wild pack of misfits that counts as one. I also set into motion a plan to infiltrate our shady government, the Magikai, to determine what, if anything, is rotten in Denmark. Or wherever their headquarters actually is. Credit where credit's due, Nadia—or Ever, as she's calling herself these days—got us that particular gig. We start later this year.

The downsides? Well, let's see. Ran into my ex almost-mate. The one who abandoned me nearly two hundred years ago and whom I've vowed to kill. Accidentally helped him destroy the head of the Claw, an evil magical organization of which he has now become the new leader. Let said boyfriend slip from my grasp. And made what could be a terrible deal with the Bone Reader. How was your holiday season?

I have until Halloween to hunt Damien down, although now that he's the Claw's new leader I might want to speed things up. Just like me to let things get down to the wire. This is what a couple centuries of dillydallying will get you. My favorite mysterious, magical entity, the Bone Reader, gave me Damien's location. The only issue is the price he charged for the information. I have to turn a new Were. Something that I've never seen done and have no knowledge about how to accomplish. That's the Bone Reader, though. Big ask, big price tag. And because of his magical ability to bar you from achieving your aims until payment is completed, I'll have to tackle that before I can handle Damien.

Combine that with the fact that I had a lovely Christmas with my friends and the vampire coven I accidentally acquired and we've got a recipe for grouchiness. That may sound great, but going from a jovial hall in a Vegas mansion full of tinsel and trees to back on my own in Sacramento is a jarring change. It's no wonder I'm in such a foul mood.

"I need a drink!" I announce, as I throw myself, with all the drama I can muster, onto a stool in Elios's bar. The old, or at least elderly-appearing, cursed satyr raises a brow at me from his spot near the register.

"Well, that much is obvious. May I assume it's going to be some confounded concoction that no one in their right minds would actually want to consume?" Elios grumps as he circles a dirty towel vigorously on the bar top. I'm one thousand percent certain he knows it's not doing anything for cleanliness, and at this point it's more habitual than anything. And the speed of the towel swiping increases when he's annoyed. That, I can definitely confirm, since as an intuitive I can read emotions. I've been here all of ten seconds and I've already got his goat. Get it? Satyrs, goats? No? All right then, moving on.

"Someone woke up on the wrong side of the bed this morning, huh Sunshine?" I tease, flashing him a flirtatious smile. I have a proclivity for learning the meaning behind names. Elios's is particularly fun to poke at, since he's not exactly known for his sunny disposition.

Elios growls, the sound out of place coming from a male who isn't a shifter. And wouldn't be, even if he weren't cursed to look like an old, human man. He walks a few steps over and shakes the dirty towel in my face, but I can already feel his annoyance ebbing.

"Don't try to butter me up, you crazy Were!"

See? This is what I like. This back-and-forth banter at my neighborhood bar. Just the thought of my patterns being disrupted is enough to send me right back into Grumpsville. Listen, I'm happy with a vacation as much as the next gal, but this upcoming trip will be anything but.

"Hey. Is that a frown I'm spying on that face?" Elios actually attempts a smile. "Can't have that. I've seen you angry, annoyed, frustrated, flirtatious, and downright enraged. But not depressed."

He gives a sigh, throwing the towel over his shoulder. He begins pulling garnishes and liquor down. For once, I don't pay much attention to what he's making as I ponder my situation.

The Bone Reader, with all the powerful and ancient authority his services afford him, told me I'd need to go to the place I least want to go, if I'm to have any hope of turning the new Were I promised him. I'm more than happy to pay up and get on with hunting down my ex, but given that I have no knowledge in the 'create a new Were' department, I'm screwed. My family and I were born the old-fashioned way. You know how it goes: two Weres meet and fall in love. The secret to turning a non-Were into one of us has been lost for a long time.

My second and larger problem is *where* the Bone Reader has suggested I go. The place I most loathe. That can only mean the Isle. You see, there's a very, very good reason why I want to murder Damien. It's not just some dramatic breakup story. Actually, I suppose it is. But not the kind where he made eyes at some other female or just started ignoring my calls. Nope, he went full-scale on this thing. I'd thought he and I were going to be mates. The 'die for each other and live for each other' kind so many shifters long for. Instead, we got ourselves on the radar of some rather dangerous individuals. The Collectors, they called themselves. A group of elite magicals who operated secretly, gathering other magical beings as possessions and using them for all sorts of evil and illicit purposes.

And my dear old half-mate, Damien, dumped me in the woods to fend them off myself, while he got away. Not very gallant. And unfortunately it resulted in my being forcibly detained for a number of years. One can see why I've avoided bringing up such painful memories until now.

"Surely one of these will perk you up." Elios slides a wooden tray over, bearing three drinks sitting in curved glasses. One is a vibrant pink, one blue, and the third a light cream color.

"What are these?" I eye the glasses with suspicion.

"Poco grande glasses. The kind you give to drunk people on cruises in locations where they're going to get horribly sunburned and hung over."

I stare at the beverages for several moments, my brows scrunching.

He lets out a sigh of exasperation. And again, I know that's what it is. Intuition and all that.

"Well, if you don't want them, I—"

"Hey now, I didn't say that!" I protest, grabbing at the tray before he can take it back.

"In that case, stop scowling and start drinking!" He snaps the towel against the edge of the bar top.

"All right, all right. Pushy male. I just can't figure out why you're being so nice to me all of a sudden." I survey my choices again, then pick up the blue beverage.

Elios mumbles something unintelligible and goes back to wiping down the bar with furious circles.

"Elios." I try to make the threat clear in my voice.

"Well, word may have slipped that you took out the leader of the Jeweled Claw. Now, I keep myself to myself, but we all know they were a problem group. And here I thought they'd been dealt with years ago." He's looking down at the bar while he talks, as if the towel wiping requires serious concentration, and I can feel the mix of apprehension, nostalgia, and sadness rolling off him. "I have my reasons, all right," he finishes.

He's not the only one who thought the Claw was gone. Imagine my surprise to discover them, and now have my backstabbing ex as their new Crown—which is the ludicrous title they give their leader.

"*Elios.*" This time I drawl his name, prolonging each and every syllable in a manner I can tell he finds grating.

"Maybe I care about you and your sorry hide!" He waves the towel, small brownish drops flying, mercifully missing the drinks he's just supplied me. He sighs and drops the sopping cleaning rag on the bar before leaning across it toward me. "I suppose. That perhaps. Maybe. I could admit to a bit of a soft spot. *Favoritism* might be a better word, when it comes to some of my patrons. And I'd prefer to have you not dead. There." He grunts.

Coming from him, it's practically a declaration of love.

I reach across the bar and grab his hand.

"Thank you."

His eyes widen a bit, and it's another reminder of what has been an unfortunate side effect of my newfound family and realizing I actually do care about others. I've gone soft.

The drinks are sweating a bit already, and I move through each for a taste test. Elios may purport to hate serving anything that isn't cheap beer or straight hard liquor, but he's got a knack for it.

Sunshine spills across the floor as the door of the Lusty Lute opens. I scowl toward the cheerful outdoors and the clean scent of winter air unfettered by the dustiness of the bar. Three shadows walk in, their faces obstructed by the brightness, but I can tell who they are well enough.

Todd, Lynx, and Aggie stride into the establishment and make a beeline for my barstool.

The first is a tall and muscled male with deep brown skin and eyes that fall somewhere between caramel and copper. An intimidating bear shifter who's probably more mature than the rest of our group combined. Lynx is just what he sounds like, a feline shifter. His mate joined him for Christmas with the vamps and was heavily pregnant. She gave birth just a few days after he returned, so I'm sure he's had his paws full.

My final visitor is a teenaged witchling from a rare light-magic coven. Typically that means she'd have lesser magic, or at the very least have to work much harder for it. It generally pays to slay when you're a witch, and those practicing light magic don't kill any creatures to power themselves. The vegetarians of the witchy world, if you will. Agatha is special. Her key—that is, the specific talent each witch possesses—is a doozy. Aggie is a stripper. Not the glitter and glam kind. The 'sucks all the magical ability away from you temporarily, and if you're a shifter leaves you stuck in human form and sapped of strength' kind. A truly terrifying nemesis for those in the magical world. I, being a Were who has her head on straight, have offered to permanently house the dangerous witchling. Because who doesn't want someone capable of siphoning off all your power as a house guest? To date she hasn't given me an answer.

"Never!" Aggie squeals, throwing her arms around me. "Oh, you don't look nearly as down in the dumps as Lynx said you were and ... oops." She grimaces and casts a side-eyed glance toward the feline.

Lynx, for his part, is wildly waving his arms in a 'nix' gesture behind her.

"Give us away, why don't you!" he hisses, literally, at her. "Not that I was spying, Never. I simply called the vamps after the rest of us had left from the holidays to check in on you."

Just great. I've been so mopey my vamps even spotted it. While chasing the Jeweled Claw, and Damien, the trail led us to a Vegas vampire coven. After their lord captured me, I challenged him to combat, based on a doozy of a loophole in their laws. Winning freed me, along with Lynx and Aggie, from torment and death. But in doing so I became the lady of the coven. I had intended to find a way out of it, but honestly, the bloodsuckers are growing on me.

I'm fairly certain I know who to thank for blabbing my mental state to the feline. Hugh. I first mistook him for some sort of vamp butler, but he's much more than that. He's a historian. And a valuable one. I keep meaning to ask if he was a lawyer before he was turned, because he has a vast knowledge and grasp of all magical rules, laws, and even rumors pertaining to vamps. He came off as subservient at first glance, but I'm learning he's more than capable. If I weren't intent on keeping the coven, he'd be a decent choice to take over the duties of leadership.

"Have you given any more thought to my offer?" I ask Aggie, who is chittering away at Elios.

Mere months ago, I wouldn't have even considered opening my house up to guests. Now, though? I may be gone quite some time, anyway, tracking down information for the Bone Reader. A responsible house sitter can't hurt. And since Aggie's witchy friend Chrys, whose key is intense protection spells, has warded my house, I know she'd be safe there.

Aggie twists a piece of merlot-shaded hair around her finger.

"I have decided to accept."

"Excellent. We'll get your room set up, and before I go, we can—"

"But, as terms of my acceptance, I want to come with you for whatever it is you're doing." She juts her chin out, arms pulled back, and I have to try hard not to laugh at her attempt to look forceful. She's determined, I can feel that much, but I can also tell she's nervous.

And she should be.

"Absolutely not! This is going to be a dangerous trip. A long trip. Very likely not a comfortable one." I, too, am upset at that part. I do love the amenities afforded to me in this century. I try to think of anything else to dissuade her. "And violent. Bloody and vengeful and revengeful, all in one." Aggie may have an ability to harm other magicals, but that doesn't mean she likes hurting people.

"Precisely why you need some powerful sidekicks," she counters, entirely undeterred.

Her green eyes flash, and she stamps a small foot on the concrete floor of the bar.

I laugh, setting my half-finished third drink back down on the wooden tray to sweat liquid down its sides.

"And just who might those sidekicks be? Let me guess, our resident feline and bear shifters?" I cast my gaze over toward the dynamic duo.

Lynx and Todd are fellow enforcers. We all take contracts to hunt down, capture, or rescue, as the case may be, various magicals for the Magikai. And the Magikai is the governing entity that oversees us all.

Lynx holds up his hands in protest.

"Not me, oh no. Fiona would skin me if I left her with the triplets."

I raise an eyebrow at Todd.

"What about you, bear boy?" I tease.

"I'll accompany you to Vegas to get the vamps squared away, but then I need to get back to here to California as well. I have some business to settle with my brother. He will expect to see you again soon."

Todd's brother, Rex, is the ruler of the northern California bears. I can assure you I'd love to jibe him about the names. Rex got kingly for a name as the slightly older twin, and Todd got ... a fox? It hardly fits. Then again, not all magicals have the same interest in the meaning of names as I do, even though they are powerful things in their own right.

Either way. His brother and several of the bears helped us pull off a maneuver that tricked the Jeweled Claw and allowed us to get close enough to take out their former leader. In exchange, I promised some use of my abilities to Rex. I'll get around to it.

I roll Aggie's idea around in my mind. It has plenty of company with all the loose marbles up there. As much as *I* loathe where I'm going, in theory she should be safe there. After all, I eliminated any threat on the Isle long ago. The only ghosts there are for me, not her. Then again, I haven't told any of my friends about the place, or what happened there. Some secrets aren't meant to be shared. On the other hand, there is someone else I've thought of asking along who could always serve as a witchling babysitter of sorts, if I need someone to keep an eye on her.

"All right, Stripper, looks like you and I are going on an adventure!"

Aggie squeals, clapping and bouncing up and down in her seat like I've just bought her a car or something. I regret my decision. After a brief catch-up, and once I've sucked down all three beverages from Elios, we stand up and prepare to head out.

The satyr leans over the bar again to collect the tray of drinks and the payment I've thrown down.

"What in the seven circles of Hell!" He sputters as his hand closes around the iridescent dragon scale and ivory dragon fang I've set on the bar. "So it's true, then." His eyes are wide as he stares after me.

The thing is, I didn't take out Ekaitz, former ruler of the Jeweled Claw. Damien did. The sapphire dragon was capable of breathing acid rain and had been leading the Claw for who knows how long. After the kill, though, Damien cast the blame on me so he could cement himself as the group's Crown.

As for the Magikai, who had sent me after the Claw in the first place? They didn't feel the need to set the record straight. Seems they're tired of me running rampant, below the radar and out of their control. So my carefully constructed layers of secrecy are blown, and

I'm becoming rather infamous in the magical world. 'She who hath slain the dragon,' or some such nonsense. I may as well get ahead of things.

"Tell your friends." I wink at the barkeep and throw a hip swing into my steps as I exit the bar.

2

Two's Company, Three's a Crowd, Four's a Headache

The following morning I'm in a chipper mood as we get close to the vampire coven grounds outside Vegas. Todd's driving. The bear hates being cramped in a small vehicle. I have been navigating, much to his both spoken and unspoken chagrin.

"Stop! Scenic overlook!" I shout as I fling an arm across his field of vision.

"There's no need to yell," he grumbles as he shoves my hand away, "you're in the passenger seat. And we do *not* need any more delays or pictures in front of trees."

He keeps on driving while I cross my arms and scowl at him. Is it possible I'm delaying just a smidge? It's more than a little likely. But who's running this show?

I had Todd take a path from Sacramento past Lake Tahoe, and then down through some very fun nature areas to get to Vegas. Did it add time to the drive? Yes. Did we camp out under the stars? Also yes. Look, I like my technology as much as the next spoiled magical. But sometimes it's nice to go old school, run beneath the moon, and howl at the local wildlife. This is especially true when you're drawing out each and every minute before traveling to your most hated destination on the planet.

I even convinced Todd to stop for caffeine this morning. Our choices were limited, given that we started the day in the middle of nowhere, but I had him pull through a small town that had what I'm going to generously refer to as a coffee shack. But I digress.

As Todd weaves his truck up the serpentine road that leads to the mansion's grounds, I notice something is off.

"Um, is it just me, or has my mansion completely disappeared?" I question, tapping the empty coffee cup against my chin.

"Looks like she had time after all!" Aggie bounces up and down in her seat, smiling toward the giant skyline of absolutely nothing ahead of us.

"Just what does that me—"

Todd slams on the brakes, and I'm thrown forward. Thank the moon for seatbelts. I'd survive being thrown from a car, but I would have owed Todd a new windshield and an ass-whooping.

"Hell's bells, bear! What was that for?" I rub my head, even if it is uninjured, in protest.

Todd just puts the truck in park and gestures with an arm out in front of us.

A petite and very familiar witch is standing maybe a foot from the front of the vehicle, grinning and waving. Aggie's friend Chrysanthemum, or Chrys. She's got medium-toned brown skin, springy corkscrew curls that are a stark white, and soft-shaded violet eyes. She had joined our little Christmas get-together this past month, and we'd discussed her putting a protective spell over the vamp grounds. The only thing is, we had yet to settle on a price.

Hugh, my local knower of all things paperwork-related, comes jogging up behind her, his textured brown hair lifting at the ends as he moves.

"Lady Never," he says, sweeping into a bow, "wonderful to see you. We have several rooms ready and have brought in food for you and your guests." It's been an adjustment for them, having to get a kitchen up and running. Vampires survive primarily on blood and alcohol.

"Thanks, Hugh." I yell from the truck.

Before the situation can get away from me, I get out of the vehicle and turn toward Chrys.

"And just what is this full-grounds protection going to cost me? Not that it isn't very impressive," I grumble, begrudgingly. Aside from the Bone Reader, with whom I'm already in deep, I like to know what I'm paying before I get the product.

"Well, I talked to Aggie about it." Chrys glances at her witchy friend, uncertainty seeping from her. The witchling gives me an anticipatory grin. "Aggie said you'd probably come around. I mean, she and Nadia had such a huge adventure with you. An underground villain organization? Training with a Were? A dragon?" Chrys ticks the items off on her fingers, then spreads her arms out wide. "And a vampire mansion to boot! Come on, I need in."

"In on what?" I press.

"Your trip! You guys are bound to get into some seriously crazy scenarios, and I'm so there."

"Oh no. Absolutely not. I am not getting tricked, bamboozled or otherwise cajoled into another adventure in babysitting," I counter, turning to stride away from them and toward my mansion, which I assume will make itself visible once I'm far enough into the grounds.

I whip around as a hand wraps around my arm.

"Please, Never," Aggie pleads, "we helped out before! You might need us!"

"And we definitely won't need a babysitter," Chrys adds. "Aggie's nineteen, and I'm twenty-one. Adults, see?"

I press a hand to my forehead, kneading at it.

"May I suppose that if I continue to deny you, the price of my vampire defense spell is going to cost me an absurd amount of money?"

"That's exactly the case. You can pay me off with this trip, or mission, or whatever you're calling it. *Or*, I can drive this coven into debt so steep even a magical couldn't climb their way out." She smirks, victorious.

"You'll both excuse me if I fail to consider a mere two decades of life as evidence of maturity. That being said ... fine. Fine. You can go."

Aggie squeals again, jumping. Chrys grins, the little blackmailer.

As we enter the gardens via the front lawn, the mansion makes itself visible. A couple of the vamps hold the double doors open for us. The girls head up the stairs, and I can hear their chatter growing dimmer. In truth it's not a bad idea, having Chrys come along. When my fellow intuitive Were, Ever, went back home to Colombia, I could tell it bummed Agatha out. Now she's got a witchy friend to keep her company until Ever makes her return. Given that Chrys isn't a light-magic witch, we may run into some roadblocks there, but we'll figure it out.

A fellow intuitive Were, a stripper witchling, and now Chrys. I've become some sort of young magical mentor. Who knew?

Come meet Never-she kills, she fights, she suppresses her feelings, and she thinks she's a role model.

I make my way up to my own rooms. The vamps have stocked the armoire with a whole variety of fancy labels. I've got my pick of ball gowns, handbags, and heels. Even though they know I'll just shred the things if I shift while wearing them. The joys of being lady of the vamps. I ignore the more intricate items and instead throw on a pair of soft sweats and a fitted tank top. What's leadership if it doesn't earn you the right to walk around in pajamas any time you want?

As I exit the room to head back downstairs, a vamp appears from the shadows. Sneaky little thing. She's wearing a tailored crimson pantsuit, and her fingers have one or two rings apiece. She dips into a bow. As she comes up, her eyes linger on the pajamas. I can feel the judginess.

"Did you not find any of the other clothes to your liking, Lady Vicious?" The vampire lord I got this gig from gave me that nickname before I turned him to a pile of ash. He meant it to be mocking, but the vampires have taken a liking to it, as have I. "We have an extensive inventory of clothing. I'm sure we could find something that's less, well, casual."

"These are perfect, thank you. But I would kill for a drink, if you've got one handy."

She just dips into a bow again. Don't get me wrong, I do like the authority. Who wouldn't? But the vamps are a bit too formal around me for my taste. I'm trying to get them to loosen up. She leads me down the stairs to the ornate dining hall. Two vamp leaders ago, the Vegas coven was built out near the canyons to resemble a medieval castle. It's needlessly intricate. Within minutes, another vampire is handing me a crystal glass.

"A limited release Napa cabernet. Incomparable vintage. Several thousand dollars a bottle. We own all the known remaining inventory," he states, then stares at me.

"Um, nice?" I supply. He just bows again and backs away as I drop into a blush seat lining a large banquet table.

Hugh makes his way into the room, seating himself across from me. I swirl the glass of red wine before taking a long sip. It's good, but I'm a cocktail gal through and through, which I know serves as an endless disappointment to the vampires.

"Hugh?" I ask.

He's out of his chair and at my side in a matter of seconds.

"Yes, Lady Never?"

"Come with me to the library." I stand, still holding my glass, and the vamp historian follows me.

I'm beginning to get my bearings in this gigantic behemoth of a home. The library is sprawling. It's got vaulted ceilings and books from top to bottom. It's even two levels, a set of stairs leading to a balcony that runs the inner perimeter of the room, and ladders to help you reach high books on the lower and upper levels. The only thing I don't care for is that there aren't any windows. Vamp castle, sunlight, and all that. There are plenty of candelabras, and

I honestly don't know how the books have survived with fire as a primary lighting source. I mean, they built an entire modern castle and didn't think electricity might be a good idea in the book room? Moon's sake. I've solved it for now by having battery-operated floor lamps placed around the room, but it does clutter the decor.

Hugh comes to a stop next to me as I take everything in. The vamp has hair in varying shades from gold to brown to auburn. I can't say why, but I picture his eyes as a leafy green before he was turned. The whole look makes me nostalgic for an early fall day, when summer loosens its grip and the slight chill in the air is pleasant and welcome. Right now, Hugh's eyes are a deep crimson. He's a bit taller than me as a human, although I tower over him with fur. It's not his physical features I appreciate him for, though; it's his mind. And trust me when I say I am not looking to complicate my current situation by getting romantically mixed up with my number two vamp. I have some sense. Sometimes, anyway.

I've asked him here for an entirely different purpose.

"Hugh, my friend, I have a favor to ask of you."

He doesn't respond. Just makes a noncommittal sound from somewhere in his throat that lets me know he's heard me.

"I'd like you to come with us on this journey," I begin, ramping up for a convincing speech.

He beams at me.

"Me? I can't say I'm not pleased," he says, redundantly, given I can feel that emotion coming from him, "although I would ask why. I was actually going to ask you if I could accompany you, but I envisioned it being hard to convince you. Especially now that you've got the two females going along already."

That does tip our entourage from a stealth mission to more of a family vacation size.

I nod at the vamp.

"Fair question. Easy answer. Research. You, my academically minded vampire, come in quite handy with paperwork. And that is a skill I'm in sore need of at the moment."

I give him the bare-bones portion of the plan.

"And that's the gist of it. We've got a pretty packed agenda, but only a few objectives. Find the information on turning a Were, locate someone to turn, and get that pesky payment to the Bone Reader out of the way, then get rid of Damien. Before Halloween."

I don't specify why I've set that particular deadline. That's for me to know.

"Which gives us several months," Hugh clarifies. I nod. "But you've had this plan in the works for quite some time, right?"

I nod again, beginning to feel a bit like a bobblehead toy.

"The Damien part, not the Were part." I confirm.

"Right. So you have a task that, as a vampire coven–ruling enforcer, you weren't able to accomplish for years and years. And you want it done within the next several months. Except now, you've added to your task list needing to find a long-lost secret of a dwindling magical species, and you're not at all daunted about your timeline."

"Exactly." I smirk at him. He slaps his forehead, pulling his hand down his face as he speaks.

"Excellent. Very well. I suppose we'd best get on with it, then."

I clap him on the back.

"That's the spirit, Hugh! If you wouldn't mind packing your stuff and then booking us some flights for tomorrow morning, it'd be much appreciated."

I head for the exit, planning to put on my fur and take a stroll around the gardens. It's always empty during the day, when the vamps prefer to keep inside and in the dark.

"It might help if I knew where we were going!" Hugh calls after me.

"Germany, for starters," I toss over my shoulder. You can't fly directly to the Isle. As far as humans are concerned, it doesn't exist. We'll need to take a more roundabout travel path. I've avoided most of my fellow Weres for decades, but I did locate someone who will help us.

Hugh catches up to me as I hit the front doors, hissing as I begin to pull them open. I shut them again, blocking the rays of light coming in.

"Have you given any thought to how you're going to tolerate this trip?" I demand, "Because I can't commit to nighttime travel only."

"Understandable. I do have a supply of spelled ointment that will allow me to survive in the sun well enough. But it's from lord Costas's private stock, so I've kept it reserved."

Stealing from his former lord? I like his style, so long as it doesn't extend to *my* things.

"Good. Anything else before I grab some me-time?" I start pulling off my sweat pants, folding them by the front doors. They're soft, and there's no need to shred them. A small hint of embarrassment comes at me from Hugh's direction. Shifters don't care about nudity as a general rule, but vampires don't shift. Then again, given the lustful activities that were constantly going on in Costas's coven, I doubt it's anything he hasn't seen.

"I have one last question. A request, really. And I think it would benefit us both. It could cut out one of the steps in your plan and hasten things along," Hugh states, still averting his eyes.

"Then I'm all ears," I respond as I fold the tank top, furred ears sprouting from my head as my bones crunch and realign. It does hurt, but this pain is different. It's freedom. I sigh, shaking out my fur.

"If we manage to find this Were-creating process, I'd like for you to turn *me*," he states.

"Excuse me!" I blurt. "A vampire wanting to shed his bloodsucking ways? That *is* one I haven't heard before."

Hugh ducks his chin, and I can tell I've made him uncomfortable. Damned intuition. Now I'm beginning to feel guilty. Can't have that.

"Hugh, I'm not even sure that's possible. I've never personally seen anyone turned. Even when I've heard about it, the individual turned was always human. Someone who stumbled into the magical world and wanted in. I've never, not once, not a single time, heard of it being used on a being that already had their own magic. It might not work. It could be dangerous, deadly even," I caution him. No point in attempting this if he's not all in.

"I understand that," he states, lifting his chin. Resolute. "And I still want to try."

"Why?" I lean in close, sniffing for answers. All right, so intuition doesn't smell. My Were nose could still pick up something. But the vampire doesn't budge.

"I'd prefer to keep my reasons to myself, for the time being. But I assure you my motives aren't a danger to you." Complete and honest truth. That's all I need.

"Deal." I hold out a paw for him to shake, his hand comically small against it, now that I've got my fur on. I turn, intent on taking a run on the grounds. It's been too long since I tasted the freedom of the wind.

"Lady Vicious! We have a call for you!" Another vamp bustles in, holding a cell phone on a silver tray, of all things.

"Tell them to leave a message. I have business to attend to," I snap, pushing at the front door. Hugh and the other vampire flinch at the ray of sunlight that makes its way in, but neither leaves.

"It's urgent!" insists the vamp with the tray. "It's the Crown of the Jeweled Claw."

"Hell's moon!" I curse under my breath, shutting the door. It seems I'll need to save my run for another day. I pick up the phone and growl into it, even as I put my skin back on.

"What do you want? You have some nerve calling here," I snarl into the phone as I grab my pants off the floor. No need to put them on, since I get clothes when I shift, thanks to a rather expensive spell. I wait several seconds with no answer, all the more annoyed that I'm completely unable to read whether Damien's plotting or penitent on the other end of the line. My intuition doesn't work on him.

"Well?" I growl into the phone.

"I just needed to explain some things to you. At the mansion with Ekaitz, when I killed him. Look, I know you think I double-crossed you somehow, but that's not—"

"That's exactly what I think!" I snap. "Because that's what happened! As you might recall, it's not just that you offed your boss. You also left me alone with him to get acid-rained on, went after my intuitive protégé and witchling friends, lied to me about your plans, and then you announced to the Jeweled Claw that *I* was the one who murdered their beloved Crown." I tick the offending actions off on my fingers.

"I didn't intend for anything bad to happen to you—you've got to believe me."

"Believe you? I'm number one on the Claw's hit list, thanks to you. If you wanted to help, you could call your underlings off. Also, thanks to you, I'm quickly becoming infamous in the magical world."

"And that's bad?"

I squeeze the phone so hard it starts to crack at the edges. *Calm, Never.* I take a deep breath, air whooshing into the receiver. I pace the entrance of the mansion, longing for a priceless vase to smash.

"Yes, it's bad! I prefer my privacy."

"You're an enforcer for the Magikai! They run the entire magical world. Surely your existence hasn't exactly been a secret."

That does it.

"Get me something breakable," I instruct the nearest vamp. He scurries off toward the dining room.

"You're not taking responsibility for any of this! It's not about whether my life was a secret. I just kept a low profile outside certain circles. Off *your* radar, for one. Which is my right. I don't have to explain myself to you."

The vampire comes scurrying back in, balancing a good dozen crystal champagne flutes on the silver tray. I hope they were expensive.

"Never. You need to calm down. Now." Damien's voice is sharp over the phone.

My vampire hands me the first flute. Just in time. I throw it onto the floor, the glass shattering with a satisfying noise that echoes in the entrance hall. I reach for another.

"Give me one good reason I shouldn't come to your headquarters right now and shove this phone right down your—"

"You couldn't find us if you tried."

Insufferable. Intolerable. Controlling. Aggravating Were. There aren't words. Little does Mr. Self-Important know that the Bone Reader already gave me his location. I thought the price of turning a new Were was steep before, but I'm just angry enough at Damien now to consider it more than fair.

"We'll see about that. You're on my list, Damien Onasis. And your time is running out." I hold the phone out, about to click the disconnect button, when I hear him again.

"You can't run from this, Never. From me. Our meeting a couple months ago, when you were chasing the other intuitive, it did something to me. Kicked our half-mating status into high gear. I think it started when we slept together, and—"

I bark out a laugh. He can call it what he likes, but our little rendezvous involved an abandoned store in Sacramento, ripped clothes, bad decisions, and me running out on him afterwards. Hardly a fairytale romance.

"Never! Are you even listening? Look, you've played games long enough. I get that you were mad at me when I left you years ago, but I had no idea you'd been taken by the Collectors. It shouldn't matter, though. It's been two hundred years, and enough is enough. We need to sort this out, once and for all, so we can be together."

"Mad at you? *Mad at you?* That doesn't even begin to describe how I felt. You betrayed me! You let me get pulled from my home. They took away my ability to shift on my own. They used it against me. The males that ran the Collectors were violent and sadistic, Damien. Do you have any idea what I went through, because I—"

"It doesn't matter! It's in the past. Now, I'm coming to get you, Never, and I'm sick of this chase. Stop running from me, from us."

I'm almost glad he interrupted me. I was saying too much.

"There's no need. I'm not running. I'm just biding my time. But make no mistake, I'm coming for you," I sing-song into the phone, a smile spreading across my face. Across the room I feel a few responses of unease and fright. I glance over to where Hugh stands, the witches entering at his side. I must look positively unhinged. A veritable madwoman. I need to calm down.

"Never, you need to calm down."

It's one thing for me to think it. Another for him to say it.

"You don't rule me, Damien! I'll be calm when this is finished." I crush the phone, throwing it to the ground beside the shattered glass.

I stride past Hugh, the witches, and the other vamps scattered across the entrance, no doubt drawn here by my outburst. Aggie's mouth is in that surprised little 'o' expression she does whenever her emotions slap of shock. Chrys, however, smirks.

"Boy trouble in paradise?" she asks.

"You could say that. Change of plans. Hugh, we leave tonight. I'll take care of the flights. You three meet me back down here in an hour."

I want to make it very clear I'm not running, not in the way Damien thinks. He's decided this is a chase. I'll show him. It's a race. I just have to find that Were-turning magic and get Hugh changed before my time is up. And before Damien can stop me.

3

From the Woods

"That was the coolest flight I've ever been on! It was like a traveling hotel. Did you have any idea they put actual small beds on planes?" Aggie is chattering away behind me, gushing to Chrys. I glance over my shoulder at the two witches.

Chrys, I gather, has a little more worldly experience than my favorite light-magic stripper. But she also seems a genuinely good person, aside from the whole dark-magic bit. She smiles back at Aggie, and even though I can feel through my intuition a trace of disbelief at the other witch's naivety, her response is nice enough.

"It was a very smooth flight. Thank you, Never. You're shaping up to be just as cuddly and sweet as Aggie described you to be."

I whip my head back around with a scowl, but Chrys is grinning, perfect white teeth showing as she winks. The comment rankles me, even though I can feel the sarcasm. She just laughs, the sound deeper than I would have expected from her smaller frame.

"Oh you *are* going to be a fun one to poke at. Aggie mentioned you didn't like to have your good deeds discussed."

"It was merely for my own convenience. I need everyone well-rested for what's coming next. If I'd put you in economy, you'd probably have come off the flight whining, red-eyed, and exhausted. That wouldn't do," I grump.

"What about Hugh? He's always red-eyed," Aggie questions.

I see Hugh hide a chuckle behind his hands. Traitorous vamp. He's supposed to be on my side. And currently he's sporting hazel eyes, thanks to some concoction Chrys brought along. Everyone else in her family has a key pertaining to poisons, but that doesn't mean they don't sell all manner of magic, including vanity potions. She did warn us, though, that the effect is short-lived. I can already see a ring of rose-red at the edges of Hugh's irises.

I clap my hands together.

"All right, crew, let's make our way to the rental car area. I can't wait to get my paws on the autobahn," I announce, moving forward.

"She's hell on wheels. Todd won't even ride in the backseat when she drives because he says it makes him carsick," I hear Aggie whispering to the others behind me.

My German is rusty. I've let quite a few things fall by the wayside in the couple hundred years I've resided in Sacramento, and languages are unfortunately one of them. I really should get back on that. I step up to the counter, fully prepared to be shamed when the man helping us hears my horrid accent and has to transition to English.

"Allow me, Lady Never." Hugh slides in front of me. He clears his throat.

"*Ich habe ein Auto auf den Namen Never reserviert.*" Useful little bloodsucker. He slips into what my ears find to be a flawless accent.

The two of them get the details sorted out, and the man behind the counter turns to grab our keys. Hugh then hands him the mansion's black card. Soon enough, the human passes the card back, alongside folded paperwork and a set of keys.

"There, all set!" Hugh states, handing them to me.

"What was that?" I demand.

"Rusty, if I'm being honest. I've been lax on reviewing my conjugations," Hugh admits, straightening his shirt and running a hand through his hair.

"You didn't tell me you spoke German. Are you fluent in any other languages?"

He smiles, and I can feel the humble but pleased attitude coming at me. I have to say, my intuition does not pick up humbleness in magicals very often. A refreshing change.

"Actually, I know seventeen languages. Although I'd really only consider myself truly fluent in ten or so. With the rest I'm merely conversational."

I gape at him.

"Would any of those happen to be romance languages?" Chrys questions, leaning in close to the vampire. His embarrassment hits a peak, and it's lucky for him vampires don't blush.

"Well, technically yes. That is to say. Fluent in French and Italian. Conversational in Romanian, although I really didn't get interested in that until after I'd been turned. So I've only learned on paper; I've never had much opportunity to practice that one in person."

"You, my vampiric friend, are chock-full of fun surprises," I state, poking him in the chest and grinning as he moves to fix the wrinkle in his shirt.

"Like a piñata!" Aggie giggles at her own joke. "Except he's full of historical facts and languages instead of candy. Not quite as tasty. I mean, not to say you're not tasty, Hugh, that is to say ..." She trails off, blushing furiously.

I'm about to say something reassuring to the witchling, or pile on with an equally inappropriate jab, who knows? Even I'm surprised at times at the words that come out of my mouth.

"Look at that perfect blue baby!" I shout. See? Didn't expect that, did you?

The rental car they've pulled around is a sports car, as I requested at booking. It's a gorgeous shade of cerulean blue, and glistening from a fresh wash. I can hardly wait to get my paws on it. Do I know one lick about the mechanics of cars? No. Do I like the ones that look sleek and go fast? Yes.

"Looks like it should take us about three hours to get to our destination," Hugh states, unfolding a map.

"I'll make it in two," I promise, putting the car into drive as the others pile in.

"Is that a *paper* map? How old *are* you?" Chrys questions, leaning across the center console to stare over the vamp's shoulder as Hugh buckles himself into the passenger seat.

He folds the paper.

"This is a current and up-to-date version, I assure you."

"Seatbelts on!" I warn everyone as I gun it and we go flying from the parking lot and out onto the road.

Two hours and exactly three minutes later, we're exiting the car, which I leave parked in a small grocery lot.

"That was exhilarating!" Chrys says, purple eyes wide and alert.

"That was terrifying," Aggie moans. She gets on her knees and kisses the pavement. "Thank goodness we made it."

I roll my eyes at the witchling.

"Your dramatics aren't fooling anyone! Come on, we've still got a ways to go before we meet our contact." I wave my arm, beckoning the others.

"Are we going into the Black Forest?" Aggie questions, keeping close to me. I sense she's concerned. She really shouldn't be; after all, a stripper is scarier than most things we could find.

"No. This is Harz. Different forest entirely. But I do believe the packs around here like to stick to smaller towns near nature, as a general rule. Now hurry up, let's not keep our contact waiting." I stride into the trees.

Over the holidays, I put in a call to an old acquaintance, Silva. Weres are a bit of a dwindling breed in the magical world, but there's still some true packs out there. Ever, my little intuitive protégé, came from one in Colombia. Silva leads the German packs, and as far as I know is the only lone female Were ever to do so.

At about an hour into our hike, I'm itching to throw on my fur. As much joy as technology brings, the continued presence of humans can be a bit of a drag. We'd be making much better time if I wasn't having to walk around in trail shoes. Then again, maybe we wouldn't, since witches don't have enhanced speed. A small squeal pulls me from my thoughts. I tense as Aggie grabs my arm. Hugh moves to his left, positioning himself between Chrys and the individual who has just emerged from the trees.

Stunning and dangerous. The first would be obvious to anyone with eyes, and the second I know from personal experience.

"Hello, Silva," I offer our visitor. She dips her chin toward me.

"Never." I can feel the hesitation as she responds. It's not the name she knew me by when we were first acquainted. "It's been a long time."

"It has."

I brought us to Silva because she can help, but before my recent call, I hadn't spoken to her in well over a century. Bad memories. The Were in front of me is fair-skinned, though not nearly pale enough that you'd guess her fur color is a stark white with auburn tips. Her eyes, both as a wolf and in her skin, are a striking canary yellow that ought to be impossible. I imagine it's one of those inexplicable traits that humans are willing to overlook, because she doesn't cover them. In her skin she's an inch or two shorter than me, with an hourglass figure humans would have to spend years in a gym to even attempt to obtain. A Were queen. Not that the title means the same thing as it did back when I was growing up.

She bends one knee and tucks it behind her, dropping into a slight bow.

"I'm happy to help a fellow royal, and an intuitive. I heard you found another like yourself? Is that true?" Silva lifts her chin, yellow eyes locked on me as she awaits a response.

"I did. She's already been tagged by the Magikai, though, so no hope of recruiting her." I hedge around a more detailed answer. I'm loath to admit that I had to make a deal with the head of the Magikai that means that, if I make it through my quest against Damien alive, I'll have to go work at their headquarters while training Ever.

A branch snaps behind us, and I hear the murmur of hikers approaching.

"Better get off the main trail. I have some things to share with you." Silva turns, her long ash-blond hair lifting in the breeze as she runs into the trees. We follow, held up a bit as Chrys and Aggie climb clumsily over logs and fallen branches that Silva, Hugh, and I can clear with ease. Even a powerful witch's key is no substitute for heightened shifter abilities.

The sun has gotten low enough in the sky that the woods are beginning to grow dark when Silva holds up an arm, drawing us to a halt. I tense, waiting for whatever comes next. She shakes out her blond hair, fur cascading down her back. I take it as a sign to relax, and do the same. Silva howls as she finishes the change, and from the trees, Weres, in their skin and their fur, join us.

The ones in their skin are murmuring to one another; those in their fur are silent. While Silva and I have mastered speaking with a muzzle, it's not a particularly simple skill. Weres in times past didn't bother very often. Not when we could be in our fur the majority of the time.

I hear "princess" being thrown around. Technically, I am. It's what allowed me to challenge the vampire lord of the coven I now rule. Being royalty. Although I haven't been back to my own pack in ages.

One of the Weres in her skin runs forward, a smile on her face.

"Princess E—"

Silva snaps, long teeth clicking together inches from the other Were's face, silencing her.

"Never," Silva corrects her.

I dip my head in thanks. Curiosity slides over my skin from Hugh and the witches. But now's not the time. They'll learn more than I'd like, soon enough.

"Were you able to arrange us transport?" I ask Silva.

"Yes, and we overpacked supplies. It was hard to plan without knowing the coordinates of where you're going." A sliver of offense, but she covers it well.

"I'll take care of that," I respond, not giving anything more away. Hugh, Chrys, and Aggie hounded me half the plane ride with questions about our destination. All I've said is that I can get us there. And that's enough.

Deep in the forest, Silva's Weres have set up a bonfire, with large logs pulled up around it for seating. All kinds of foods have been set out on a wooden banquet table under the trees.

"Don't worry. I have guards around the perimeter of the clearing," Silva states as she passes by me toward the food. She's not concerned, but I can't help it. Ever since I left the Bone Reader's place, I've been on edge.

I don't let myself relax, but I do try to enjoy myself. I'm sitting on a log, stuffed with food, by the time the moon has risen overhead. The witches are dancing around the bonfire with several of the Weres, who have turned this whole meeting into an event, complete with music. Hugh's been going through our packs, checking and double-checking our supplies. Chrys runs over to him and tugs him away, pulling him into the dancing. At first his movements are jerky and awkward, but as she twirls around him, a smile breaks out, and he loosens up a bit. Maybe bringing the witch was a good idea after all.

I approach the queen.

"Silva. Thank you again, for all your help. We'll be out of your fur at first light. Speaking of which, anywhere I could rest for now? Away from the noise?" I can only take so much fanfare and togetherness.

"Certainly. If you follow me over this wa—"

A yelp sounds in the forest. Several of Silva's Weres tense, snouts and noses raised and sniffing for danger. The music comes to a squeaking halt.

"There!" Hugh yells, pointing toward the trees. I look just in time to see the glint of an emerald armband flicker between some branches.

The Jeweled Claw is here.

4

To the Sea

Hugh hisses, canines and nails lengthening. Whatever magic turned his eyes wore off hours ago, and they glimmer red in the dark. Chrys and Aggie stand flanking him. The purple-eyed witch is already sweeping her hands through the air, no doubt trying to create some kind of defensive barrier. Sapphire and amethyst colors glint in the trees, joining the emerald and ruby armbands as the Claw circles us.

The Weres stand facing the forest, our backs to each other as we monitor the threat. Aggie looks toward me.

"Not yet," I tell her, and her hesitation drops away, replaced by determination.

Several of the glinting armbands form a line. A row of magicals bursts through the trees. I don't even try to sniff out what they are.

"Now!" I scream at Aggie. She lunges forward, arms out. The witchling manages to knock five of them flat at once. Two wolves and two felines fall to the forest floor, gasping. Their fur falls away and they're stuck weakened and in their skin. The fifth individual must be a warlock; he looked entirely human already.

"Abomination!" he screams at Aggie as he tries to lift his hand against her and nothing happens.

I hate that she cringes, fear and doubt flooding her. This won't do. I stalk toward the five of them, standing directly over a now shivering warlock as he stares up into a mouthful of sharp teeth.

"Jealousy is an ugly color," I chide him, "but I think I have a solution." I cut off his scream with a snap of my jaws.

"That was amazing!" Chrys crows from behind me. Approval. Of all the times to get an actual read on her.

"We don't call her Lady Vicious for nothing," Hugh grunts at her side as a wolf shifter collides with him. Aggie strips the shifter, who falls to the ground.

The fight is in full swing, and I have to say we're giving even the best bar brawl I've seen a run for its money when a voice echoes across the trees, tugging at my memory.

"Mate!" Damien steps into the clearing, wearing his grey fur and showing his teeth. The strutting, admittedly handsome, muscular, peacock of a male.

I move toward him, claws dripping a trail of crimson into the leaves as I walk. I punctuate my words with swipes and blows to his entourage as I stride closer.

"I. Am. Not. Your. Mate."

He snarls in response, and as he dips his muzzle down I get a good look at his eyes. I tense, taking a half-step back before I can stop the prey-like response. Something is wrong. His eyes roll, whites showing. Crazed. He reaches for me, claws extended. When I pull my arm back, they rake cuts through my fur.

I hiss in a breath, leaping back as he swipes again. I kick out, taking his legs out from under him, but he manages to land in a crouch. He launches himself, hitting me in the chest as we go rolling head over tail through the melee. As we skid to a stop he manages to get the upper hand, or paw, and my back is slammed into the dirt. Leaves and twigs press into my fur as those wild, white-rimmed eyes stare down at me. Saliva drips onto me as he opens his jaw over my neck.

"Damien, don't!" I could kick myself. What did I think he was going to do, when I'm out to kill him? Play nice?

He leans close to my ear.

"Mine," he growls.

"Like hell!" I protest. I get my legs pulled up and kick. He grunts, his hold loosening, but it's not quite enough to dislodge him. He yowls as I kick again, twisting. I begin to roll us over, determined to get out from under him.

"Never! Stay down!" Aggie screams. I fight my instincts, going limp underneath Damien. For a brief moment his eyes clear. Then her magic hits him, and he's thrown off of me. I run for the witchling. When Damien stands he's human, and naked, but doesn't appear any less pissed off than before.

Stumbling, he runs at Aggie as I pull her behind me. Before he reaches us, one of Silva's Weres barrels into him, but a Claw shifter follows. Soon enough there's a pile-on, and I can't tell who's who, with all the limbs kicking and clawing.

"This way!" Silva's voice reaches me across the clearing. I grab Aggie and shout for Hugh and Chrys. Grabbing our packs on the run, they reach the Were queen before I do.

"In here!" Silva waves us toward her. She's holding open what looks like a cellar door, hidden under a pile of leaves. I grab the witches and push them through first.

I cast a glance back at the clearing. Damien is up and fighting; human, but protected by his Claw minions. I'm not one to run, but if I try to fight him now, I'll just be a hindrance. Blasted Bone Reader. Turning Hugh had better not take long.

"This is impressive. Is it a full tunnel system under the trees?" Hugh asks after we've made it down, staring above us at the roots and dirt that line the dark tunnels. Silva holds up a flashlight, her white fur and yellow eyes illuminated in the dimness of the tunnel. She shakes her head.

"Not a full system. The Harz Mountains are far too large for that sort of undertaking. But the tunnel helps us. We have it to distance ourselves from the humans quickly and discreetly. In the past, it aided us against monster hunters, but now it's just an easy way to have your fur on and not risk a run-in with tourists."

I hear crinkling, and Hugh shoves his map under the light of Silva's flashlight.

"Where do we let out?" he asks.

She squints, staring down at the map with intense concentration. I'm glad that at least she's easy for me to read. I have no doubt that she's being forthright with her intentions to help us. I can't feel even a hair's width worth of deceit. I do feel a sense of indebtedness. Of owing. Silva had a mate, a lifetime ago. He turned out to be a villain, one of the Collectors I escaped from. I have to hand it to the Were queen; she was fiercer in her retribution than most when she found out what her chosen mate was up to: buying and selling other magicals. She ran him out of the pack and became the first female alpha ever to seize control in her own right. Still, she didn't track him down and kill him. I got that particular task.

Hugh rolls up the map, nodding enthusiastically as Silva repeats her instructions to him.

"And when you reach the edge of the forest, you'll continue north. There's a boat waiting for you in Vejers," she informs us, naming a tiny, coastal Danish town. "Now hurry. We'll hold off the Claw and contact the Magikai when it's done, but I'm betting several will slip away from us. You'll need as much of a head start as we can give you."

Silva passes flashlights to each of us.

"Go ahead. I'll catch up," I tell the others. Weres move much faster with their fur, but I'll be traveling at the speed of witches. I let the change wash over me like water, closing my eyes at the familiar and painful sensation of rapid bone-crunching alterations. I sigh as my muzzle is replaced by a straight nose and full lips. The others are already making their way into the dark tunnel.

I turn back to Silva and reach out a hand. I wrap my fingers over her forearm, and she does the same to me. We lock eyes, our stares unblinking. An old Were tradition.

"I appreciate this, Silva. I know the cost this may have to your pack."

"It's the least I can do. After what happened all those years ago ... I should have been paying attention. I should have followed him. Even when I ran him out, I couldn't stand the thought of killing him." She offers the excuse, and I feel the anguish tearing her apart, even though her expression remains neutral.

I shake my head, not taking my eyes from hers.

"He was your mate. At least your chosen mate. I couldn't have asked you to kill him. Don't tell Damien where we've gone, although I'm betting he'll figure it out soon enough, and I'll consider us even."

The anguish relaxes a little, giving way to relief.

"Thank you, Never."

"Don't mention it." Really. I'm being as civil as I can, but I have no desire to dredge this up again.

"About Damien. He seems ... wild. Out of control. It reminds me of my own mate, back when everything happened with the Collectors."

"Damien's not my mate," I snap.

"Even so. Something is wrong with him," Silva insists.

"You've got that right. He's a controlling, lying, backstabbing maniac." I state, tallying off what might not even be his worst qualities.

She just shakes her head.

"No. I mean something *else* is wrong with him. Just, be careful," she cautions.

Silva's put her pack in jeopardy for us. And her pack relationships. In the name of that, I bite my tongue and hold back any further arguments. Silva turns, white and auburn-tipped fur shining.

"You know, Never, I didn't seek out a mate after what happened with my last one. I've turned down dozens of potential suitors. Some wanted the authority in the pack, and some wanted me. But I wasn't interested in any of them. I've been a strong ruler to the Weres here, but I was afraid. Afraid of making the wrong choice again. I'd been so fooled that first time around. Lately, though, I've had reason to reconsider my stance. All thanks to a particularly charming magical. I think ... I think I might actually be willing to try for happiness again, even if it doesn't look like I always expected it would."

I square my shoulders, drawing myself up to full human height, defensive in the face of her confession.

"And just what does that have to do with me? Because if you're suggesting that the situation with Damien is any different than expected, I have news for you; it's not."

She rolls her eyes and gives an overburdened sigh. Here less than a day and already driving her to the edge of her patience. I'm telling you, I have a way with people.

"That's not what I'm saying. I can tell that you're well and truly done with him. And I'm glad you seem to have opened yourself up to other friendships and relationships. I'm just saying, don't close yourself off to the possibility of a mate. Just because things went poorly with Damien doesn't mean you have to be alone. There are options. And you know, your old pack is still out there, if you wanted to seek them out."

She's up and through the door, shutting it overhead before I can cobble together a response. I know I'm not alone. I have more people in my life than ever before. Todd and Lynx, the dynamic enforcer duo. Ever, who is the whole reason I'm rushing this mission, along with not wanting to die. The witchlings and even Hugh. Heck, I'll even count the Bone Reader as a friendly acquaintance, problematic as he may be. Who needs romance? I squash down the tiny part of my heart still hopeful enough to disagree.

I walk down the tunnel, not bothering to put on much speed. I'll catch the others even without it. As Silva's words echo in my head, I find myself growing more and more annoyed. What is she suggesting? That I pick up a new boy toy on this journey? I'm busy enough, thank you. Besides, I like the love-'em-and-leave-'em strategy that I've adopted in the centuries since things with Damien went south. *Poorly,* she said. Hell, she doesn't know the half of it. *Crashed and burned* is more like it. All because he set fire to it himself. It's no wonder I haven't gotten close to anyone since.

But all my internal convincing doesn't do anything to remove the niggling loneliness at the edges of my emotions. No sense acknowledging it. Even if I had ever wanted to get closer to any of the males in my life beyond a casual fling, I'm not sure it's possible.

Like it or not, I am almost, sort of, halfway, not quite mated to Damien. It doesn't matter what I've done since. He's still alive, which means that bond is still in place. Darned magical details getting in the way. My unfortunate run-in with the Collectors happened before we went through with the official ceremony, but we made promises to each other in the woods. Those were binding enough that I can't read him with my intuition, and we can both feel enough of each other to know the other's still breathing. If my suspicions are correct, I can't have a real mate as long as Damien's alive.

Which puts me right back at square one.

Once I catch up to the others, our trek through the tunnel is uneventful. No Claw chasing us down. Where things begin to get interesting again is when we make our way to the beaches of Vejer.

"Darned sun," Hugh pouts, the flopping sunhat he's wearing utterly ridiculous on what is otherwise a dashing facade. He's got some magically spelled sunscreen, but even magic isn't a miracle. His skin is turning a garish shade of red anywhere that the sun does manage to hit it. His bad luck is that it's an atypically bright day for winter. The red spots are fading as fast as they appear, but they've got to hurt. We walked through the night and, for our trip to the coast, got our hands on another vehicle this morning. A small red thing, nowhere near as impressive as the blue sports car I'm going to get an enormous fine for leaving in a parking lot.

"It'll be sunset soon enough, and then we'll sail through the night," I reassure the vamp, somewhat tempted to tell him he's being a big baby. I'm trying very hard to be Nice Never on this trip. I'm asking all three of them for an awful lot of help, and they're not even getting paid. Well, the witches are getting a European adventure, and Hugh hopefully gets fur instead of vamp fangs, but that's a huge maybe.

"Do you see where being a Were could be a distinct advantage in cases like this?" He gestures toward the bright sun that my intuition can tell he finds offensive. "What I wouldn't give to be able to go to a museum, the library, the park, without risking having my skin burnt clean off."

"You're preaching to the choir there, pal. I'm the first one to claim Weres are the best of the magical options. Although I have to admit, you vamps are growing on me." I bump him with my hip and his scowl transfigures into a smile.

"All right. Point taken, Lady Never. Every magical tends to like their own. I just don't think I was cut out for vampirism. Not that I realized there were other options when I was turned."

Now, that is a story I'd like to hear. The four of us lie on our bellies behind a sand dune, staring down at the beach.

"While we wait for the signal from Silva's contact, why don't you tell me about that," I press, and I feel his cold reluctance. "For the sake of education, of course. For all we know, your background could play a role in whether I can make you a Were or not." I mean, it *could*, but how the hell would I know that? I'm just being nosy.

We lie in silence, monitoring the beach for the purple car we were told would arrive. After a few minutes, he sighs, relenting.

5

Museums & Mistakes

"I was a scholar once," Hugh begins. "A lifelong student, I'd have referred to myself as. I worked at a museum. I've always been a fan of the past, although my special love was languages and how they evolve over time. How they impact the interactions of different people throughout history."

A cloud of dust kicks up below us and I hear the thrum of a motor. I tense, claws digging into the sand for a moment. False alarm. A blue vehicle comes sliding onto the beach at far too high a speed for the environment. When the driver gets out, though, it's a very human man with a woman, scantily clad in a bathing suit in spite of the chilly temperature. I turn back to Hugh.

"We'd been preparing for a special exhibit. I was in charge of its organization. Scrolls, books and texts on loan from all sorts of places. Other museums, universities, bookstores, and private collectors. Each an example of a now-dead language, or at least those that have been so thoroughly altered over time that they hardly resemble what they once were. I recall the thrill of it all. I stayed late one evening to unpack the items and begin setting them up. I am, and was, a bit of a perfectionist. I'll admit to that much. I didn't want just anyone handling the documents, many of which were particularly fragile."

"And let me guess, a coven of vampires found themselves with a hankering for books but sadly unable to visit a library during opening hours?" Chrys drawls from her spot in the sand. She's pulled her bouncy, spiral curls up into a headwrap to keep them from dangling into the sand. She's smiling, and I can tell she's being sarcastic, maybe trying to lighten the mood.

Hugh frowns, affronted. Maybe he should be the one with intuition. Might help him read the room a bit better.

"No. Although," he admits, "they *were* there for a book. That night, several men and women, all dressed elegantly in clothes more appropriate for a gala than a dusty back room full of ancient artifacts, came strolling through the museum doors. My initial thought was perhaps they *were* looking for an event. The museum had played host to several such fundraisers. Maybe they had the wrong venue, or the wrong date. I'd been absorbed in preparing the exhibit, and it was completely possible I'd missed something on the calendar. One of the men approached me. I remember he was pale, notably so. Sickly, almost. And yet, I wasn't put off by it. He was handsome. Black hair slicked back, suit well-tailored, and the man himself well-spoken. Without so much as providing an excuse as to their presence, he began asking questions about the texts. I, a complete fool, answered them. I was so excited to have someone demonstrate an educated interest, and this was in a time where a human's first thought wouldn't have been to worry about foul play."

Hugh stops for a moment, placing one hand on his head, ruffling his hair. I feel the fear trickle into his emotions. Just a little hesitation at first, but soon enough a flood of it.

"They were after a specific document. A spelled one, although I obviously didn't know it at the time. The text referenced the location of some extravagant holding of wealth or another. I honestly can't recall—isn't that odd? To them, the contents of the document were of the utmost importance, but afterward I was far more focused on what their greed cost me. Anyway, I showed it to them, and before I could lock it back in its glass case, they grabbed it. I chased them and got thrown over a second-floor landing onto the tiles below for my trouble. I'd broken my neck. They could easily have left me. But the vampire I'd spoken to about the document decided my academic interests could be helpful to them, in a historian-based capacity. Believe it or not, dredging through ancient texts and artifacts isn't a favorite pastime of most vampires, even if it is necessary."

I believe it. Your average vampires like shopping, drinking, debauching, and flirtation. Not reading legalese.

Hugh stares down at his hands, nails sharpening to points.

"I awoke changed. Many new vampires talk of the immense hunger they feel the first few years. Learning to adapt to that. For me, it was more difficult to be restricted to the night. To give up all the things I'd once been interested in. Costas wasn't the leader of the coven when I was turned. He overthrew the vampire who had done it. Costas didn't care as much for my particular role, but he kept me on regardless. As hard as becoming a magical was, I soon found myself with plenty of time to pursue my hobbies. In place of the museum, I was determined to learn as much as I could about all magicals."

"Is that when you decided you'd rather be a Were than a bloodsucker? Because if so, I have to congratulate you on your good judgment," I tease, thumping him on the shoulder.

One of the witches tugs on my arm.

"Never, look!" Aggie points to the sand, where a purple vehicle has parked some distance from the other cars. An individual steps out. The few humans on the beach don't react, so he's got to have spelled his appearance somehow. I can see him clearly, though, and I feel my teeth extending as a low growl builds.

"Oh no. Absolutely not!" I snap as the magical clicks a flashlight off and on toward us three times, which is the signal Silva warned me to watch for.

"What's wrong with you? That's our ride!" Chrys insists, picking up her pack and making her way down the dune. Hugh follows her, his steps barely indenting the shifting sands. Aggie's the only one who waits, staring at me as I struggle against the fur and claws threatening to break loose.

"Are you getting a bad read on him?" she questions. "Something with your intuition?"

"No," I admit. "Nothing like that. But he's an elf. I don't trust them." I glare down at the long-haired magical.

Aggie sputters beside me.

"Well, that's prejudiced! Look, as I remember it, witches weren't your favorite either, but here I am. And you've even brought Chrys along. See? Proof that silly, misplaced stereotypes can be wrong." She gives me a shake, and when I don't move she stands up without me. The witchling dusts the sand off her outfit as she steps after the others.

"Aggie, don't!" I grab at her and she stumbles a bit, turning toward me with a scowl. "I'm not wrong in this. You don't understand. The last time I had dealings with a grey elf—"

"May have been a bad apple. Did it ever occur to you that in your line of work, tracking criminals, you may have seen more than your fair share? Look, I support you in a lot, but not this. I'd say the same thing to magicals who think *you're* bad news just because Weres are scary-looking when they shift."

Shows what she knows. Weres are gorgeous. Not our fault everyone expects us to look like oversized, fluffy forest creatures, like wolf shifters or bears.

Her nose and cheeks are red as her indignation grows. Below us, Hugh and Chrys have already reached our contact. No use arguing with the witchling now. I follow her toward the others, and the elf plasters a smile on his face when he sees me. He's anxious, and it puts me on edge.

The witchling has a point; I could be reading into this because of my own experience. I chide myself. It doesn't work. I scowl at him even as I reach to shake his hand.

"You're Silva's contact?" I demand.

"I'm the one assigned to take you to the boat," he confirms, truthful so far.

"Let's see it," I respond. I can feel the disapproval from Aggie. And worse, I can feel my own guilt in response. I'm not used to having to explain myself to anyone. And I loathe the idea of digging into my past. Even if this boat *is* supposed to take us directly on a trip down memory lane.

"A speedboat?" Hugh protests as we make our way to it, our packs in hand. "This thing is supposed to take us who knows how far across the ocean? Never hasn't even told us how we're supposed to find it yet."

The elf just shrugs.

"No time to search for a better vessel," I hiss into Hugh's ear. "If you forgot, we have the Claw on our tail. Now, let's get loaded and get moving!" I instruct, jumping into the boat.

The witches and Hugh hop in, while our elf shuffles his feet.

"We can't leave yet," he states. And yet he's growing increasingly impatient. Something isn't adding up.

"Just why not?" I demand.

"I left something in the car." A lie. He gulps, eyes widening as I exit the boat and stalk closer.

"Try again."

"I need to check in with our destination, so they know to expect us," he offers. A second untruth. I asked for the boat, but I haven't told anyone our destination.

I lean in close, making each word out of my mouth a threat.

"Where we are going, no one is waiting. That blasted isle is cursed. The Magikai made sure of it. So there isn't anyone there that you'd have as a contact. Is there, Claw lackey? Now tell me, what did you do to Silva's real contact? And how long do we have until Damien arrives?"

His face twists into a sneer, defiance replacing impatience.

"Minutes. Then you'll all be under our control."

"That won't be happening. No male controls me, least of all your two-timing pup of a leader."

The sky overhead has grown dark while we've wasted our time awaiting a contact who isn't coming. At least all the humans have left. The rest of the beach is empty. I lengthen my claws, scraping them down the side of the elf's car as I stalk closer. The squeal and screech of nails on metal.

He ignores the insult, at least outwardly.

"Truthfully," the elf starts, "I don't know why we bother. Our last Crown wanted an intuitive to help him weed out any among our ranks who were disloyal, and to use his closest troops to take the Magikai by surprise. But thanks to you, they already know all about us. This Crown is insistent we retrieve you as a replacement, but I'd just as soon put you down."

He looks down his nose at me, although he has to tilt his head up as I get taller, fur running down my arms.

"You're welcome to try." I show my teeth, shoving my muzzle down into his face. He cringes away.

Deception. It hits me square in the snout, and I move with no time to spare as he pulls a pair of short, silver swords from behind his back. Anyone's guess how he managed to smuggle those under his shirt.

I grab his wrists as he brings the swords down, stopping them inches from my fur. You have to be *very* careful when disarming an elf. They often have enhanced weapons; otherwise, why bother in this day and age with things like swords or bows? There's no point unless they'll maim or kill your magical opponent. He shoves against me, but I keep my grip firm. I squeeze around his wrists, but he withstands the pressure, and we stare at one another, deadlocked.

"I'm not sure why the Crown bothers with you," he seethes, glaring up at me. I manage to shove him backwards in the sand, but his feet just slide over the top of it. He doesn't even lose his balance.

"He thinks you're some valuable asset. Some coveted mate. But we've been tailing you since the Claw first went after that other intuitive. And that's not what I see."

"Do enlighten us," I snap.

"You're a disgrace to the title of Were royalty. It's no wonder you hide out as some Magikai mutt for hire. You'd never make it as a free magical. You're a sloppy, lewd, drunken mess—"

"Don't forget my beautiful blue eyes," I snark.

"He's just stalling you, Never!" Aggie yells from behind me.

"You heard the witchling, if you've got anything else to say, you'd best get on with it," I prompt the elf. Let it not be said I can't be polite, giving others a chance for last words and all that.

His nose crinkles as his glare deepens.

"I know about this isle you're trying to get to. Who the Collectors were, and what they did to the magicals they held there." I have no idea how he knows, but memories claw at me. "You may think you're some big bad Were enforcer, but I know the truth. No magical escaped that place unscathed. You're nothing but a used-up, past-her-prime whor—"

I'm thrown off balance as someone collides with the elf. His swords drop to the sand, useless. Aggie dives after them, scrambling to pick up the blades. Behind her in the sand, Hugh is clawing and biting like a feral animal. And it's working. Chrys is right behind him, arms out and somehow managing to manipulate whatever shield she's working so that all the elf's return blows are blocked.

"Chrys! Catch!" Aggie yells, tossing her the blades. The violet-eyed witch drops her shield just long enough to snatch them both, handing one to a frenzied Hugh. In tandem, they swing the blades, and the elf is dispatched before I can shake off my shock.

They walk back toward me, Hugh slicking his hair back from his face. Crimson stains his shirt. He offers Chrys and Aggie a hand into the boat before getting in himself. I jog after them, fur melting away.

"Um, excuse me! What was *that?*" I demand.

"He insulted you," Hugh responds, then turns back to the boat as if that's that.

"Found the key!" Chrys declares, popping up triumphantly from an open compartment under a seat in the boat. She tosses it to Hugh, and he tries to start the boat, but the motor just sputters.

"Never, can you push us off while Hugh works on the engine?" Chrys asks. I glare at the water, but I hop over the side in water up to my knees.

"Hugh, I haven't once seen you lose it like that. Explain," I demand as I get to pushing.

He huffs.

"Very well. You are the *lady* of the Vegas coven."

I just blink at him, and he rolls his eyes.

"I may be trying to make myself a Were for personal reasons, but that doesn't mean I dislike everything about the vampires. I do appreciate the level of respect they have for their leaders, at least those who deserve it. No one insults you in front of me. And how would our coven look to the magical world at large if we didn't defend our lady?"

"Hugh, you're gunning for a promotion," I grunt as I push the boat, feet sliding in the sand. If I say anything else I'm likely to get all emotional, and no one likes a crying Were.

6

Party Crashers

Hugh hasn't managed to get the engine going, and several figures crest the dune where we hid earlier.

"Now would be a good time to get this thing moving!" I call out. Chrys grabs my arm.

"Put on your fur and get us further into the water. That'll at least get some space between us and them," she instructs. As much as I loathe wet fur smell, I put it back on to give myself some height and muscle.

I shove us several yards out into the surf, and behind us growls and curses sound. Seems the Claw found their elf friend.

"I told you! I *told* you that I didn't trust that elf. But did anyone listen to me? No," I grunt as I shove the boat. "What I wouldn't give for a mermaid, or a sea serpent of some kind. Even a kelpie would do if it could push this damned boat."

I'm chest deep in the water by this point, already bothered by the scratchy feel of salt and sand. I just *know* I'm going to be left smelling like seaweed. The witchling offers a hand, but I grab the side of the boat. As I heave myself into the small vessel, it rocks precariously. Aggie's face pales as she clings to the sides.

"This thing won't sink, right?" she asks, eyes focused on me.

"No. It shouldn't. I've almost got this figured out back here," Hugh throws over his shoulder as he fiddles with the motor.

"*Almost* may not be good enough!" I yell as several individuals join the fallen elf on the beach. I'd recognize Damien's tall, grey, furred self anywhere.

Jeweled colors glint in the dark, and I imagine they've all got those ridiculous Claw armbands.

"You're no better than a bunch of groupies!" I yell at the offending magicals. A few seconds later a rock, of all things, comes sailing through the air. It dents the side of the boat when it hits.

"They're going to sink us!" Aggie wails. She takes a few shaky breaths. "We can get off the boat. I'll go strip them, and then—"

The witchling goes quiet as Chrys throws an arm in front of me.

"No need. I've got it." She shoves each of her sleeves up her arms and rubs her palms together.

Duh, Never. You've got a defensive spell witch onboard.

Chrys stands in the boat, taking a moment to steady herself. Then, she drops into a crouch, arms out as though she's in the middle of some type of squat workout. Another rock hits the deck by her feet, cracking a seat.

"Chrys. Any time now," I hiss at her. The Claw members are running down the beach and toward another docked boat. At least they don't seem to have any shifters who can fly. One or two stay in the sand facing us, lobbing rocks. A small one, just a pebble really, smacks me on the forehead, but a small trickle of blood gets in my eye.

"That does it! I am going back to shore and I am dismembering some Claw trash," I seethe.

"Just. Wait," Chrys grunts as she begins to lift herself out of the squat, shaking like she's lifting a heavy weight. As she stands, a wall of water rises around the boat. It's semi-transparent, and I can see the rocks hitting it and falling like they've come in contact with a solid wall. Damien and the others are speeding toward us in a boat now, as I hear our own engine sputter to life. I scramble over the side, double-checking that we don't have a rope or anchor dragging behind us. My wet fur sloshes water onto the deck.

"Hold on!" Hugh yells as we're propelled forward. I lunge, snagging Chrys around the middle before she can go toppling into the sea. We're hit with a splash as the top portion of her water wall falls onto the boat, but she corrects it quickly, throwing it back up around us.

Now listen, I'm a nosy Nelly. A curious Were. But I also understand the importance of timing. So I keep my trap shut and hold the witch in place as she controls the cylindrical border of magicked water around us. Damien and the others are gaining, but a few yards from us their boat slams to a halt, the front dented and the engine smoking. I see Damien stomp his furred foot like a petulant child.

"Dammit, Never!" he screams over the roar of our engine and the waves.

"That's my name, darling, don't wear it out!" I shout, receiving a snarl in response. "On second thought, don't use it again at all, you two-timing dog." I'd like to throw myself into the water and pull his boat under, but I'm busy holding Chrys, so I settle on an exaggerated smile instead.

"Never!" Damien yells again. I blow him a kiss, waving with my one free arm.

"Ta-ta, darling! Let's not meet again, shall we?" We'll have to, of course, but by then my goal is to have one freshly turned Were so that the Bone Reader's magic won't prevent me from killing him.

Chrys drops the water wall once our pursuers are out of sight. After a while, Hugh turns the engine off entirely, letting us bob and dip on the waves. We're the only boat I can see.

"Just us and the open sea," I muse, unsettled by this entire endeavor.

Chrys is slumped against the side of the boat, and Hugh offers her a water bottle.

"Thanks, leech." She grins, winking as she takes the bottle. The corners of Hugh's lips twitch, and I swear he's about to smile. He might even be blushing, if such a thing were possible for vamps.

"Ugh, Never. I have to tell you, you've got the absolute *worst* taste in guys!" Aggie accuses as she drops down in the seat next to me at the front of the boat. She holds a water bottle out toward me and then untwists the cap of her own. I clink mine with hers before taking a sip.

"No arguing there, witchling. By the way, what other provisions did Silva have our host prepare for us? Don't suppose they managed to pack the boat before the elf offed them?" I lean over Aggie, eyeing the cooler. I scrunch my nose, sticking my tongue out at it. "Blech. Water and light beer. What I wouldn't give to be sitting at the Lusty Lute with Elios preparing me a cocktail while he rants about all my flaws. Bless his cantankerous heart."

I lean back, eyes closed, as I picture that comforting sight.

"There's something very wrong with you, you know that?" Hugh quips from his side of the boat. I swipe at him, not really intending to make contact.

"You, vamp, are dangerously close to insubordination." He freezes for a moment. "For the record, I prefer this more assertive version of you, Hugh. I'm almost convinced you'd do well as a Were."

I smirk at him before settling back into my seat.

"So, witch. Care to explain to me how someone with a key for defensive spells seems to have also acquired some sort of elemental control?" I roll my eyes toward Chrys, who is shoving a granola bar, courtesy of our cooler, into her face.

"Sure," she offers, cheeks puffed out and crumbs escaping as she chews. "It's the same skill. I don't have to have control over the water. Just the defensive spell. I weave the water into the shield or wall I'm creating. Simple enough, in theory. My key gives me the ability to do it, but the physical part of drawing and pulling the water is taxing. Hence, why I normally just go for your old-fashioned, average, invisible to the eye, straight-up magical shields. In this case, however, I was protecting something very precious to me. My own ass."

I let loose a deep laugh.

"I knew I liked you on day one, witch." I toast her with my water bottle.

"Now that we've sorted all that out, would you please tell us how exactly we get to this island? I must admit to being less than thrilled at the concept of floating aimlessly in the open ocean," Hugh says, carrying his maps over toward me.

I swipe one of the maps, spreading it across a seat as Aggie leans over me with a flashlight.

"Where's the island?" she asks, leaning closer until the flashlight touches the paper as she scans it across the North Sea.

"It's not on the map. The *Isle* is spelled."

"You have *got* to be kidding me!" Hugh fumes. He tugs at his hair. "Lady Never, I would love to hear how we're meant to find an isle not on any map that's magically warded in some way. Did you happen to bring a spelled item that will allow us entry?"

"Yes. I brought myself."

Time to share at least some of the truth about the blasted Isle.

"Years ago, long before the days of fast food and air conditioning, there was a group called the Collectors," I begin. Let no one say I don't know how to set the stage. I give the group the bare-bones version. Damien dumped my butt in the woods, the Collectors 'collected' me against my will and took me to the Isle. And there I remained for a number of years, thanks to some shape-shifting dampener. After the Collectors' little operation was ruined, that is, after I blew their whole secret wide open, the Magikai stepped in. With all that had gone on at that place, they chose to conceal it from prying eyes, lest powerful beings or items were to fall into the wrong hands. So, they hid it using very powerful shielding spells.

I plow through the whole thing, ignoring the swell of emotions from the others at certain points. And I'm giving them the trimmed down and cleaned up version.

"But they obviously needed some way to go back if they wanted to return to it for some reason. Thus, a loophole was born! The only ones who can find the Isle are the ones who have been there. The coordinates may as well be burnt into my brain," I finish with a frown. "Ironic, isn't it? Those who haven't experienced it can't find it, and those of us who would just as soon forget the place, never can."

Hugh sighs as I jot down the coordinates in pen on his paper map.

"Well, that's helpful to our present mission, at least. Now all we have to do is locate what or whoever the Bone Reader expected you to find there and turn me into a Were. Then you're free to turn right back around and chase down the Crown of the Jeweled Claw. That part should be simple enough, given he's been on our tail since we left Sacramento," Hugh grumps.

I'm fairly certain he needs a nap. Poor vamp's getting cranky.

After a rousing meal of granola bars and mixed nuts, we settle into shifts. I take the first, following the map of the stars easily enough on a clear night. The witches take the next shift as a pair, Aggie rubbing her eyes as I rouse her. As I curl up on the deck to rest, I try to ignore the fact that I'll likely awaken to the nightmare that's haunted my dreams for years.

7

Isle of Nightmares

Our small vessel emerges from a curtain of fog as a new day dawns. The air is, to nobody's surprise, frigid. I cling to the warmth I pretend is coming from the soft yellows and pinks that light the horizon.

As long as I'm lying to myself, I'll say it's the chill and nothing else that has my teeth set to chattering as the edge of the Isle comes into view. It's been years and years, but I know without a doubt we're at the right place. This place deceives you. It looks unassuming. Pleasant, even. Sea grass blowing in the breeze, soft green against the sands.

"You can see how the air around the Isle waves and shimmers in spots," Hugh points out, standing up so fast that the small vessel sways and water laps over its edges. "A clear sign of magical defense."

Chrys nods her head in confirmation, her curls held back from her forehead with a turquoise and navy headwrap this morning. Her violet eyes flicker, and Agatha's deep green eyes do the same at her side. Using their witchy powers to determine the magic's perimeter.

"He's right," Chrys offers. "The work of quite a few powerful magicals. Witches, for sure, but also something else."

"I can't place it. Warlocks, but additional layers of protection on top of that," Aggie states.

Doesn't matter to me how the Magikai managed to seal the place off. The Isle of Tears, The Isle of Lost Hope, The Isle of Nightmares—it has many names. At least it did, among those who ruled it and lived on it. In a way, the Collectors were more dangerous than the Jeweled Claw. Damien's organization has a clear goal: overthrow the Magikai, subjugate the humans, rule the other magicals with an iron fist. Simple, right? Evil, but easy enough to wrap your head around. Not so with the Collectors.

I've figured out, in all my years as an enforcer, that when the bad guys have a clear endgame I have a much easier time getting in on their plan and disrupting it. It's the ones who seem evil just for the sake of it who you have to really watch out for. With the Collectors, their lifestyle *was* the end game. There was no clear plan. They were a well-connected and gloriously wealthy group. And that's 'wealthy' compared to magical standards, folks, not human. This underground network of all kinds of magicals bought, captured, and sold spells, enchanted objects, and their fellow magicals alike for their own various whims. Near impossible to stop, because they made careful choices and stayed off the radar of the wrong people. They bribed and bought off the others.

We all know I like to stand out, but when I lived on the Isle, I was just one of many. As our boat pulls up to shore, I remind myself that the difference is *I* did something about it. And yet, I could have gone a thousand years without seeing this place again.

The soft swish of waves against the shore, and the whisper of the sea breeze through the grass, create a comforting and picturesque scene. When I was trapped here, there was always noise. Screams, sobs, begging, but noise. Despite my reluctance to come here, I launch myself from the boat before Hugh even has a chance to tie it off. I put my fur on in mid-air, the change ripping over me at a speed that's fast by even my own standards. I'll be damned if I set one, single, solitary appendage on this place without my fangs and claws.

"You look ready to fight the island itself," Chrys observes as she walks up next to me. The statement is accompanied by the odd sensation of neutrality. As someone who has wave after wave of people's emotions coming at her constantly, it's always surprising when anyone manages to make a statement that truly doesn't have an emotional motivation behind it.

It's disconcerting.

"You do look rather ferocious, Lady Never, or perhaps your Lady Vicious moniker would be more appropriate here?" Hugh raises one brow and tilts his head, gaze questioning and teasing.

"Let's just get this over with."

I kick at the rocks along the beach, unable to keep myself still as the others gather their packs from the boat. I don't bother taking mine. Doing so would be to admit that we might have to sleep on this wretched plot of land, and I'd rather not face that possibility until we come to it.

When I hear them all shuffling in the sand near me again, I begin walking toward a series of small cottages.

"This way," I instruct the others. They fall into step beside me, silent.

The Isle used to be grand. A large stone castle dominated its center. On the grounds of the castle was a magnificent garden complete with several intricate fountains shaped like various magicals. Beyond that there had been a massive stable, but it had housed imprisoned magicals instead of horses. Under the grounds of the castle was a dungeon where the Collectors kept even more of their precious finds. If we walk far enough, to the other side of the Isle, we'll reach the small stone cottages reserved for holding the most valuable prisoners. I lived in one myself for a while.

Maybe I'll get lucky and we won't have to go that far.

On the side where we've docked is a village. Or at least what used to be one. These cottages have thatched roofs and facades of whitewashed stone. The whole place is only a few streets wide. The Collectors didn't have nearly the same issues with humans that the Jeweled Claw does. They used them. Had them carry out a lot of the day-to-day labor around the Isle so they could focus on their more illicit pastimes. As we get close, I see the worn walls of the village, white stone gone grey in places. They dot the sands, poking up above the beach grass. I make my way toward them, curling and uncurling my claws as I go.

"Be prepared for anything," I throw back at the others. The Isle may look calm and serene, but my time here was anything but. I won't be fooled again.

Once in the village, we start down what would have been its main street. Quite a few of the houses are in disrepair: roofs falling in, windows broken, stone worn down. But several near the center of town appear to have been kept up. Fresh white paint on the stone, shutters in blues and blacks. Roofs well maintained. I sniff the air, scenting for who or whatever is responsible.

We're nearly through to the center of town when a voice sounds behind us.

"*Tere!*" someone calls. I spin, crouching into a more defensive stance and lifting my claws. A human man and woman are standing in front of the house we just passed. They look similar to each other. Both are tall for humans. They've got fair skin, soft blue eyes, and strawberry blond hair. The man's is cut just above his chin, and the woman's falls in waves to her shoulders. They both go wide-eyed, the woman flinching as I turn.

"*Kas saame sind aidata?*" The man takes a couple of steps toward us, eyes scrunching. The rising sun is at our backs, and it could be that or the presence of magicals that has him struggling to take in what's in front of him.

"He'd like to know if they can help us," Hugh strides past me and toward the couple. "I can take care of this, Lady Never, if you don't mind. Estonian isn't one of my better languages, but I think my conversational skills will get us through well enough."

I lower my claws and gesture toward the couple, but before the vamp can reach them the woman grabs her partner's arm, shaking it.

"*See on tema!*" she yells at the man, and then she sprints toward us. I tense, readying for this strange woman to launch herself at me, but she comes to a stop maybe a foot in front of me. As she stares up at me, I can feel her emotions. Wonder. Now, that's something I don't often get when in my fur.

"*Vabastaja*." She whispers the word, awestruck as she tilts her head to stare up at my muzzle. She reaches one trembling hand out as if she's going to pet my nose. I flinch back.

"They're saying—"

"I know that one," I cut Hugh off. I've heard this particular word before. The villagers here chanted it when I escaped the Isle.

Hugh turns toward the two humans, both of whom are now standing in front of me, staring and whispering.

"*Kas sa räägid inglise keelt?*" Hugh asks the pair.

The man begins nodding enthusiastically.

"Yes. We speak English. My name is Ardus, and this is my sister Meeri. We're guardians of the Isle. We have seen the texts about *Vabastaja*, but I never thought we would see her with our own eyes. It is an honor." He sweeps into a bow, his sister dropping into a curtsey.

"Um, Never," Aggie speaks out the side of her mouth, "What exactly happened last time you were here?" When I told them about this place, I kept the explanation down to a simple *and then I got away*. She's oozing with concern and curiosity.

I ignore the witchling in favor of our hosts. I'm more than content to put that answer off as long as possible.

"We've come looking for something very important. Magical information. A set of instructions on how to make a new Were; a creature like myself." I gesture toward my own fur.

They turn toward each other, all excited whispers.

"They're debating the most likely place to find what you're asking for," Hugh translates. Even compared against our fair-skinned hosts, he's notably pale. At least he's not burning and crisping on the spot. Thank the moon for magic sunscreen and cloud cover.

"They're saying how the villagers in the years since you left have guarded the Isle and maintained things like the gardens, but otherwise left the areas outside the village untouched, as they were instructed by the Magikai."

Oh goody. That means it will all look just like I left it. A smoldering pile of ash. Hugh joins the conversation, and I do my best to wait patiently for several minutes. Not my forte. After what feels like an eternity, Hugh turns back toward me.

"They're assuming whatever we need is probably a text, but there are a few magical objects that weren't cleared out as well. They're mainly in the remains of the castle, but there's a particular cottage behind the gardens they think we should look through as well."

As much as I loathe the Isle, I suppose a bit of an explanation is in order. Let's make this quick. We all remember Damien, my almost-mate and dashing but dastardly ex, right? When he first dumped me in the forest and into the Collectors' paws, I was young and dumb. I thought he'd come back and help me. More fool me, right? Instead, I was given a fast and thorough education on how depraved some individuals can be. It sucked big time. Once I realized I'd have to free myself, I got to work. I found a way around the shackles that were meant to take away my ability to shift. Presto chango, I managed to put on my fur in spite of their silly little chains, and I ran amok. I freed all my fellow prisoners, burned the castle, and murdered a good number of the Collectors as well. This came with the added bonus of liberating the small human village on the Isle from their forced indenture to the Collectors. Hence, *Vabastaja*. Liberator.

It was only *after* this particular display, during which I more than broke our kind's law against exposing ourselves to humans, that the Magikai found me. Leave it to them to come in once all the work's been done for them. That's when they first offered me the enforcer deal. Unkai, my favorite sky-dwelling mythical being and one of the few Magikai I could honestly say I don't resent at least a little, told me at the time that they had shut the Collectors down for good. I would have thought the villagers would all be gone by now, but it seems I was mistaken on that front.

That about catches us up to the present day.

I press one paw against my head, running it through the fur there.

"Let's get this over with."

Perhaps not the level of appreciation our hosts are hoping for, but I'm in no mood to play pretend. We tramp uphill toward the building I least want to see. I keep my gaze focused on the two blond heads in front of us, refusing to look up at the castle remains.

"We are here," Ardus announces after several minutes. The Isle isn't big in size, just in terror and bad memories.

One side of my lip curls as I growl at the stone facade. The structure is damaged; burnt out on the inside. And yet, more of it stands than I had hoped. I wanted the whole thing to be nothing more than a pile of blackened ash. Instead, I'm getting soot-covered walls. Vines have woven their way into the structure. I peek into an opening that used to be an intricate glass window and see the burnt wood and ruin I was hoping for. Still, parts of the place are preserved enough that I can see specific rooms.

I pull my head out of the window and kick the structure. It hurts even my Were feet.

"Stupid stone wall!" I yowl, clutching at the foot. "I hate this place!"

Aggie and Chrys giggle behind me, and Hugh places a hand on his temple.

"Really, Lady Never? A temper tantrum?"

I grit my teeth. "Trust me. I'm allowed."

The siblings lead us around the side of the castle.

"The front entrance was badly damaged, and has since fallen in on itself. This is the only safe way to get into the castle."

We walk around the left side of the exterior, and I bare my teeth as we pass the entrance to the dungeon: unassuming wooden doors set into the dirt, as if it's nothing more than a cellar. But I know better. The siblings don't take us through that way, and I breathe a sigh of relief. A little farther down the wall, they instruct us to climb through another empty window casing.

A quick search through the areas that used to be the great hall, a dining area, and the kitchens yields nothing of value. I doubt the Collectors would have left their prized possessions out in the open where they entertained, but it was worth a shot.

"There are several huge piles of rubble behind the collapsed staircase, I'd assume the remains of the second floor. We ought to look there," Hugh instructs, the siblings following him as he clambers over some fallen beams.

"Never, are you coming?" Aggie calls back as she and Chrys go after the others.

My throat's gone dry, tongue heavy in my mouth. Must be the dusty air.

"I don't think there'd be anything useful back there, anyway!" I call, cursing myself for a liar as the words escape. The second story is where several of the Collectors kept their personal rooms. Some of them preferred to remain on the Isle near full-time instead of traveling. They used their chambers to *entertain* their preferred guests, a.k.a. the unfortunate souls trapped here.

"This looks like something!" Hugh calls, holding up a dusty old chalice that glints gold as he rubs the surface with the edge of his shirt.

Chrys grabs it, eyes flashing. Where a Were scents things out, witches use some sort of visual voodoo to suss out magic. At least that's my observation. Magical species don't go around handing out all their secrets, so it's never been clear to me how it works.

"This may have had magic placed on it at some point, but it's just a gold chalice now," she says. Hugh shrugs, tossing it back into a pile of ash.

"What about this? It holds magic." Aggie waves a fancy glass orb in the air, colored smoke swirling inside it. Hugh holds his hand out and Aggie passes the orb over. He turns it in his grasp, squinting into it. Then he shakes his head.

"No good. It's a somson orb. Magical, and we should take it with us, but not Were-related." He tucks it into a satchel he carried with him from the boat.

"Jackpot!" Chrys yells, stumbling as she climbs over a large pile of beams and stone in the back corner. "You guys need to see this!"

I join the others, offering Aggie a hand as she slips trying to climb over a burnt armchair.

"Thanks, I—"

"Let's just look at whatever Chrys found and get this over with," I snap, angry at no one in particular.

"It's a stockpile of stuff!" Chrys throws her arms out to where silver and gold glint at her feet, dusted in ash. "All kinds of weapons, some of which are spelled. Maybe this was some sort of armory? Then again, why would that be in some bedroom on the second floor? There's even some cracked canopy bed over here." As she rambles on, I feel my chest go tight, the air too thin.

I can tell I shouldn't take another step toward them, so of course I do. I refuse to be called a coward, even by myself.

"Whoever lived here was twisted," Chrys continues. "Look at this thing! It's enormous! I don't envy whoever this was for." She holds up what looks like a cat o' nine tails, but it's got the length of a bullwhip. There are bits of sharp metal embedded in the braids.

Aggie's eyes are flickering as she and Hugh peruse the rest of the pile.

"Nope. Some of it's more durable or deadly than a regular human weapon, but that's all," Hugh concludes, adding a few smaller weapons to his pack regardless.

I finger the silver chain around my neck. At its end is a vial with a glowing blue liquid gifted to me by the Bone Reader. He'd told me it was for Damien, and I've imagined it holding all kinds of destructive abilities. I'm tempted to shatter the vial on the castle grounds and see what happens.

"Let's get out of here and go look in that cottage they mentioned. This is a waste of time," I grouse, turning my back on the group as I make my way toward the exit.

"I'm keeping this. Check it out!" Chrys calls. I block the witch out until I hear the snap of the whip, small bits of metal clinking against one another.

I'm across the room before I know what's happened. I yank the weapon away from Chrys, ripping the strands apart as I pull them loose from the handle.

"What the hell!" Chrys demands, cheeks going red as she stumbles back.

I keep ripping and yanking until I've shredded the thing, useless bits of leather and metal falling to the floor.

"Um, Never?" Aggie squeaks out.

"What!" I round on her, lip curled up over my fangs.

"Your paws." She points down, and I realize I've cut them open in several spots. She pulls a t-shirt from her pack. "Here, I can wrap it."

I wave her off.

"It's fine, they're already healing up." The wounds begin to sew themselves shut, a few crimson drops all the evidence that they were even there. "But thanks, witchling," I add, to take the sting out.

I turn to the siblings.

"Where else could the Were information be?"

They point toward the gardens, and the small cottages beyond.

Looks like I'll get to see my old digs after all. Joy.

8
Breaking & Entering

The cottages behind the castle are in various stages of disrepair, much like the castle itself. We pass the fountains in the garden as we walk toward them. One is completely destroyed: melted metal and decay. The second is pristine, a rising phoenix in flight that holds up the basin of the fountain. Once we pass them, we reach the cottages. These are spherical stone structures, each just a single room.

"That was mine." I wave at one that at first glance looks just like the others. I look around and see that I'm no longer walking behind our hosts. I've frozen in front of the crumbling mess of stone and wood that once made up my prison.

"Oh, Never." Aggie squeezes one of my forearms, and I can feel the sympathy. Smell the saltwater as the first tear snakes its way down her cheek. I move to shrug her off, but stop as my eyes catch something in the dirt of the cottage.

I kneel down, and sitting in soot is an item I have long since written off as lost. I scoop it up in one paw, gently wiping the dirt from it. To the untrained eye, it looks like a marble, green and blue weaving around each other within the small glass sphere. But it's not. It was a gift from a friend. The one individual on this blasted Isle I could stand, although I won't see them again. Come to think of it, paws aren't the best way to transport this particular item.

"Here. Keep this safe," I instruct, passing the sphere to Aggie. She nods several times in succession, placing the item reverently into the pocket of her pack. Perhaps I ought to tell her it's not powerful, just sentimental. But I suppose that has its own power sometimes.

"Which cottage?" I ask the siblings.

Meeri points to the last one of the bunch, a lone building sitting so far from the castle that by the time we reach it I can see the ocean behind it. Smell the sea air, feel the breeze. Whoever was in here had the best of a bad situation, if there even is such a thing.

"We do not think your Magikai cleared this building," Ardus explains as he pushes open the door. Other than some crumbling and neglected stone around a gaping hole on one side, it's intact. "In fact, this cottage is an oddity. We have avoided it for the most part. It was not even listed on the map the Magikai were given. Our ancestors have maintained the Isle for generations, but this building only made its way into writings a few dozen years ago. Like it appeared from the sea."

So it was spelled. It has to be a strange experience, a human at the very edge of the magical world. Tied in by necessity of where you live, but with no actual interaction with magical beings.

"Who else lives here, other than yourselves?" I ask, recalling that there was only a faint human scent to the village.

"No one," Ardus confesses. "We've always had the ability to leave, but Meeri and I stayed with our family. Our father felt it was his duty to guard this Isle as long as he was able. We took over the task when he passed away last year, but we've questioned whether it might be time to leave."

I know my opinion on the matter. I don't want to spend a single, solitary moment longer on this sandy prison than necessary. I can scent magic on the dwelling, but it's Chrys and Aggie, with their flickering eyes, who come up with the answer.

"Concealment spell," Chrys states with one curt nod. "Witch work. A very talented witch with a defensive key, similar to mine, did this, or was told to do it."

"The Collectors had magic to keep people contained and subdued. Not hidden. At least not while on the Isle. There would be no point," I counter.

She rubs a hand on her chin, lips scrunching.

"Then whatever is inside was valuable enough for someone to take the time to conceal it before they escaped."

That's enough for me. I push the door all the way open.

The others pile in after me, and Hugh's jaw drops open, revealing glinting fangs. He turns in a circle, taking in our surroundings. Other than the collapsed portion of wall, it's all full of books. So many shelves and piles that I'm surprised it all fits inside.

"I don't know who lived here, but I have to say I approve of their hobbies," Hugh says, running a finger over a row of books. Aside from a notable layer of dust, they're all in much better condition than I'd expect for being so near the sea, with a massive hole open to the air. With more than a tinge of reluctance, I let my fur fade back into skin. If the answer we're seeking is in a book, it won't do to shred it with claws. I can only imagine the Bone Reader laughing me out of his icy cave if I return to him begging out of payment for a reason so ludicrous.

I pull a book at random off a shelf, turning toward our hosts.

"And no one has disturbed this home?"

Meeri shakes her head as Ardus answers, a sense of duty wafting off him. They take their roles seriously.

"No, Lady Never. We merely maintain."

I turn the book I've chosen over in my paws. Leather-bound, heavy, thick paper. The cover is a deep brown, and when I flip it open I see something scrawled in ink on the first, otherwise blank, page.

"Property Of" is written in scrawling text. And beneath it, a symbol stamped onto the page. A glistening, purple dragon scale.

"Seems someone pilfered this from a dragon hoard. I don't envy them the consequences if they're ever caught." I chuckle to myself, passing the book to Hugh, who cringes.

Dragon tempers are notorious. Oh, they're as even-keeled as any sane magical on a good day. But it's decidedly *not* a good day if they realize someone has stolen something from them. All dragons hoard.

Rare objects, jewels—I've even met a dragon that hoarded plants. Whatever the hoard, dragons are fiercely protective of it, in the way most shifters are with their mates. Do not, under any circumstances, touchy-touchy the dragon treasure. Big mistake. Huge.

"This one has a scale, too," Aggie calls over, holding out a green leather book and opening it to reveal the same marking.

"And these," Chrys adds in, holding a grey book in one hand, a purple one in the other.

A sense of unease creeps over me. I pull book after book off the shelves, opening them to see the same symbol, then stacking them in a pile.

"Hell's bells." I put a hand up to my forehead and squeeze. That pesky headache has made an appearance. "More dragons."

Listen, it's not that I mind the magicals. Truly, I don't. They're not ones you often come in contact with. They tend to be solitary in nature, preferring to venture forth primarily to gather items for their hoard. Various sizes, shapes, and abilities that are quite interesting to learn about, if you're lucky enough to meet one when it's in a good mood. Still, Damien's predecessor at the Claw was a dragon. Very hard to kill. It required Damien tricking me, and procuring a magical object that I'm still not certain the origin of. So you can understand why they're not the top being on my list to come in contact with.

"Let's split up the shelves and start looking through. Anything about Weres, or turning humans into any magical being, save in a pile on the table." I point toward the wooden piece of furniture in the center of the room.

By sunset, I'm staring at the table, where we've got five books stacked up, none of which mention Were creation. Aggie snagged a 'how to' text on saving up power for spells without dark magic. Chrys managed to find a book with poisons even her family might not be aware of. Should make one heck of a Christmas gift. There's two I've added. One that describes Were history, but nothing on turning new ones. And another cataloging unique and ancient magical species, including several I don't recognize. I'm hoping to find the Bone Reader in it somewhere. And his shifty, shadowy friend. Hugh's taken one on magical law. Bore and snore.

"You know, you really ought to be more interested in all of this, given that you're the one who actually works for the Magikai," he sasses when I roll my eyes at his keeping it.

"I'm freelance. Not the same," I snipe back.

Every single book in the cottage has had the same dark purple dragon scale stamped inside the cover. If we can't find what we're looking for here, I have a pretty good idea of our next step. But I am nothing if not a master of avoidance.

"All right, kiddies, let's break for dinner," I announce as Ardus and Meeri return from the village, each carrying a platter. The smell that wafts from the food is tantalizing. Meeri sets down her tray, with multiple loaves of homemade bread, potatoes, and carrots. Ardus lowers his to reveal a whole chicken and a roast. Mouth-watering.

"A serious improvement over boat granola bars," I declare.

Chrys heaps her plate high with potatoes, carrots, bread, and nothing else.

"What about chicken?" I ask, eyeing the vegetable-heavy plate.

She rolls her eyes.

"I don't eat meat. You haven't noticed?"

I have not. And that says something about my level of distraction, because she was at the vamp mansion with us all Christmas.

"I already have to fuel my magic with living things. This is my way of balancing it out," she says by way of explanation.

Dinner is a silent affair, the only sounds chewing and clanks of utensils on plates. We finish up eating, and maybe an hour afterward have only added one more book to our pile: *Weaving Elemental Magic Into Your Key.*

"Seems like we may be here for a while, at this rate," Hugh states as he places another book back on the shelf where he got it.

We all have our own methods. Chrys has been tossing them into a pile, Aggie stacking hers on the floor. I've been shelving mine just like Hugh, although with a tad less reverence.

"Just great," I growl toward the stacks, "a sleepover on the Isle of Nightmares. Goody."

"I know you said it's not traceable to anyone who hasn't already been. But do you think if we're here too long the Claw will find us?" Aggie asks as she thumbs through the pages of a text bound in blue leather. It's on the tip of my tongue to remind her she doesn't need to feign nonchalance with me; I can suss out nervousness a mile away.

"You don't have to worry about the Claw or their Crown," I assure her. "I have no plans to rest as long as we're here, so you've got a guaranteed watch. And tomorrow, whether we've found what we're looking for or not, we're leaving."

"That hardly seems like the best course of action!" Hugh protests, snapping a book closed and sliding it onto a shelf.

"I gotta side with the bloodsucker on this one," Chrys says, nudging the vamp with her elbow, "seems like a waste after we've come all this way."

"I don't think we're going to find what we want regardless. There are shelves and shelves of books in here. So we didn't think to look for any more, right?"

Their heads bob up and down in response.

"And we can tell from the fact it was protected and the way the books are all shelved with care that the dragon here was meticulous. Then there's the busted wall, which is likely how our draconic friend escaped. Have we seen one, single, solitary book amidst the rubble of that wall?" I lean toward the others, eyes wide, as I scan between them and the rubble several times.

"Wait, you're saying that there were books there, too. Which means he took some with him. And that might include the one we need. You want to follow the dragon," Aggie gasps.

"Eureka, someone gets it!" I tap my finger on my nose. "And *need* to, not want to."

"How are we supposed to find a dragon, though?" Chrys pipes up. "He ... or she, or they, didn't leave a forwarding address as far as I can see."

"Let's not get ahead of ourselves. We should still go through each book, just to be sure," Hugh insists. I'm beginning to notice that his red eyes blink faster when he's feeling intense about something. One thing's for sure, if and when we do find this book-hoarding dragon, Hugh and the magical will be fast friends. Bonded over books. Chrys may have some competition.

We call it a night once the sliver of moon is high overhead and Meeri and Ardus have long since retired to their home. Chrys is asleep, using a pile of books as a pillow. Hugh has draped his coat over her as he scans more texts.

"You all can take a break. I'm used to keeping odd hours at the mansion. I'll take a nap closer to sunrise," he insists.

I'm more than happy to leave him to it, but I have no intention of sleeping. I exit the cottage after Aggie knocks out, dozing with her head on the dinner table. It's not as if I have a destination, but I throw on my fur and wander regardless.

My steps take me toward what used to be an enormous stable. When I arrived, it had been converted into magically shielded stalls. A holding place until the Collectors figured out what to do with you. The barn is nothing but a ruin at this point. It didn't fare quite as well as the castle. I scowl at it, almost offended that there isn't anything left to burn. Instead I pick my way through the wreckage, hoisting and throwing a few beams from one end of the ash pile to another. I get to a few galvanized steel beams buried under some soot. Yanking one free from the pile, I squeeze on each end until it begins to bend.

I jump as I feel a soft brush against my arm. Turning my head, I see the witchling snuck up on me somehow. This is what focusing on your crappy past gets you—jumped when your guard is down. Yet another reason to leave it behind.

"Never, what happened to you on this Isle? That elf on the beach knew more about it than we do."

"Nothing I couldn't handle. A mere blip of time in a four-hundred-year existence. Breaking out of this joint was a cakewalk compared to handling a couple witchlings, tracking down another intuitive, or trying to find a way to get Hugh to go from team leech to team Were."

She doesn't believe me. Hell, I don't believe me.

"You know, it seems a little silly for me to feel like I need to tell you this, but you're not alone. You've got people who care about you now. And we're not going to judge. We've all got a past."

Maybe so. We do all have a past. But I've been running from mine for years. It's part of the reason I didn't go after Damien until the literal last minute—or last year, I suppose it would be. Avoidance. I've become a veritable professional. Aggie walks around so she's staring up at me. She puts a hand on the steel bar and pries it from me, dropping it into the soot.

"At some point, you're going to have to deal with this. Have you ever considered therapy? It could really help you process your trauma." Smarty-pants, know-it-all witchling.

"Oh yeah, that's just what I need, a magical shrink."

I bark out a laugh, but she just frowns.

"You don't have to tell us everything. But you should know we didn't just come out here for some sort of adventure. We came here to help, because we believe in you. We care about you. And I'm just saying, it might be nice if you could trust us, even a little." She's got her hands on her hips, bottom lip jutting out.

"I trust you with my life!" I snap back.

"Maybe so. To protect you in a fight. But not to open up to. We can't be there for you if you won't let us in. If you ask me, I think you're burying years of trauma somewhere deep down, and if you don't face it, I'd be willing to bet it rears its ugly head in violent ways at unfortunate times." She examines her nails rather than looking at me; they're a vibrant shade of hot pink. I can feel how difficult all this is for her to get out.

"You may notice I *didn't* ask you," I grouch, but I can't quite make the sharp tone stick. I walk a circle around the remains of the barn. "I'm just not ready to deal with it. One unfortunate incident at a time."

For now, Damien's a convenient excuse. Then there's the matter of turning Hugh, sorting out what to do about training Ever and the Magikai. None of these are fun tasks, but if I keep piling them on, I'll have a list so long it near-guarantees I'll never get around to dealing with the Isle. Never sounds nice.

Get it? Never? Not the time for jokes? Fine then.

9

Dragon GPS

I end up sitting in the sand and watching the black waves under the stars for a while. I make my way back into the cottage as the moon sets and the first rays of daybreak hit the horizon.

Hugh's sitting up against a stone wall, head lolling onto a shoulder. Chrys is leaned up against the other, and they're both under his coat. Aggie's back at the table, her head on a rolled up sweater, which she happens to be drooling on. I am determined to move through the rest of the stacks with as little noise as possible. We only need one cranky, sleep-deprived individual on this misadventure.

I manage to follow through with my plan for all of one row of books. As I begin another with nothing more promising than *Witch and Were Disputes of the 1700s*, I let out a low growl and snap the offending title shut. Aggie stirs, mumbling before she turns her head and drifts back off.

Hugh and Chrys have woken up, giving each other a single wide-eyed glance and jumping away from each other, before joining me.

"I'm beginning to doubt this blasted book was ever here. Remind me again why we're on the Isle in the first place? Just because you hate it, or some such ridiculous reason?" Chrys demands, yanking another book off the shelf and discarding it with barely more than a glance.

"Precisely," I respond. "The Bone Reader told me I needed to go to the place I least desired if I wanted to find the secret to turning a new Were. The Isle *is* that place. But I'm beginning to think this is less of a one-stop-shop situation and more of a marvelous, magical scavenger hunt."

Chrys groans.

"So the Isle is clue one, and what? The actual dragon might just be clue two? How long do you have to get all this sorted out again?"

I tap one finger on my chin.

"Let's see. Math. Well, I promised the Magikai I'd be back to train Ever by the first of November at the latest. And I am magically bound to destroy Damien by October thirty-first, latest. But I won't be able to until I've paid back the Bone Reader. So, all that considered, I'd say sometime between today and Halloween."

"Magically bound?" Hugh asks, shutting a book and joining the conversation, his interest piqued. "I thought we had a timeline because of some personal reason, not a contract."

"It's a personal contract, and one I'm not willing to budge on given the centuries of work I've already put in," I admit.

"And you haven't managed to complete things yet? Cauldron's boil, Never, what have you been doing all this time? Damien can't be that hard to track down; you're an enforcer, for goodness' sake! And now he's practically stalking you! You know what, it's fine. My family's got all kinds of antidotes to things. What's the penalty if you miss the deadline for Damien?" Chrys questions.

I've been keeping that particular detail to myself. Better they think I'm being picky about the timeline because I'm just a difficult magical than the real reason. As long as we're getting everything out on the table though...

"I die."

A gasp comes from across the room. Seems the witchling is awake.

"Lady Never—"

"Well, that was dumb!" Chrys interrupts. "Who in the world tricked you into that raw deal?"

"I, um, made it with myself," I admit.

"You what?" the three of them chorus in unison.

As far as I know, it's not something that's done. The whole process of creating these contracts involves spelled paper and ink, and a witness, among other things. It's not like they're free to create, either. Those items are expensive. Plus, the contracts are just as likely to promise rewards for fulfilling a contract as they are penalties for breaking them. There's no reason for anyone to make such a binding promise to themselves. But two hundred years ago, I had to be extra about it.

"I was young! Younger. And I was angry. At Damien, and the Collectors, and myself. I'd shown pretty poor judgment up to that point. The contract made sense at the time." I'd been so besotted with Damien that I'd made a monumental error, given that my intuition should have saved me from it. I spent one two-hundred-year lifetime behaving like a lovesick fool; it seemed fair to spend another two hundred years doing the opposite.

"That is without a doubt the most idiotic thing I have ever heard," Chrys chides, then smiles. "But it's also just the sort of thing I could picture myself doing. I guess we'd better get a move on."

"You two want to say anything?" I turn toward Hugh and the witchling.

Hugh runs a hand across his face. "I need a drink," he says, pulling out his water bottle of O-negative. "We're nearly done with all the books, and I doubt we're going to have any further success. I'll go get Meeri and Ardus, see if they have any ideas." He throws on his sunhat, wrapping his coat around him like a cape before he exits.

"And you?" I raise an eyebrow at the witchling.

"I still think you need therapy," she blurts, blushing and covering her mouth with a hand not a second later. "Sorry, that was rude."

I shake my head.

"No. You're right. I dish it out; I should be able to take it. Let's get it all out."

She pauses for a second, balling her hands into fists as I feel her convincing herself.

"All right, then. Never, that is the most bull-headed thing I have ever heard. You put yourself in a real mess, and now the rest of us are involved. But if you hadn't, your life might have been very different. And I wouldn't have a gotten a sister out of it. So, I suppose I can't be that mad."

She launches herself at me, squeezing me into a hug. I squeeze back for maybe a second before I'm prying her off.

"Okay, all right, enough! Let's get the rest of these books sorted."

Meeri and Ardus join us for breakfast, bringing in a tray of pastries and coffee, thank the moon.

"Blessed caffeine, how I've missed you," I croon, cradling a ceramic cup against one cheek.

"Does coffee mean something different to magicals?" Meeri asks Chrys out the side of her mouth.

"Only to caffeine addicts," the witch responds as she pours herself a cup. Over in the corner, Hugh is discreetly refilling his blood bottle from the supply we brought along.

"Where do you get all of this, anyway?" Aggie questions, biting into a croissant.

"When the Magikai allowed our ancestors to remain on the Isle and watch it for them, they spelled some crops. We're able to grow all sorts of things that wouldn't typically be able to take root here," Ardus explains, grabbing a croissant for himself.

"What about the rest of it? The things that can't grow?" I ask as I pour myself a refill.

Meeri shrugs.

"The Magikai have a few different individuals who show up to drop off supplies, once every month or two. We don't have much contact with them. They leave the boxes on the beach and go."

I feel the fur rise on the back of my neck. I swallow the change back down. It wouldn't do to shatter my coffee cup.

"What kind of magicals? Any Weres, like myself?"

Meeri shakes her head.

"Not that I've seen. At least, when we've met them there's been a warlock, a vampire, and someone who identified themselves as a raiju."

"Unkai. A Magikai representative. Keeping tabs on things," I supply.

I feel the tension drop from my shoulders. No Weres. No chance Damien could follow us here. It's a silly fear, and yet he did say he'd been working with someone from the Magikai at one point.

He's just lying to you, you idiot.

But I can't quite convince myself.

Hugh clears his throat, blood bottle back out of sight.

"Speaking of making one's way *to* the island, we were rather hoping you could help us with another matter. Whether it's possible that the Magikai kept tabs on the locations of those who made their way *off* of it? As they did with Lady Never? And if so, whether you might have some record of it here."

Meeri shakes her head again, strawberry-blond waves shining in the early morning sun. I note our resident vamp has kept to the shadowed edges of the room.

"They wouldn't leave something like that with us. Although ..." She taps her chin.

"The maps?" Ardus questions.

"What maps?" Hugh prompts, his eyes going from muted pink to a deep crimson as the blood does its work.

Meeri twists her hands.

"When the Collectors were here, most of the villagers weren't allowed on castle grounds. The majority didn't even know there were magical creatures here until *Vabastaja* freed them and burned the

castle. But there were a few tasked with care of the, um, prisoners."
She shoots a glance over at me, chewing her lip. I feel trepidation
slapping against my intuition.

"No offense taken. That's one word for it," I reassure her. She
smiles, her relief washing over me like a wave.

"They took some things. The Magikai confiscated most objects
they deemed powerful, but there were some smaller items, and some
papers left behind. Nothing like what you all were looking for,"—she
waves her hands—"but it could help you now. When the Collectors
put bindings on people, they wanted to be able to track them down
even in the rare occurrence of escape. So they made the items they
used traceable."

"Medieval, magical GPS," Chrys offers. Meeri gives the witch a
tentative smile, some of the apprehension falling away.

"We've never used one, but if the dragon you're seeking still has
whatever was used to bind them, you should be able to track them
down. The maps are all labeled with a description of the individual. If
you don't mind waiting, we can retrieve them for you," Ardus offers.

"That would be perfect, thank you," Hugh states, and the siblings
scurry out the door toward the castle.

Hugh clears his throat.

"What? Huh?" I ask, taken off-guard.

"I was asking if there's anything else we should be doing while we
wait," the vampire responds.

I can't think of anything. All that comes to mind are those
wretched chains. Every involuntary resident of the Isle had their
own version. Imprisonment and torment in all styles and fashions. I
myself had a matching set of wrist cuffs with a chain looped between
them.

*Restraints for the fashion-forward magical. Have you tried our
ankle option? Comes complete with the ability to repress shifters from
changing form.*

I shake my head to snap myself out of the morbid advertisement playing in my mind, forcing a chuckle.

The others are staring. I sigh.

"Did I make the mistake of saying any of that out loud?"

"No matter, Lady Never. I'll go down with Meeri and Ardus. Perhaps a helping hand will speed things up."

"Yeah, me too. I mean, the sooner we find those maps, the sooner we get out of here, right?" Chrys adds. Hugh holds the door open as the two of them all but flee from the cottage. I can sense their unease. Sometimes I hate intuition. It'd be nice to be able to believe the lie that they don't find me that odd.

"I'm going for a walk," I announce to Aggie. She just nods and murmurs a response, slurping coffee.

I wander down toward the sands on the back side of the cottage, opposite where our boat is pulled ashore. Once there, I stare out at the water, listening to the repetitive cycles of waves crashing, rolling up the sand, and drifting back out again.

"It would be relaxing here, watching the water, if the rest of this place weren't so creepy." Aggie shivers as she walks up next to me, then looks with a frown back toward the castle. As if she can feel the lingering evil. Perhaps she can. After all, as a stripper she'd be more equipped than most to be aware of magic.

"It was once much worse than this," I say, not bothering to elaborate.

We stare out at the waves for a while longer.

"Never, what did you do with *your* um, bindings, as Meeri put it? Do you have them somewhere? Because if those maps fell into the wrong hands ... "

Little light-magic witch is always looking out for me. Standing up for me. Perhaps some secrets have been kept long enough.

"I had a pair of wrist cuffs, complete with matching chain. Gorgeous but restrictive accessories." I wink at her, although I doubt I've pulled off nonchalance, "and I tossed them into the sea."

"Right. That's good, then."

We go back to the companionable silence. I've almost forgotten she's there again, lost in my thoughts, when she speaks next. I can feel the intense consideration she puts in each and every word. As if she's trying not to spook me.

"What happened to the Collectors? What about the one who caught you? Or the one who had the room in the castle with … the stuff you shredded?"

I can see the wall of flames in my mind's eye as clear as the day I escaped. Feel the desperation and the rage as I tore through the castle grounds, freeing others and mauling my way through the Collectors to get to the one I really wanted. As long as we're sharing, may as well dump all the baggage on the table.

"I burned this place to the ground. The magicals I freed killed a lot of the Collectors on their way off the Isle, and I'm told the Magikai caught up with the rest. But the one who imprisoned me and the one who lived in that room in the castle were the same male. A grey elf."

I don't have to look up to know she gets it. My intuition informs me when the "aha" moment hits her. Tying together why I was so bothered by the elf on the beach. I surge forward, determined to get the rest out and done with.

"I wasn't going to let him get away. And I had more than a small grudge, after years of being stuck here. I boxed him. If there's any justice in the world, he's still down there, drowning in the sea for the millionth time or so."

"Boxed?" Aggie squeaks. Sometimes it stinks, not being able to let others give you the white lie of approval and support. I don't say anything, because she doesn't say anything. But I can tell she's a bit disturbed. After all, boxing is a terrible way to go. And I'm not in the least bit sorry about it.

"Hey, you two! We've got the maps!" Chrys's voice carries from the dragon's cottage. Trance broken, I move to follow her.

"Thank you for opening up." Aggie's quiet words almost don't reach me.

And now we get to the benefit of intuition. She truly cares. Even if she doesn't approve. That's something I never had with Damien.

As we enter the cottage, Hugh and Ardus are dumping armfuls of parchments onto the table. The resulting stack teeters, threatening to spill onto the floor. My stomach squeezes as I recall that each of these papers represents a magical whose life was ruined or taken by the Collectors.

"Phew! That's a lot of people to go through. We've got the Claw, and you all had the Collectors. Tell me, is there a time where magicals *weren't* at each other's throats?" Chrys demands, giving voice to a question I don't think has a good answer.

"Why ask me?" I counter.

"Because you're so old? You probably remember when magic first appeared in the world."

"Watch it witch!" I bop her on the nose with a rolled up parchment, even as her teasing washes up against my intuition. "I've maimed people for less. But no, in my recollection there's no time in magical history where there haven't been notable disputes."

Old, she says. Please. I'm in my prime.

Meeri pulls the top parchment off the top of the pile, having to stand on the chair and then her tiptoes to reach. She clambers back down, holding the sheet up for us all to see.

"Here"—she points to the top right corner—"is where a description of the magical and what they are bound with is recorded. Then down here"—the bottom three-quarters of the map—"is where you find them. But keep in mind, this only guides you to the bindings. If the individual you're searching for has dumped them, this won't be of much use."

"At least it's a starting point. We appreciate it," I tell her with sincerity.

Hugh holds a hand out, and Meeri passes him the parchment. His eyes scan the text on top, left to right, vibrant red irises flitting across the page. He looks up after a few moments.

"Right. This documents an ankle cuff used on a seelie. And the silver dot on the map sits at a spot on the edge of the east Scottish coast. Perhaps they remained there—"

"Or more likely they wrenched off that anklet the moment they reached the shore," I supply.

Hugh sighs and hands the parchment back to Meeri, who accepts it with a murmured thanks.

"It is a long shot that the dragon would still have the item. I can't think of many magicals who would want to keep something that represented their time imprisoned here. But we really don't have any other options, Lady Never."

"Just *Never*, Hugh," I remind him. "And you're right. Let's divide up the pile and get to work."

10

Hiding In Plain Sight

The stack looks tall, but it's nothing compared to the bookshelves we went through. Within an hour we've tackled a good quarter of the pile. And have jack squat to show for it, if anyone's keeping track. Except perhaps a better understanding of the depths of the Collectors' depravity.

Hugh sighs, one elbow on the table as he leans against his hand, rubbing his forehead.

"I've got another pixie net here. You said they used one for a whole group? They were smuggling thousands of them, if that's the case."

"A unique find over here. Enchanted necklace to bind a siren. What did they do, keep her in a giant water tank?" Chrys huffs, tossing the parchment into our 'useless' pile.

"As a matter of fact, they did have several of those for aquatic species. I've got a Were over here, which is shocking, considering I never met another me while imprisoned. Looks like they tossed their cuff somewhere in Spain, or they're still running around with it." I roll this particular parchment up and tuck it into one of our packs. Who knows when a little Were networking might come in handy?

"I'll go make some tea and sandwiches," Meeri offers, shuffling out the door. Her eyes are bloodshot. She and Ardus have worked themselves into the ground trying to help us. When all this is over, I'll have to send them one heck of a thank-you basket.

"I think I have it! I think I have it!" Aggie's bouncing up and down in her seat, waving a parchment around.

"Let me see!" I insist. Hugh snaps the document from the witchling's fingers, spreading it out on the table so we can all look.

He traces a finger under the paragraph of text in the top corner.

"Spelled rings. Count of ten. Used to suppress a male dragon. Collected alongside his accompanying hoard of texts. This is it!" There's so much excitement clogging the air I want to fan it away. Even positive emotions can be overwhelming to a sixth sense like intuition.

His finger moves further down the page. The map on this parchment shows the North Sea and surrounding land. He taps the page at the same time I see it. A silver dot, and it's sitting smack dab in the middle of the water, not far north of our current location. And nowhere near any landmark.

I growl, stomping around the perimeter of the small cottage. I'll never be able to pay the Bone Reader back at this rate.

"Wretched hornswoggling paper! Promising and not delivering. Cursed fustilarian parchment!" I shake my fist at the thing.

"Muckspout," Hugh accuses, a grin spreading across his face.

Aggie and Chrys are glancing between us. Concerned and perplexed, respectively.

"Did someone break Never? Because that made no sense to me," Chrys states, leaning back over the offensive paper and scouring the thing as if it will supply new information.

"Old curse words," I explain, "I like them almost as much as I like names. When you're a centuries-old Were, you have to change with the times. Which has meant moving on to newer things."

"Like jackass. Jerkface. Douchebag." Chrys supplies with a grin.

I tap a finger on my nose.

"Exactly. But there's always a space for the classics."

Aggie's turned her back to all of us, rifling through the 'useless' pile.

"Wait a minute! Ugh, I *know* I saw it. Just wait—aha! *Here* it is!" She rips two parchments from the pile, waving them in the air. "Now, look at this."

She slaps both parchments on the table, overlapping our dragon map. The first is one of the pixie nets, and it's also sitting in the North Sea. The third is a witch. Listed as 'key-concealment and deception.'

"So they threw their bindings in the ocean. An excellent decision, if I'm speaking for myself," I start.

Aggie shakes her head, wine red waves flopping loose and green eyes shimmering.

"Not that! Look at where they are. In the North Sea. In the *exact* same spot as the dragon. Now, what are the odds they're all sitting together and dropped their bindings at the same place, or that the ocean waves would have left them there without them washing onto a shore?"

I feel the prickling sensation of my hair standing on end.

"She's right. And with that witch's key, it's possible—"

"They're on another hidden island somewhere in the middle of the North Sea. Which would mean they could still be there, and we've got the only way to find them," Chrys finishes, violet eyes flashing.

Hugh is nodding along with the witch's suggestion.

"It's certainly worth a shot. What have we got to lose?"

"Fuel. You're the unofficial boat master here, Hugh. Based on this map, do you think we can make it to that island and back to the mainland on either side? I don't care if we make landfall in Norway, Denmark, or the UK, as long as we've got the gas."

"It's iffy," he admits.

Meeri and Ardus start whispering to each other, all eagerness and joy. Which seems out of place.

"We can help!" Ardus announces. "We've got a boat. The Magikai provided one for the residents here, in case we ever needed to escape for any reason. You'll take it, and you can just leave us yours. The next time they show up to resupply us, we'll simply ask for fuel."

"This is perfect, thank you!" Aggie gushes, throwing her arms around the siblings in a hug.

I hold up a hand.

"Just a moment, witchling. I'm not sure if this is our best course of action." I feel physically ill at the thought of having to trek back to the mainland in our own boat, refuel, and turn back around without running into the Claw, but ... "I have to admit, this particular adventure isn't exactly sanctioned by the Magikai. It's taking place strictly off their radar, and I'd prefer it remain so. Is that something you two are all right with?"

The siblings look at each other, then back at me, heads bobbing up and down.

"For *Vabastaja*? Anything."

Truthfulness. I let out a sigh of relief. Who knew a centuries' old fan club could come in handy?

"Good. In that case, I think we could make this work. When was someone from the Magikai last here? The more of a head start we have to get to the dragon's island and off it, the better."

Ardus grins.

"They arrived only a few days before you. So we won't see them again for a number of weeks. They won't need to know about the change in boat until then. Or even longer, if you'd like. We could wait to request the fuel."

"No need. I don't want to leave you two with no other way off this place. A few weeks is plenty." If we haven't found the dragon by then, we're in deeper trouble. I may have months left to catch Damien, but he was spiraling last time we met. I'm not chancing that he'll hold onto his slipping sanity that long.

We grab up the papers and books we plan on taking with us. A whole duffle dedicated to the books. I have an idea of how to use those.

It turns out the boat is being kept in a shed near the shoreline. A bit dusty, but otherwise in working condition. It's sitting on some wooden frame, preventing the bottom of the boat from scraping the floor.

"No wheels," Hugh and I blurt out at once.

"Ah, yes. When it was initially left here, there were quite a few more people on the Isle. We would have been able to move it down to the shore. Will that be a problem?" Ardus asks, his emotions already preparing to apologize.

I stretch my arms, rolling my neck as it gives a few satisfying cracks.

"No sweat for a Were. Hugh, my good male, grab me a rope."

The plan is to pull the entire thing, frame and all, across the sand and into the water. That way we don't risk damage to the bottom. Hugh ties two pieces of rope, one on each side of the wood frame, and my end is fashioned into a makeshift harness. I've thrown my fur on, muscles tensing as I flex my arms.

The others scramble to the back of the frame, ready to push. Although I doubt if anyone other than Hugh is going to make much of a difference.

"All right!" Hugh calls up. "On the count of three. One, two, three!"

I lunge forward, the ropes snapping taut. At first, nothing happens, but after a few moments there's an ear-splitting squeal as the wood slides across the concrete floor of the shed. I pull, but instead of moving toward the doors, the whole thing is turning toward a wall.

"Hold it! Hold it!" I yell. "How are you all divided up back there?"

Chrys calls back.

"Hugh, Ardus, and myself on the left side of the frame. Aggie and Meeri on the right."

"No good! Give Hugh a side to himself."

We get back in position. On try two we actually get out the door. Thank the moon it's a downhill path to the seashore. I'm huffing by the time we hit the water, the waves refreshing. I free myself from the rope harness, which Hugh pulls back up onto the boat. The wood frame falls away as the boat moves further into the waves. As I swim around the side, Chrys lowers a single rope and the witches pull me in, over the side. I shake off like a wet dog, a similarity I normally wouldn't want pointed out, but it is what it is. Then, I collapse against the side of the boat.

"This counts as all my workouts for the week," I announce, breathless.

Meeri and Ardus are waving from the shoreline. Next to our pile of luggage, I spot a bag that smells of fresh baked goods.

"They cooked for us?" I ask, scenting the air.

"Sure did! Try one of these filled pastries!" Chrys shoves some sort of jam-filled croissant into my hands, taking a large bite out of her own as she waves to the siblings on shore. I take a bite, and it's heavenly.

"You know. I have to admit, the reception on the Isle this time was much better than my previous experience. Nowhere near enough to make me want to ever return. But, I would be happy to help Meeri and Ardus get settled in Sacramento, if they're ever so inclined," I announce as I shove another bite of pastry into my mouth.

Aggie smiles, helping herself to a cream cheese option and snagging a second one, which she takes over to Hugh where he's steering our boat.

"I would love that! I've made so many connections since I met you, Never," she gushes.

Sometimes I forget that I'm not the only half-reformed loner of the group. Aggie's never been close to the other witches in her light-magic coven, given her aggressive key. Chrys is the outcast defensive spell caster in a family full of poison masters. And Hugh's obvious. A vampire who'd rather be a Were. A whole pack of misfits.

"How long until we hit the dragon's island?" I ask our intrepid navigator. Hugh's got the map spread out in front of the captain's chair.

"If we keep going at this pace, I'd say we'll make it by sundown. Maybe sooner if we're lucky. Now we just have to hope your Crown and his Jeweled Claw lackeys aren't trolling the surf, waiting for us to appear. You do realize it's possible they could have decided on that strategy once we vanished."

I run a hand down my face.

"Yes, and it's also possible the dragon burns us all to a fiery crisp, or kills us using whatever his particular power is, before we ever hit the shore. But we don't make our decisions based on ifs, Hugh. Besides, we'll just have Aggie take care of the Claw if it comes to that."

"I'm always ready to strip!" she pipes up from her seat.

"And here I thought we'd decided to keep our clothes on," Chrys states with a giggle. "If we can defeat the Claw or a dragon just by showing some skin, I'm willing to volunteer. That'd be a lot simpler than using magic."

"I do appreciate you ladies being prepared to take one for the team. But how do we know they wouldn't be more interested in a sunburned vampire wearing nothing but a floppy hat?" Hugh chimes in.

"Hugh, I didn't realize you had such a sense of humor," I tease him. The four of us dissolve into giggles, and the farther out to sea we get, the more I feel I can breathe. As much as I dislike the open ocean, it's better than the Isle by far.

Hugh keeps an eye on the map, and when we're within what he judges to be an hour or two's distance, I pull out the book duffel.

"All right, team. We need to figure out what we're going to do once we get to this island. Dragons aren't always hostile magicals, but they're not team players either. They need a reason to engage with, or make deals with, others. My thought is we offer these books up as a gift, and hope that gets us an audience at the very least."

Hugh answers from the captain's seat. He's looking rather ridiculous, covered in long sleeves and pants, a blanket pulled up over him, and the floppy sunhat holding it in place. He's also wearing sunglasses and a generous amount of vampscreen.

"He may not even consider it a gift. He'll just see it as being given back what he's owed," Hugh warns. "At best, we're just returning his own possessions to him."

"Well, then, he can damn well consider the act of *delivering* them the gift," I snap. "I note he didn't make the flight back himself, even though dragons don't ever abandon their hoards. So I'm sure he'll appreciate the full gravity of what a visit to that Isle is worth."

At least he'd better.

Hugh's even more accurate than I anticipated. The sky is putting on a dazzling display for sunset—warm pinks, gold, and orange—when we see a black mass in the distance. The closer we get, the clearer it becomes. Rocky outcroppings dotting the perimeter. Truth be told, this island is less welcoming at first glance than the Isle. Then again, looks can be deceiving.

"We may need to circle around. Look for a safe place to bring in the boat," Hugh advises. "Then we can worry about locating the dragon."

We're maybe a quarter of the way round the island's western edge when the dimming light above flickers. I squint up and see the black outline of wings.

"Hugh! I don't think finding the dragon's going to be all that difficult!" I call.

Now we just have to hope it wants to talk to us before frying us to a crisp.

Who sent you?

I grab at my head, shaking it as the words echo and boom in my mind.

Who!

Aggie squeals, and Chrys curses.

"I take it I'm not the only one having their mind invaded, I can only assume by our draconic host?" I ask the group. The girls give a shaky nod. They cringe, hands slapping over their heads as the voice sounds again.

I will have answers! How did you find this island?

That does it.

"Maybe if you'd come down here and chat instead of playing mind games, we'd be able to tell you!" I scream at the sky. My eyes water as I squint again, trying to get a better look at the dragon circling overhead. The sun setting on the horizon makes it impossible.

The form overhead does another loop, then pins its wings and swoops downward. The boat rocks, water sloshing over the edges as the dragon lands. I hear a squeal as Aggie jumps up. I move myself in front of the others, and Hugh abandons the helm to stand by the witches. I stalk toward the dragon, or as close to stalking as I can get with only a few steps of room, throwing my fur on as I go.

"What do you want?" I demand, claws out and ready.

There's no need to yell.

I can't believe it. I'm being mentally chided by a dragon.

"If I hadn't yelled, you wouldn't have heard me from all the way up there," I argue back.

The dragon's mouth opens, revealing a row of sharp, pointed teeth.

"You're lucky you made it this far. I could have incapacitated you from the sky. Now, I suggest you state your purpose for trespassing in my home."

11

Hot Springs & Hotter Shifters

His voice is low and smooth, resonating through me even without him using his mental ability. Pushy beast. Pushy and handsome, if anyone was wondering. Not that I'm distracted by a pretty face.

"We're not here to fight," I assure him, determined to backtrack on my earlier, snappy words. I'm nothing if not diplomatic. Okay, that might be a lie. Alright, it's *definitely* a lie. "We're here to give you something."

He stares at us, eyes flitting between me and the others. He lifts his snout in the air, sniffing.

I have to admit, he's spectacular. Scales of grey so dark they would look black to human eyes adorn his back. The undersides of his wings have near-translucent whirls of purple, a softer version of his deep purple eyes. Both are several shades darker than Chrys's violet. He's a Western dragon, no doubt about it. He's also not nearly as large as the few dragons I've come into contact with. A good foot taller than a Were at least, but not much more than that. Although his wingspan is impressive.

"We'd like to stay here, as guests on the island. Just passing through," I assure him. We can get into the details later. First things first; we have to actually make landfall.

"Guests?" I register surprise in the word, and indecision. We have one chance to make an impression on this powerful magical if we don't want to get kicked out of here at best, roasted at worst. Or whatever it is this particular dragon can do.

"Guests who have come to return something to you," Hugh states, stepping forward with slow steps and holding one of the books aloft.

The vamp barely has time to duck as our host lurches forward and snaps his fang-filled jaws in the air above Hugh's head.

"Where did you get this?" the dragon demands, swiping the uplifted tome from Hugh's hands and clutching it toward his chest.

Emotion pours from the dragon, sloshing into me. And this particular feeling is one that's hard to describe. Dragons and their hoards? There's a bond. They love their objects. Not like someone loves a mate, of course, but also not like humans when they use the term for things like, "Oh, I just love this new song," or "I love avocados." I mean, maybe you do and that's your business, but you get the gist. They're protective over the items, but not in the miserly way one might imagine. No, what I get from a dragon around its hoard is a deep and abiding sense of reverence and appreciation. You can bet that, whatever a dragon hoards, he or she is an expert on that item.

"Fifth century. Leather-bound. The only copy of its kind. A collection of tales and poems from a region that predates today's Eastern Europe." The dragon rattles off the information, and I get small waves of excitement from Hugh. As anticipated.

"We've brought more," I offer, reaching down to grab the duffel. I'm itching to leave my fur on in the face of a dragon, but this is one of those occasions where the unassuming human look might benefit me. Take away any lingering details that make him think we're threatening him. I let my skin wash over me as I hand the duffel over.

The dragon leans down to take it from me. He sniffs as he draws in close and wraps a claw around the handle of the bag. He doesn't move to pull it away. Instead, he sniffs again, putting his scaled snout so close to my hair that I'd slap him if he were any regular male. In fact, I'd slap him anyway, if I wasn't fairly certain he has the information on Weres that we need.

"You smell familiar. Almost like—" His vertical pupils dilate, and something begins to spill from between his fangs. A soft fog that flows from his jaws like a waterfall, lingering in the air around my feet.

The fog rises, forming a wall around me and blocking my view of the others.

"Never!" I hear Aggie call from beyond, but when the grey recedes I don't see her. I don't see any of my friends. I'm not even on the boat anymore. I'm back on the Isle. I turn, fur spreading down my arms as I see the castle looming above me. It's on fire, but it's whole. I remember this night. It's when I burned the whole thing to the ground. The front entrance of the castle is wide open, and from the blackness within strides a lone figure I haven't seen in ages. One of the Collectors. A grey elf carrying a seven-tailed bullwhip. He snaps it, and the metal clanks together like a perverse wind chime. I feel the sting as the tip of one strand hits my muzzle.

"Hello, pet."

The voice sends a chill through me. The kind that has me longing for the warmth of the fire, which for some reason I can't feel even as the castle is engulfed in flames.

"I threw you into the sea." The words come out hoarse, my throat gone dry.

"I came back for you. And this time I'll make sure you don't get away." He's standing in front of me, one hand reaching toward my face. My heart is racing, hammering so loud in my chest that it drowns out my own voice as I start to scream.

And then it's gone.

The scene in front of me snaps back to the boat, like someone shut the vision off with a remote.

My heart rate is so high that it feels more like a vibration under my ribcage than a steady rhythm. As the fog recedes from around my feet, I can't help clutching at my chest, sucking in lungfuls of air as I look at the others around me. I've put my fur back on, and my claws leave shallow cuts in my own hide as I grab at my heart.

I need a moment, but all I get is an onslaught of emotions, thanks to my blasted intuition. Confusion and concern. Worry.

But from the dragon? Understanding.

I manage to catch my breath as I stare him down.

"What did you do?" I demand. I clench my furred fingers at my side, claws digging into the skin beneath. My arms are shaking.

Instead of answering, he holds a claw out to me. I scowl down at it, but I want my answer. I place my hand in his. I realize while doing so that his scales are steaming hot, and my hand is ice cold. The dragon's voice is deep and soothing when he speaks again.

"I think you and I have something in common."

"Could it be our all-expenses-paid trip to a certain Isle from which there was almost no escape?" I tease, unable to put the humor in my tone that I would like. I shiver, struggling to get warm. The dragon's eyes flick down as I shake.

"You all may stay on my island for now. Guests, as you requested. I'll guide you into an area where you can leave the boat." With that, he shoots into the sky and flaps above us. Hugh scurries back over to the captain's chair, and he steers us underneath the dragon as we're led around the rocks and into a sandy cove.

I shiver in silence as the others chat.

"He's shorter than I thought a dragon would be," Aggie whispers out the side of her mouth toward Chrys and me.

"It's not all about size, dear, it's what you do with it that counts." Chrys winks at her, and Hugh bursts into laughter. I manage a half-hearted giggle.

The witchling's eyes go wide, jaw dropping open.

"You all are *lewd*!" Aggie squeaks, the accusation a full octave higher than normal.

The boat slides onto the sand, and Hugh hops off, tying it to one of the many jutting rocks. As the rest of us clamber over the side and drop onto the beach, the dragon lands in front of us. Behind him I can see the entrance to a cave. As I lean closer, a light grows from within. A slew of pixies shoot out of the entrance, descending upon us. They're glowing blue and squeaking as they speak to one another in minuscule, high-pitched voices.

I wave one away as it pulls at my fur. Chrys is swatting at one that's trying to dive into her spiraling curls.

"At least this explains the pixie net," I mutter, another shiver running down my spine. Our new host walks over to me, offering me his arm.

"Come with me. I think I can help with that." I weigh my options, and decide to take him up on his offer as I loop my arm through his.

"What about my friends?" I question as I allow the dragon to lead me further up the beach and into his lair.

"They will be safe within my walls, and I won't harm them, as long as they don't try to take any of my books."

I almost swear to him they won't, but I realize I can't guarantee it. Hugh's a history nut. He's likely to find dozens of things he wants to have. And if he stumbles on the Were text we need? Well, let's just say I'm not making any promises.

The dragon leads me through a large stone arch at the back of the cave and down a narrow tunnel. As it opens to another cavernous area, we find ourselves at the edge of a pool of water. I know what I've said about Weres and water, but this is different. It's crystal clear, and I can see it's shallow enough for a Were to stand with their head above water. Steam is wafting off the surface.

"Hot springs," the dragon offers. "It will help you with the symptoms."

"Symptoms of what?" I ask as I wade in. I put my skin back on, since no one likes the smell of wet fur. Soggy is not my best look. The dragon watches for a few moments as I kick around in the water, then steps in after me.

"So," I try again, kicking my way back to him. "Are you going to tell me now what exactly it is that you did to me? I've filleted people for less, just so you're aware."

I glance up when I feel an almost sheepish guilt coming from the dragon.

"An accident. I have worked for years to gain ironclad control over my abilities, but some memories evoke volatile responses. I know the Isle you saw, and your scent reminded me of it."

"Your dragon ability is what, then? A way to dredge up the worst things that have ever happened to someone and force them to relive the experience?"

He wades through the water, walking the perimeter of the pool. He tucks his wings back but keeps his scaly form. I find myself distracted by the thought of what his skin might look like.

"Sort of," he offers. "I can immerse people, human or magical, in their worst nightmares. Or their wildest dreams. Either way, the experience is fully captivating for most. I'm so good at it that the visions are near-impossible to tell from reality."

He feels certain, not prideful. With more than a hint of regret.

"You've got that right. It certainly *felt* real. The last dragon I met was a storm dragon who liked to melt people with acid rain. I'm hoping this experience goes better, but I have to warn you, we aren't off to a great start." I move the conversation toward one of my favorite topics, names. "So, what should I call you? Are you a dream dragon, or a nightmare dragon?"

"I call myself Nahum," the dragon responds.

"Nay-hum." I roll the word around on my tongue, liking the taste of it. It's an old name, and a rare one. "Comfort. Comforting.

Comforter. I suppose that could fit, at least if you're handing out more good dreams than bad," I reason to myself as I slide my hands back and forth through the water.

"Since my escape from the Isle I've rarely used my abilities, for good *or* ill. But I'd be happy to demonstrate if you'd like. After my mishap on the beach, I owe you that much."

As he steps toward me, he folds his wings in front of himself, blocking my view. When he pulls them back again, aside from the flight-giving appendages, he's in his skin.

I have to bite my tongue to avoid an appreciative whistle. Even by the lofty beauty standards of magicals, he is something else. His skin is a cool-toned medium brown, stubble on his sharp jawline. Black hair that's longer and natural on top, and faded on the sides. He's in the water up to his waist, and I just barely resist the temptation to look down.

Come on, Never, you're four hundred years old. Not some lovesick Were-pup howling at the moon for the first time. Get a grip!

He smiles when he notices me looking, and I *know* he notices because I can feel his awareness of my gaze. A dazzling white smile, I might add. My cheeks have to be blazing red, and still I can't stop myself. Perhaps his waking nightmare had more of an impact on me than I thought. My usual confidence is replaced by an unbearable awareness of my own sopping-wet silvery hair, tangled at the ends, and how my fair skin is leached of any warmth. I blame the nightmare.

He takes another step forward, reaching his hand out toward me.

"A good dream might also warm you up."

Oh, I'm plenty warm. I feel my pulse speed up as his hand gets closer. At the last second I slap his hand away.

"No. Thank you." I add the last words on hastily. No sense in angering the male we need to help us. I clear my throat. "I'm Never, by the way. The red-haired witchling with the porcelain skin you saw on the beach is Aggie, the vampire is Hugh, and the violet-eyed witch with the springy curls is Chrys."

He nods.

"So that's why the witch screamed 'Never' at you. Is it—"

"My given name? No. And now another question for you. When you force these nightmares or dreams on people, is it correct to assume you can see what they're seeing?"

He dips his chin in affirmation. Another small slap of apology hits me.

"I have no control over that part. I can't choose to not see. Believe me, I understand that it's violating." Another small smile, close-lipped this time.

"But you spoke in our minds."

"Yes, but that's just a general dragon trick. I can push the words in, but I can't pull anything out. The dreams are the only way to do that. You can't imagine what it's like, having this window into people. Digging through their deepest secrets to see what makes them feel joy and fear."

"You might be surprised," I grumble, crossing my arms over myself as I lean against the rock wall of the pool.

"Oh?" He mirrors my movements, his wings disappearing as he leans against the wall next to me.

I sigh. What's that saying? Give a little to get a little? Fingers crossed it applies to my current situation.

"I'm an intuitive," I respond. I've done this enough times that I've got the reaction down pat.

Three, two, one.

His eyes go wide as the word sinks in, realization dawning.

"Feel free to be impressed," I tack on, preparing myself for any eventuality. Shady shifters tend to respond in a negative way to my ability. The rest start to consider how they could use me, but always with a lurking sense of unease at what I might unearth.

"This is wonderful!" the dragon gushes, throwing himself forward and wrapping me in a hug. His chest slams into me about the same time that his sense of joy does.

"I'm sorry," I murmur, face squished against rock-solid dragon pectorals. "Has the meaning of intuitive changed over time? Because I'm certain I just let you know I can read you like one of your own books."

He nods, grin still plastered on his face as he pulls away.

"Apologies. That was a bit overenthusiastic of me. Yes, you can read me. But it also means you can understand."

12

Let's Make a Deal

It's on the tip of my tongue to ask Nahum for an explanation when a few blue pixies come zipping into the cavern, circling the dragon. My personal experience with pixies is that they're snide, snarky, and enjoy a good prank. One might even call them mean-spirited, if they found themselves on the receiving end of a pixie's sense of humor. These pixies, though, have thus far been perfectly well-behaved. Nahum whispers to them, and I see their tiny heads nodding before they fly back down the tunnel.

The dragon turns back toward me, still so close I can feel his breath on my neck as he leans down to speak.

"You all must be tired. The journey to this island is not an easy one. Perhaps I *could* extend you some true hospitality. We can discuss the purpose of your visit tomorrow. For now, the pixies can get you settled."

He strides toward the shallow end of the hot springs, scales rippling down his back as he exits the water. I twist my long hair, squeezing excess water out before I join him. We move back down one of the tunnels and into the larger cavern we walked through earlier. The others are seated, leaning against their packs. They're eating some of Meeri's pastries.

"Could you please show our guests to their rooms?" Nahum's voice booms and echoes in the high-ceilinged cavern. After he speaks, there are sparks and swirls of glowing blue light as the pixies zip toward us.

Chrys frowns as a few begin pushing her toward one of the many tunnels. I imagine it's easy to get lost in a place like this. Another pixie begins tugging on Hugh's sleeve.

"Come on, then!" it urges him in a high, squeaky voice.

A swirl of pixies circle Aggie like a small tornado, her hair lifted by the breeze. She just giggles, then leans down and holds a finger out. One of the pixies flits down to perch on it.

Surprise buffets into me from where the dragon stands, and I turn to see the whites of his eyes showing.

"A light-magic witch?" he questions.

I frown.

"How did you know that?"

He gestures toward our glowing companions as they lead Hugh, Aggie, and Chrys down separate tunnels.

"The pixies. They're very nature-centered. They can tell she doesn't steal her magic from that source. She's likely made a whole pack of new friends."

"That's not entirely fair. It's not as if Chrys *wants* to suck the life out of frogs and squirrels; that's just the nature of the gig." I'm not sure I agree with what I'm saying, but Chrys has stood by us so far. I defend my own team. Before the dragon can pose a counter-argument, I throw out another question.

"Going for a bit of divide and conquer? It seems to me you like separating us."

"I told you, I will not harm you and your friends. I'll admit I'm not used to visitors, but I'm not some evil monster you need to worry about, and I know now that you can tell I mean that. After all, if I wanted to hurt you, you've already seen how easy that would be."

He does have a point there. He could have just thrown us all into a nightmare; used it to confuse and torment us. From my small taste of it, I have to admit it very well would have worked.

"If I may be so bold, perhaps I could show you to your room?" Nahum holds out an arm to escort me again.

"Do you know," I muse, taking it, "the last time a dragon offered me his arm, it didn't turn out so well."

"Ah yes, the storm dragon. That's a story I look forward to hearing. Would you be willing to share?"

I could lie. After all, *he* doesn't have my abilities. Just a veritable army of pixies roaming around. Then again, where's the fun in that? I already know Nahum is intimidating; it's time he knows who he's dealing with. I summarize our situation for him.

"Let me see if I'm getting this all correct. You set out to rescue another intuitive Were. Your ex was after the same Were, but secretly working for the Claw. Which he is now in charge of, after murdering its leader and blaming it on you."

"You, sir, are one sharp dragon. That's exactly right." I don't add that I'm now on a mission to off that particular ex, which will require Nahum to give up one of his precious books. All because I made a shady backroom deal with an ancient magical entity in exchange for information on Damien's whereabouts. A bit pointless, considering he's been following us, but a deal's a deal.

"Well, that's a shame. Ekaitz was always an interesting dragon. I've never met anyone else with acid rain as an ability."

I tense, shifting my stance a bit. My claws itch to break loose. Were they friends?

"Always sad when magicals go to the wrong side, particularly when they're so unique. Although, I gather my present company is anything but ordinary as well."

"You got that right." I tip my chin up and wink at him. This has to be the cheesiest pile of baloney, but in the name of honesty I've got to tell you folks my heart may actually skip a beat under his heated gaze. Those purple eyes of his are proving dangerous.

"You're not upset, then? He wasn't some long-lost dragon relative?"

Nahum lets out a short laugh.

"Hardly. But there aren't so many dragons left. I would be willing to bet that I'm aware of most, if not all, of them. Is it the same for you? I know Were populations are limited as well."

I don't really have a good answer for that. After Damien and Ever showed up in Sacramento, I'm beginning to question that. How much of the perception is really dwindling numbers, and how much is me isolating myself from anything to do with my life before the Collectors? After all, Silva and her pack seem large enough. And Ever had a pack in Colombia. Maybe there's more of us than I thought.

"Here we are!" Nahum announces before I have time to put together a suitable response. He sweeps a scaled arm out. It's really just a small alcove, but the walls of the rock have been chipped away to form shelving. There's a mattress, blankets and pillow, underneath shelves of books.

"Pretty homey for someone who's not used to entertaining," I muse.

He rests a claw under his chin.

"True, but I have ample free time. I've carved out all sorts of rooms in this cave system." Nahum retreats back into the tunnel, leaving me with my own thoughts.

As someone who's used to upscale living, I fall asleep with ease. After all, I was raised to appreciate the open forests and sleeping on the ground under the stars. A cave isn't so bad, but whatever Nahum did to me has some after-effects. I toss and turn, shooting up, with my claws ripping out, after a nightmare where a shadowy figure shows up at the cave and slaps magical shackles on me. At first, I think it's the Collectors, but then as the figure steps into the light I see that it's Damien. That's enough sleep for one night. I stare at the rock above me until I can't stay still any longer.

I'm grumbling as I make my way back into the tunnels. A flitting blue pixie guides me down some twists and turns to an unfamiliar cavern. This one houses an assortment of cooking utensils and a wood-burning stove. There's a large table that I'm betting the dragon carved himself, alongside matching chairs. He wasn't kidding about that free time.

"Your eyes are as red as mine. Did you get the same squeaking pixie alarm I was subjected to this morning?" Hugh questions, raising a brow and handing me a glass of orange juice. I snag it from his hands, downing it.

"Coffee. I need coffee. I am not nearly caffeinated enough to deal with the day yet," I grump.

"Did the pixies trick you as well? Our host's little helpers directed me down the wrong hall six times before showing me to the dining room, doubling over into fits of giggles each time," Chrys accuses, eyes narrowed at the small blue magicals as they flit around her. She waves them away.

I feel a tap on my shoulder and twist around to see Aggie, holding out a ceramic cup.

"Praise the moon!" I exclaim as she sets a steaming carafe of coffee in the center of the table. I dive for it, ignoring any pretense of manners.

Hugh chuckles, taking the seat next to me.

"What's so funny?" I demand, taking a long sip of glorious caffeine and sighing with pleasure.

"You. Ladies and gentlemen of the magical world, may I present Never. Fearsome leader of the Vegas coven, scourge of the Claw, guardian of newly discovered intuitive Weres and witchlings alike. Brought low by one morning without caffeine."

I grin at him, taking another loud slurp.

"Hugh, my friend. You're not wrong." I turn back toward Aggie and hold my cup up. "Thanks, witch."

"Purely selfish," she assures me. "If you don't get a mug you're likely to down that whole carafe. And I, for one, am also in need of a bracing cup of coffee."

The pixies flit after Aggie as she goes to a cupboard to get one. She giggles as they dive in and out of her hair. I note that Chrys's curls are in a teal headwrap this morning. All the better to keep the pixies out.

After a few more minutes of chatter, I feel a shift in the air. Looking around at the bevy of tunnel openings, I see Nahum striding through one, his skin on and his face impassive. Not going to work on me, dragon boy. I can tell he's got a whole party of emotions fighting it out. Then again, I would too, if a random group of misfits showed up on my hidden island.

"I trust you all slept well?" We all give a nod, and with formalities out of the way he presses on. "I think now would be a good time for you all to explain how you came to be here. And why. I spent last night perusing the books you brought along. I assume you brought them directly from the Isle? Or have they been moved?"

He grabs a cup of coffee for himself, sitting directly across from me. I take another sip, warmed all the way down to my toes, but it's not from the beverage.

"We came straight from the Isle. The rest of your books are still there, untouched and being guarded by a pair of humans who would be more than happy to hand them over, if you're inclined to go after them." Good news first.

"And you brought them all the way here, why? Simply being good Samaritans?" One side of his lips rises in a sly smile.

Moon have mercy. If I wasn't mid-mission to deal with an ex, I'd be very tempted. That being said, I'm not above flirting with the dragon while we're here. Hell, with him, over him, under him, I'm open to it. But now isn't the time to get distracted.

"We do have an ulterior motive," I admit, getting straight to the point. "We need knowledge. Specifically, the process of turning someone into a Were. We thought that the key to that information was on the Isle. We didn't find it there, but we did find your books. It's my belief that you've got what we need, somewhere on this island."

He taps his fingers against his mug while he considers.

"And you expect me to, what, just hand it over? Assuming I have what you're looking for, that is."

"We would be more than willing to pay. Name your price." The idea of yet another magical debt makes me squirm. I've dug myself in deeper than a gambling addict, but, in for a penny, in for a pound. No backing out now.

"Before I make that decision, I'd like you to answer something. How did you find me? This island isn't on any maps."

"You have the Collectors to thank for that. The items they used to bind each of us have a tracking function. A multifunctional gadget for the sociopath on the go." I volunteer.

"That explains it." Nahum laughs, canines reaching sharp points even in his skin. He walks over to one of the shelves he's managed to adhere to the rock walls of the cave. After moving aside a few items, he reaches into a stone bowl, retrieving something. He walks back to the table, and dumps the items: ten obsidian rings clink and roll. I swipe one up, examining it.

"I kept them," he explains, gesturing at the rings. "A reminder, each one, to never put myself in such a position again. On the night I left the Isle—"

"The night I burned it to the ground and received no help at all from a certain imposing dragon. Help that could have very much come in handy," I snark, unable to stop myself from pointing out the obvious.

He inclines his head.

"That night. Yes. Although I didn't realize what was happening at the time. I just saw the chaos, and a chance to escape. And I took it. You'd freed a group of pixies. They flew past my cottage. I made them an offer, to free me."

Bribing pixies. If only my own way to escape had been so easy.

"What did you promise them?" Hugh questions, in full vampire-historian and giver-of-legal-advice mode.

"My protection," Nahum states matter-of-factly. "A home. They need not fear on this island. I am more than capable of keeping them safe. I make sure any threats stay away from here. I only let you all pass because you brought the books. They're my weakness. Just like before. But this time I'm not sorry for it."

"Is that how the Collectors got you in the first place, your books?" Aggie questions while rolling one of the obsidian rings across her palm.

I lean across the table, as if that's going to help my intuition pick up his emotions any better. He's been honest so far, but I'm not taking any chances.

"It was a combination of factors. My hoard and my vanity." It reeks of unwanted truth. He doesn't like it. But he's not lying.

"I've built this island out to my liking, but it truly was a dank and uninhabitable place when I arrived. I simply wasn't ready to go back. Before the Collectors found me, I lived in the mountains of Europe. Deep in a forest where snow blankets the trees. Other than the natural defenses that the terrain provided, I didn't bother with any sort of security. Why would I? Dragons are loners, but we don't mind our own kind. And any other magical I didn't consider a threat. After all, if they had ill intentions, I could just drive them mad with their own nightmarish fears."

Down the table Chrys chortles, and I shoot her a look.

"What? It was funny. 'Just drive them mad,' as if it's that simple. You shifters sometimes forget what it's like to be part of the magical community when you aren't born with your biggest defenses. Even keys we don't develop until our teens."

Even mid-memory, the dragon is considerate. I feel the thoughtfulness wash over me after Chrys's outburst. In truth, it is worth a conversation. After we've obtained the book. Not that I need to add anything else to my plate. *Never's School for Wayward Witches*. Can you imagine?

"Continue," I whisper, urging the dragon on.

"They tricked me. Clever, I must admit. They sent in a contingent of humans, of all things. Magicked to forget their lives, forget themselves. I couldn't bring them nightmares, because they had no memories and no fears. I knew something wasn't right. I could have killed them, but where would the justice have been in that? They were just pawns. I chased them away, down the mountain and far from my terrain. By the time I returned, several of the Collectors were there. Pillaging my precious books. Setting some of them on fire."

He changes as he speaks. Scales overtake his skin, and pretty soon he's got a lengthy tail swishing against the stone floor. Anguish, pure and unsullied, pours off of him. There is nothing a dragon loves more than his hoard, except those who have mates. But those are rare. He doesn't want to remember the Collectors any more than I do. But I need to know this. Need to hear him say it aloud.

"Destroying my innocent pages. I brought several of them down; sent them spiraling into the nightmares of their own minds, never to surface. But I had to save the books. I took off for the nearest stream, scooping water up with my mouth and claws. I flew over the fire, dousing it as best I could. I did this until there was only smoldering and smoke. Then I landed to inspect the damage. The males and females I'd sent into their own minds were no threat to me. No one awakens from a nightmare unless I will it."

I don't mind admitting that this sends a literal chill down my spine and all the way to my toes. An endless nightmare sounds worse than being boxed. And when I think how close we came to all ending up that way! It was horrifying to endure it for moments, but to be stuck in that loop for all time? To live with the knowledge that I'd caused Aggie or the others to be trapped as well? Unendurable.

"You allowed yourself to be distracted by the books," Hugh speaks, breaking the silence. As he does, the choking fear in the room eases, and I realize the others must have been having similar thoughts to my own, pummeling my intuition with an onslaught of negative emotions.

"Yes," Nahum admits. "It was foolish. A novice mistake. But I can't change the fact that I made it. I was inspecting my hoard one item at a time, focused on determining the level of damage of each and every page. That's when they threw the net over me. Much like the rest of the items in the Collectors' vast inventory, it dampened my magic. Then, for good measure, they brought out the rings." He makes a face, grimacing and then shaking his head. "And that was the end of it, until the Isle was burning and the pixies let me out. Interesting, that one fire imprisoned me and another set me free."

"And the pixies followed you here. Like fishes circling a shark to keep them away from other predators," I muse.

"Yes, something like that. And now fate has brought *you* here."

"Not much for fate personally. I would say that a bull-headed Were who makes terrible deals with mysterious magical entities, and even more terrible dating choices, brought us here. But hey, I'm not going to argue." I shrug.

"That may be so. Either way, I owe you a debt. And I'm fortunate it's one I can pay."

The dragon stands, beckoning us toward him. He leads us to one of the many tunnel entrances.

"There's something you need to see."

13

Maybe He's Born With It, Maybe It's Another Crappy Magical Gift

I look over at Hugh as we step into the dark. He just shrugs. The four of us follow the dragon down yet another tunnel, and I'll admit they're all so similar I've no idea if we've already been through this one.

As we come up to another opening, Nahum spreads his wings wide, blocking our view.

"It took years. But I built back what the Collectors stole from me. Flew back and forth to my old mountain to retrieve some items. Scoured the world for others. I can now say with confidence that I've exceeded what I held before. I say this so you understand the enormity of what I'm showing you. I have hidden and guarded this hoard in isolation, to save it. I warn you now, do not betray me." He growls at the end of the threat, and a pleasant shiver works its way down my spine.

Something is very wrong with me that I find this more aggressive side of the dragon so attractive. Before I can delve any deeper into self-reflection, he drops his wings. I can see now where Nahum spent the majority of his excavating efforts. This is, by far, the largest cavern we've been in. And carved into the walls are shelves upon shelves of books. Enough that we'll be here for weeks if we need to scour them all for our answer.

"Oh my." Hugh's voice is hushed, his eyes wide. He looks like he's in a trance as he walks into the room in front of us.

I look back at the dragon just in time to see him in his skin and buttoning a pair of jeans. Sly shifter must have spare clothes piles all over this cave system. An absolute must for those who haven't paid to shift back with clothing, and I'm the only one I've ever met who bothers. He's kept the wings.

"How do you keep the books dry?" Chrys asks.

"Magic. How else?" The dragon shrugs. "I have a few individuals on the mainland that I purchase various objects and spells from."

"Impressive," Chrys acknowledges, following Hugh around the perimeter.

"I, um, don't suppose there's any helpful how-to's on light magic in here somewhere? Just to peruse. I wouldn't take it," Aggie assures the dragon as she makes her request. Before he can answer, the pixies have swirled around her, tugging on her sleeves and leading her to a shelf on the right side of the room.

"You're all right with her looking through those books?" I question, tilting my head toward the witchling.

"Consider it part of my payment to you."

He reaches out and grabs my hand, pulling me along behind him. Instead of the familiar urge to swipe my claws first and ask questions later, I move at his side without even the itch of fur threatening to break free.

Perhaps it's that I've let Damien go after all these years, or perhaps I'm just hard up after a very long dry spell, but this dragon is doing something to me. I bring my free hand up and slap myself, trying to snap my mind from its less than clean thoughts. When I do, Nahum winces.

"Don't do that, please," he requests, a grimace marring the line of his perfect cheekbones.

"Oh please, Weres can take pain," I assure him. "Moon knows I saw enough of it on the Isle. And as an enforcer. And with the Claw." Maybe I should stop.

Nahum drops my hand and reaches into the stacks. He turns with a book in his hands, faking casualness. Silly dragon; tricks are for those who aren't in the presence of an intuitive. This book is important. He rests against the bookshelf, and even though he's the one backed against the stacks, I feel boxed in.

I lean forward, reaching for the book. He's holding it clutched close, and as I lay a hand on it his wings flash out, wrapping around us both. I don't let go of the book, and as he holds it against his chest I can feel his heart hammering.

"I have never. Never. Lent one of the books in my hoard to another of my own free will."

"That's fine. *Never* is kind of my thing." My whole mouth has gone dry, and I run my tongue across my lips. His eyes dart down, following the movement. "You let me borrow this book, and I'll consider us even," I inform him, giving a small tug to the leather-bound volume that he has yet to relinquish.

He chuckles, and I can feel the vibration in his chest.

"You'll forgive me if I hold my own life, and the pixies', for that matter, at a higher value than a single volume. Even if it is one of my treasured possessions. No, you and I are just getting started, Were. I owe. And I intend to pay."

He releases the book, and I stumble back as he pulls his wings behind him again. I turn and let out a breath, feeling the need to fan myself.

"A whole book on adding longevity to defensive shields for witches! Mind if I take notes from this?" Chrys calls from across the room. Nahum walks over to her, and I really do fan myself with the book he left me before I join them.

"Of course. But no markings in the actual book, please. As a matter of fact, that particular text was gifted to me by the very witch who shielded this island. She came with us from the Isle but left soon after."

There's one mystery solved. That explains the third item on the map.

"May I assume she also shielded your cottage of books during your escape?" I ask.

Nahum gives half a smile.

"Yes. She wasn't as easy to pay off as the pixies, but I have all sorts of wealth amassed on the mainland. And I was determined that even after I left the Isle my books wouldn't be at the mercy of the Collectors or anyone else."

"Yet you waited so long that the concealment spell eventually wore off." I observe.

He frowns.

"I always intended to go back for them. I just kept finding reasons to put it off."

More truths that he dislikes. A whole mess of internal conflict. Not that I can judge. I wouldn't have gone back either if I'd had the sense to avoid owing the Bone Reader.

"So long as we're here, you wouldn't happen to have any useful texts on intuition, would you?" I question.

I'm way behind on knowledge of my own kind. While I'm still not sure how I feel about it, I've been thrust back into the social aspect of the magical realm, and I would like to know as much as I can. Maybe it *would* behoove me to keep up some relationships with the other Weres. Like Silva, or even the pack I grew up with. Perhaps there are more intuitives than Ever and myself, not that I'd share that information with anyone.

"The Were section is one shelf up from the witch section." Nahum points to where Aggie is perusing books. "But you're going to want the section on rare genetic abnormalities. Multiple species have their own variants, and I house those books together."

I throw him a salute and a wink.

"Thanks, dragon."

Hugh passes me, headed for a table in the center of the room with a pile of books in his hands, spanning who knows what areas of knowledge.

"No wonder they took you to the Isle. This library is priceless," he gushes as he drops into a chair and flips open a book, dull red eyes scanning the page. I'll have to make sure he stops for a drink at some point today.

I'm reaching for a book on the shelf Nahum referenced, one with a gold foil Were on the cover, which looks promising. Hugh's words sink in, and my hand freezes. I turn back toward the dragon.

"Wait one minute. Why *did* the Collectors want you in the first place? It's got to be more than just your books. They could have stolen those and fled without putting themselves at such a great risk."

"Being a powerful dragon isn't unique enough?" He turns to me, head tilted.

"Not by half. You forget, I knew those magicals. Intimately." I suppress a shudder. "You had your own cottage. That means you were the best of the best, something guaranteed to bring an immensely high price. Why? To be willing to take on a dragon, it has to be something significant."

He sets a book down on the table in front of Hugh. His grip on it is so tight that if his claws were out he'd shred the cover. I'm getting under his scales.

"That's not part of this deal," he states, teeth clenched and words clipped. "Are you certain you want this knowledge?"

"Yes." I don't even have to consider. I want anything that gives me a possible one-up on someone. Just because he's on our side now doesn't mean he always will be.

He turns his attention toward me, advancing with slow steps. I let him loom over me, but refuse to step backward. I'm not prey. I crane my neck, staring up at him.

"Fascinating," he says. He reaches out, and he has unsheathed his claws. One hovers over my cheek, but at the last second he pulls it away. He moves a few steps back, giving me space as he assesses me.

"You were kind enough to share your own rare ability. I'm sure you understand that such a power is not always a gift."

"Yes," I allow, "it's helped me out innumerable times, particularly as an enforcer. It makes me a dangerous enemy. That being said, what looks like a gift can also feel a lot like a cage."

Nahum moves toward me again, his purple eyes flashing. This time he does reach out, clawed hand cupping my cheek as he stares into my eyes.

"I was right. You do understand."

I go still at his touch, and the only movement is our chests rising and falling.

"Yes," I manage.

"Do you trust me?"

I shove his hand away, ducking out from under his arm. I move toward the table where the others have gathered.

"Not in the slightest," I admit. "To do so would be unwise in the extreme. But I trust my intuition. And you're not out to get us. Not yet, at least. Sometimes people just need the right motivation."

"And yet you came to bargain with me."

"I recall you saying this was more of a debt settlement. Not a bargain. Still, we're more than happy to pay."

The others spread out next to me. Aggie's at my side, hopeful and apprehensive all at once. I know the other two aren't as calm as they appear. They're all ready to fight our way out if this goes south.

"You don't trust me, so I'll offer this. Will you allow me to conduct a quick demonstration?" He waits, and none of us speak for several seconds. "It will be the easiest way to show you what you're asking about. I just need a volunteer."

Aggie steps forward, chin jutting out.

"I'll do it," she states, voice shaking. Brave little witchling. But there's no way in hell I'm letting her go through with it.

"Nope. I'm the one who got everyone into this; I'll volunteer." I stride past the witchling and back over to Nahum until we're chest to chest again.

"Do we have a deal?" His purple eyes sparkle, and he holds out a clawed hand. I nod, giving my own hand over.

We shake, but instead of letting go, he grips tighter. His other hand flashes up, one claw slicing a deep wound down my forearm. I scream, yanking it back.

"What in hell's moon do you think you're doing?" I demand, covering my injured forearm with a hand to stifle the bleeding.

Aggie surges forward, arms raised and ready to strip.

"Wait!" Nahum yells, holding up his own arms, palms out. Now I see it. A purple light running along his arm. It looks like a shimmering vein beneath his skin. And it's in the exact spot and the exact length of my cut.

"No," Hugh breathes behind us. "It's not possible."

"What, what's wrong with him?" Chrys demands, fingertips sparking. She's on alert, more than ready to throw up a defensive wall even with her dwindling supply of magic. We'll need to find her some froggies to off soon, or whatever she prefers to pull her power from.

The dragon locks eyes with the vamp over my shoulder. Nahum dips his chin toward Hugh, granting permission.

"He's an empath," the vampire states.

"He's a what?" Aggie questions, turning toward the vampire and dropping her hands. The pain in my arm recedes as my skin finishes knitting itself closed. I wipe the lingering blood with my shirt. That'll be tough to get out in the wash. Oh well.

"When he inflicts physical suffering, he feels physical suffering of an equal degree," Hugh states, full professor mode activated. "But they're exceedingly rare. Thought to be extinct. There hasn't been one mentioned in all the papers I've gotten my hands on, in at least a millennium."

I flip my silver hair over my shoulder with a snort. "And so? What am I, chopped liver? Other than Ever, I'm the only one of me. And I'm four hun— ... I'm plenty old."

Hugh shakes his head, his eyes a shade lighter than before.

"Wrong. With intuitives, and most other magical variants, there *can* be more than one at a time. Even if there aren't. Dragons don't work like that. Their magic comes from the same unknown source, which balances itself out. For as long as he's alive, he's one of a kind."

I press my hands to my temples.

"So you're telling me, that as an empath you feel the pain of others?" I demand, marching back toward the dragon. "And that in all the world, for all the time you're alive, there is not a single soul on this earth that can relate?"

Nahum inclines his head.

"Well, that's a shite gift!" I yell, stomping the ground with feet that are growing claws and legs that are popping backwards at the joint.

"Never!" Aggie chides, covering her mouth. The witchling really should know better by now. I am available filter-free or not at all.

"Well it is! And I thought being an intuitive blew a big one at times. What the hell kind of advantage could empathy have?" As a fellow recipient of a gift that's really more of a curse at times, there's the slightest possibility that I'm taking this harder than I should be.

Nahum looks over at Hugh again.

"Care to field this one as well, vampire?"

I can feel Hugh's eagerness, but as always he's all decorum.

"If you insist. The ability causes him excruciating pain when he doles out injuries. But it also means he's uncommonly strong."

"That's just part of being a dragon. Isn't that kind of the defining feature of you all?" Chrys questions.

Hugh glances back at Nahum, who dips his chin once more. The vampire is giddy, but he keeps his expression in check. He clears his throat before answering the witch.

"He's not just strong compared to us, he's strong compared to dragons. Compared to anything, really. Almost indestructible."

"Well, is that the gist of it?" I question Nahum.

"More or less."

I cross furred arms over my chest.

"Why don't we go with *more*. As long as we're all opening up to each other."

"All right. The vampire is *almost* accurate. I am a bit more than what he suggests. It's not just *almost*. There is no one on this earth who could kill me."

14

Sometimes You Just Have to Scream

The room goes silent at the dragon's pronouncement. After all, how do you respond to someone announcing their immortality? And not the kind most of us magicals grasp at, but the real deal.

Someone clears their throat, and I grunt as I'm jabbed in my torso. Looking down, I see the witchling elbowing me, and I lean toward her.

"Is he telling the truth?" Aggie whispers, hand held up in front of her mouth.

I keep my voice low.

"At least as far as he knows it. If nothing else, he believes what he just said," I confirm.

When I look back up, Nahum's got his muscled arms crossed and is rolling his eyes.

"I can hear you, you know."

Aggie's cheeks go pink as she slaps a hand over her mouth.

"I have a question." Chrys raises a hand in the air. "What happens if we chop your head off?"

"Chrys!" Hugh and Aggie blurt in unison, mortified on her behalf.

Nahum just grins.

"You could try."

"So." Chrys claps her hands together, and I feel a driving need to break the tension flow over me from her direction. "Any chance we could take a look at that Were-making text? That's why we're here in the first place, right?"

"Yes. Hugh, grab the book," I instruct, pointing at where I set the tome Nahum handed me earlier.

Is that why we're here?

I wave my hand, trying to swat away the errant thought as if it were a fly. Still, I'm beginning to suspect the Bone Reader of meddling. He's a tricky entity, but as far as I've known him, he's not dishonest. He charged me a high price for Damien's whereabouts, but he would have known from reading the Were's bones that my ex half-mate would be hot on my tail. There was no need to send me on a fool's errand when I could have cooled my heels at home and waited for the Claw to descend.

So why hold that information back? And why this high a price over something I didn't need? It doesn't make sense. I'm going to have some questions for the Bone Reader when we bring him Hugh.

The frustrating and tempting dragon clears his throat, walking toward one of the carved entrances.

"I'll just grab some snacks, shall I? Let you all get on with your reading." He slips out of the room, then sticks his head back through the opening. "No writing in the books, and no tearing out pages!" he reminds everyone, real worry sliding off him.

I shake my head. If I were a softer Were, I'd find the way he cherishes these books endearing. Might be in danger of falling for the type of male who protects pixies. The type of male who has the power to decimate others, and doesn't.

I frown. All that ability, and what's he doing with it? If Nahum wanted, he could wipe out the Claw or the Magikai himself. For no higher price than some temporary discomfort. I begin to follow the dragon, taking a few steps toward where he exited.

"Never! We have a slight hiccup in the plans over here."

I turn to see Hugh, bent over our Were text. His red eyes flit back and forth as he looks at the pages. He flips through them at a rapid pace, nodding to himself as he gets to the end of the book.

"Yes, a definite problem," he confirms, more to himself than us.

I join him at the table, as do the witches. Staring down at the page.

"You're going to have to help a lady out here, vampire. I don't have the slightest clue what I'm looking at." I stare down at the dizzying letters until my vision doubles, as if that's going to make it any clearer.

Hugh sighs.

"*That* is our problem. Because neither do I. This writing is Euskera."

I wait a few moments, but it seems Hugh has nothing to add.

"And this is a problem because? It's not one of the many languages you speak?" I press. "I know it's not any I'm familiar with, and I speak five. Although I've been a bit negligent in using any of them lately."

"Euskera has an isolated language family," Hugh tries.

I just blink at him.

"It's not connected to another language. French and Spanish, for instance, are both Romance languages. If we knew at least one of them we'd have a starting point in the other. It's not like that for Euskera. Even with my skills, I can't read this. And there's very few on the planet who can." Hugh's shoulders slump, eyes dimming. True disappointment slaps me. He really wanted this.

"So we're well and completely screwed, then? Is that it? Because that can't be it. I refuse!" I stomp a foot on the stone floor.

"Never, it's ok—" Aggie reaches for my arm, but I pull it away.

"No! I will not accept this. We didn't come this far to get thwarted by a hardback. I didn't go back to the Isle for this. And I am not going to lie down and die over a translation issue. I'm not letting the Claw win." My lower lip juts out, fitting for the hissy fit I've just thrown.

The witches have wide eyes, and Aggie's mouth has dropped open. Chrys just grins, giving me a slow clap.

"Yes! Now we get to it! Let it out! That's probably what you need. It's good for you."

Since when did I agree to give my mental health over to these young magicals?

Aggie, Chrys, and Ever, when she was here. All three of them have been chiding and pressing about me dealing with my past. As if it still bothers me. It'll bother me a heck of a lot less when Damien is gone.

"Muffins!" Nahum announces, setting a silver tray down on one of his tables. Away from any of the books, I notice. Can't imagine crumbs are any more welcome on the precious pages than pen marks.

"You know, for an indestructible dragon you're a lot softer than I'd expect," Chrys says, mouth full of muffin crumbs as she waves the pastry at him.

For once, someone else lets their words slip before I can.

"Having the power doesn't mean using it," Nahum responds. "Most magicals could become brutish and violent if they wanted. But what do we call it when they do? Evil. Corrupted. Vile. Sinist—"

"My job," I break in, striding forward and giving the male a small poke to the chest. "Be careful with your words. Not all of us who use brute force and violent methods are bad. Many times we're the ones taking care of those evil entities so the rest of humanity and the magical world can sleep at night."

Nahum holds his palms up, taking a step back.

"I didn't mean it like that. That's the path you've chosen, and it's fine."

"Fine?" I snarl, teeth going sharp.

"It's good, what you're doing for people. But what's wrong with my decision? By your logic, every magical that isn't a villain, who enjoys their life without tracking the bad individuals down, is equally guilty. As if our ability gives us an obligation."

"It does! Don't you get it?" I'm yelling, but Nahum just stands there. Calm in the face of my storm. The realization jabs at me, and my stomach rolls as tears prick the side of my eyes, threatening to spill.

"But it doesn't. Didn't you get here after helping to free an intuitive the Claw were tracking down? Did you insist to her that she had to become an enforcer? Or for that matter, the Magikai you work for: do you judge all those representatives, the ones who sit and delegate without ever setting foot or paw into the real fight?" He raises a brow.

"No, I didn't insist Ever fight. I discouraged her from becoming like me," I admit. Although I sure as the moon do judge the Magikai. After this mess with Damien, they're next on my list. I've given them a couple centuries of service, caught my marks every single time, and I'm owed a bit more information about my clandestine employers.

"Then you can't guilt me into throwing myself into a life of revenge, just because it worked for you. Now, I *am* more than happy to help the vampire with the book. I have a Spanish translation somewhere, if you'll give me a few moments." Nahum turns his back, shuffling toward his many stacks, Hugh trailing after him, peppering him with questions.

Turning back toward the table, I see Aggie staring at me and Chrys with her head down, studying the book. Pretending to, anyway. Their concern stabs at me.

"I need some air," I mutter, all but running from the cave.

After several false starts, I manage to find an exit out onto the rocky shoreline. The wind whips at me, throwing my hair in my face. I sputter, dragging strands back behind my ears. White-capped waves rise and crash around the island, throwing a spray of sea water onto the shore in the process. I'm drenched within minutes, but I don't go back inside just yet.

I wander the rocky beach, black stones poking at my bare feet. If Hugh manages to figure out that text, we can be on our way as soon as the waters calm. Perhaps sooner, if the witchlings can work out between them how to keep the boat steady. Maybe there's some moss on the island Chrys could suck dry for power. And Aggie, well, I'll have to ask the witchling how she gets strength for things other than stripping.

As I pass the spot where we landed, my legs start to shake. Memories of the nightmare Nahum put me in are clouding my mind.

Get ahold of yourself. You're a seasoned enforcer. A Were, for moon's sake.

I shake my head, soggy hair slapping my cheeks. I keep at it until I'm dizzy. Until the memories recede.

"Have you ever tried scream therapy?" Chrys steps out from behind one of the large rocks.

I frown at her.

"No. But clearly I snap at people often enough. My cursing and temper don't count?"

She chuckles.

"Not even a little. You should. I think it'd be good for you," she insists.

"Show everyone how angry I am?" I huff, wiping a stray strand back behind my ears. Chrys just shakes her head, spiral curls flinging droplets.

"Wrong. To let go of some of those negative emotions. And it's just for you. Look, I understand if you feel self-conscious giving it a try. Lots of people would."

My turn to laugh.

"Listen, witch. After four hundred years and change, I can guarantee you I've all but lost my ability to be embarrassed or concerned by what others think. Although I'm not sure how we do this. I just, yell?" I give a half-hearted attempt, the sound dropping dead at my feet, lost under the echoing waves.

Chrys slaps a hand over her face.

"You need more help than I thought. Here, let me demonstrate." She pushes past me, out to the edge of the shore.

I scoff, crossing sopping arms over my chest.

"And just what do you have to be angry about?"

"This weather is messing up my hair, for one. An oblivious historian who can't take a flirtatious hint? This back-breaking adventure being the most fun I've had in ages because I'm typically cooped up around my coven full of family members who don't appreciate anything that isn't a potion or poison as 'real magic'? Take your pick."

Consider me chastised. Chrys turns back toward the sea. Her hands ball into fists at her sides, and she leans forward. A scream rips from her. Several seconds of eardrum-shattering sound. Once she stops, she walks back over to me, dusting her hands off with a smile.

"There, I feel so much better." And I can confirm she does; she's exuding contentment instead of pent-up resentment. "Your turn."

In spite of my words before, I do feel a bit silly. Who yells at nothing? I step up to where Chrys was on the shore, watching the cascade of waves. High enough to bury you in one fell swoop. Thrown down to the depths.

That thought does it. I'm swept back through memories I'd rather forget, from their end to their beginning. Damien betraying me and taking over the Claw, the organization trying to hunt Ever and myself down. Making my way across the sea after burning the Isle's castle to ash. Boxing the Collector who had tormented me. Crying out for Damien like a pathetic, lovesick fool as he left me with the Collectors and walked away.

I scream, the sound ripping from somewhere deep. When I run out of air I suck in another lungful, and yell again, venting my frustrations to the grey sky. Droplets of water fall on my face, in my mouth. My teeth are sharp, but I hold back the rest of the change, for once. As I start a third scream, something shatters within, and I drop on my knees into the pebbled sand. Once I'm done, I blink up at the sky, unable to tell whether the water streaming down my face is from the clouds above or the turmoil within.

But I do feel better. Less tense. A hand grabs my shoulder.

"See? It helps, right?" Self-assurance and empathy mingle together, spiraling off Chrys. I wipe the back of my hand across my face.

"Yeah. I guess so. You, Ever, Aggie. You three are going to soften me up if you aren't careful."

The witch withdraws her hand from my shoulder.

"I'm not trying to be your sister. Aggie may have wanted to fill a void from the lack of her own connections in her coven. I'm not like that. I've got enough relatives to deal with. But, I really would like having you as a friend. If that works for you?" She holds an arm back out, and when I give her mine she pulls. I press my knees into the sand, wiping off pebbles as I stand up.

"That may be the only deal I've made recently that I don't regret," I mutter.

She thumps me on the back.

"You did pretty good for your first time practicing a primal scream."

"Yeah?" I tilt my head her direction.

"Yeah. Not bad at all for an old, bag-of-bones wolf." She smirks.

"I'm not a wolf! And I'm not that old! I stopped aging sometime in my late twenties." I insist.

Chrys just keeps grinning, sauntering back toward the cave.

I follow her, leaving my screams lost in the sea.

15

Always Falling For the Impossible Option

"It clearly indicates that she'll have to use her claws." Nahum's voice reaches me through the echoing tunnels of the caves as Chrys and I make our way back to the library.

"It does not, you ridiculous reptile!" Hugh retorts.

"Woah." Chrys turns toward me in the dark hall, eyes wide and violet gaze flickering. "This may be the most passionate statement I've ever heard from that emotionally withdrawn vamp."

"Say what you will, but your insults are only undermining your perspective! They don't bother me in the least," Nahum insists as we enter.

Liar.

Annoyance is running off the dragon like droplets of rain.

"You're not the one who has to go through this process, I do!" Hugh insists, reaching down and swiping the large book off the table. He clutches it toward himself. Piles of parchment and paper with Spanish, English, and German scrawls litter the table beneath. "So, thank you very much for the book, we'll take it from here."

Nahum's nostrils flare, his form fully dragon as he watches the vampire try to walk off with a part of his hoard. The dragon stalks toward Hugh, wings out and expression cold. It's quite possible my vampireling has just punched well above his weight. Aggie sidles over to where we're watching from the entrance, out of the way if a fight breaks out.

Nahum stops inches from the vamp, towering over him. Rather than swipe at him, he takes several deep breaths.

"You're right. I'm not turning myself into a Were. And from everything we've seen so far, the process promises to be excruciating.

And *that* is a sensation I know plenty about. You might also note that I'm allowing you this book in deference to Never's request. She's the one I owe for releasing me from the Isle, and I take that seriously. Do not think that just because I'm not the one being turned I'm not treating this translation with the respect it deserves." Nahum slaps his tail against the stone, giving a swift nod that accentuates the horns coming off his scaly head.

"I'm not sure whether to be horrified for Hugh, or touched that the dragon is showing me all the appreciation I deserve for destroying that blasted Isle," I mutter out the side of my mouth to the girls.

"I vote touched," Aggie offers.

Chrys snickers.

"Yeah, Never, I'd go for *touched* as well, if I were you. And I'm sure that dragon would be more than happy with your decision." She devolves into a fit of giggles.

"You two are impossible!" Aggie hisses, but the side of her lip curves up in a smile. We're rubbing off on the witchling.

Across the room, Hugh and Nahum are shaking hands.

"You can come in now. All settled in here," Hugh calls as the two make their way back to one of the tables, opening the book back up.

"What's all this I hear about *excruciating*? Am I going to have to kill you after all, then, Hugh?" I joke as I stride into the room.

"Thankfully not, Lady Never. Although I must admit, the process is rather daunting. What we've learned of it thus far, anyway. I think another day or two of checking our interpretation against the various translations and we ought to have it." The vamp picks up papers from the table in each hand, glancing between them and the large book he's laid out.

"Want any help? My Spanish and German are rusty at best, but I—"

Hugh waves his hands at me.

"No, no, that won't be necessary, thank you though."

"Hugh," I slide his name, "Why so quick to turn me away? Afraid my language skills aren't up to snuff?"

"No, it's not that. We've got this handled." He's hedging. The vamp is hiding something, I'd bet serious money. And I'd win, because, of course, intuition. Still, there's nothing dark or devious about the vampire. I let it slide. After all, magic is a tricky thing. I don't want to mess up the translation, any more than Hugh does. Then I'll be stuck with an unpaid debt to the Bone Reader.

I spend the rest of the day doing something I dislike more than I can say. Feeling directionless. I make use of Nahum's cave kitchen to whip up some lattes for the girls. At one point, Aggie convinces the pixies to help us learn the layout of the tunnels better by playing a game of hide and seek. Spoiler alert, it ends with the pixies finding all of us with ease, and then leading us into a series of twisting and dead-ended pathways rather than back to the main rooms of the cave. Pesky little things. Then it's off to bed and another night of tossing and turning.

A new day dawns. After breakfast, the males head back to the library, debating the various interpretations of different words. Mid-morning, the witches decide to go off together as well.

"I've got to pull power out of something if I want to be of any use to us once we leave the island," Chrys explains. "I'll head to the back shore and see what I can find. Moss, seaweed, some crustaceans or fish."

Aggie wrinkles her nose, lip curling.

"I need to build up some magical stores as well," she confesses.

"And just how is that done?" Light-magic witches are too infrequent for me to understand their pattern of behavior.

She sighs.

"Hard work. Intellectual or physical. Dark-magic witches drain the energy from living things. We drain it from ourselves. It's more cyclical. By giving away my mental and physical energy, I receive back magic. A transaction."

"So you're off to, what? Jog around the island while repeating multiplication tables to yourself?"

"Something like that."

With the two girls gone, I decide to entertain myself in the library. I make it several pages into one on Weres when I come across a chapter on mating ceremonies.

While similar in theory, private mating promises and official ceremonies hold a few key differences. A private ceremony is a promise for the future. An official ceremony begins that journey together. While seeing the official ceremony through connects Weres, often opening additional magical capabilities, a private ceremony can stunt them. Mated individuals may be able to sense when the other is in danger, glean thoughts from their beloved, or loan each other strength. Private mated, or half-mates, are at a disadvantage. While there will be a link between them that each can feel, the channel isn't opened. Therefore any other abilities may be strained until the official ceremony is completed.

I clench my hand around the cover, moving to throw the book down.

"Are you alright?" Nahum's smooth tone echoes across the library toward me, and I realize I'm growling.

I take a breath and place the book down on the table with care. I catch the admiration coming off the dragon, and I've no idea whether it's for me or the text. Either way, I feel my face heat under his gaze.

"Yes, I just need some time outside."

Stunt your abilities? Now they tell me.

Two centuries of not being able to read that damned male, and this is likely why. For all I know, Damien was well aware of the risks beforehand. Time for some more therapy.

After checking the beach to make sure the coast is clear, I walk onto a jagged outcropping that overlooks a steep drop into the waters below. Then I yell. Chrys was right; it's good for the soul. Unfortunately, it's also chilly and windy this close to the water. When I'm finished, I find myself coated in a gritty layer of sea spray. I give the beach a half-hearted loop. I spot the girls from a rocky outcropping above where they're standing. Chrys is in front of a giant pile of shells and seaweed, muttering something. Aggie's talking to herself while lunging in circles. Best to leave them to it.

Making my way back into the cave, instead of turning toward the males, I go down the hall to the springs Nahum showed me. A nice hot soak to wash off the seawater sounds perfect. When I get to the edge of the water, I can feel the heat coming off the surface, steam clouding the air. Before I step in, I pull my clothes off and lay them out in the tunnel. No sense shredding an outfit if I don't have to, and the items can dry off while I relax.

Wading into the pool, I slide my fingers over the surface of the water. The stuff's not so bad if you aren't being boxed into the sea. When I get to the deeper side, I flip on my back and kick around for a bit, staring at the stalactites above. After a while, making my way around the pool's perimeter, I discover a shelf of rock. It's the perfect height to sit on, back leaning against the rock with my head out of the water. I close my eyes, letting myself doze. I don't manage real sleep, but it's the most relaxation I've had in weeks.

"Mind if I join you?"

I open one eye as Nahum enters the chamber.

"'Your pool. Come on in."

My other eye slides open as Nahum pulls his shirt over his head. Moon help me. Those muscles are something.

Keep it in your pants, Never. You still haven't gotten rid of the last male you got entangled with.

I chide myself, forcing my eyes shut as Nahum unzips his jeans. I don't look again until I hear the soft splash of water, and scent him getting closer. When I open my eyes, he's waist-deep and headed my way. This soak seemed like a good idea before, but now I'm finding it a bit too warm.

I wipe a sheen of sweat from my brow.

"Is it hot in here or is it just me?"

Smooth, Never.

"It could be you." Nahum smiles, straight white teeth. He's human in appearance, with the exception of pointed canines and the set of wings folded behind him.

"Do you know," I start, "with those fangs you look a little bit like the vamp. You two work things out?"

He nods.

"I think we've got everything sorted through. I don't envy him, what he'll have to go through to become one of your kind, but it should work. You all can be on your way tomorrow if you'd like. The latest storm has settled, and the witches say they can handle the tides. Although, I must admit, I've rather gotten used to there being others here. Aside from the pixies, that is. I have to say I'll miss having you all around, not that I generally want people messing about in my library."

He's rambling, and beneath the certainty he feels about everything he's speaking, I sense saudade. Another rare feeling. True melancholy and nostalgia, missing something that you fear you may never come in contact with again. For having company? For the book we might not return? For me?

Time to test out a theory. I push off the wall, kicking toward him until my feet touch the bottom, then walking through the water. The top half of my body is exposed by the time I reach him, water dripping from my silvery hair and down my chest. I don't miss it when he glances down. Intuition aside, as a Were I can scent his interest.

"Priceless books, private pools, a personal chef. You certainly know how to tempt someone dragon." I wade closer.

"Funny, I could have said the same thing about you, wolf."

"Wolf!" I freeze when I see the glint in his purple eyes, and humor washes over me. He flashes a half-smile, one fang gleaming.

"Jokes, really?" I demand, but I'm smiling.

"I was curious whether your intuition was instantaneous, but more so whether I could get a rise out of you." Nahum admits, grin spreading.

"I'll show you getting a rise." I mutter, glancing down between us. He just laughs. Aggie would die if she could hear this shameless flirting.

"You weren't wrong before, about my failure to get involved," Nahum states, closing the remainder of the distance between us. "It's a change in perspective for me, but I'm considering it. I still maintain that magicals, or humans for that matter, should be able to just live. They don't all need to make a show of vigilantism."

"What a rousing endorsement," I murmur, my face so close to his that I can see the small flecks of gold in his purple eyes.

"That being said," he continues, "you may have been right about me. You *are* right. Dragons like their solitude, and that's what I told myself over and over after running from the Isle. I wasn't harming anyone, and that was the best I could do. But after speaking with Hugh about things—"

"Traitorous little blood-drinking tattletale," I interject.

He laughs.

"Perhaps. But he's rather fond of you. And between your ranting and his explanation, I've been won over. This business with the Claw, even the Magikai. I wasn't aware of any of it, because of how isolated

I've kept myself. That ends now. I want to settle some things, sort out the best way to keep my books and the pixies safe in my absence."

"But then?" I press when he pauses for a second. I reach out, my fingers brushing against his chest and resting there as he gazes down at me.

"Then I want to make a difference. I'll start with the Magikai. The way Hugh tells it, they're a bit shadier an organization than I thought. You were on the Isle. I think we can both appreciate the risks of having mysterious individuals with questionable morals running things."

"You're dangerous dragon." I don't mean his threat to the Magikai, either.

"I gather you don't use that phrase for many beings."

"None more so than myself." I admit.

"Yes, I could see you being rather dangerous indeed." Nahum reaches out and traces my cheek with one claw.

"You do know they're not just going to let you waltz into their headquarters. Which even *I* don't know the location of, by the way." I state as I bring the subject back around to our shared interest in the mysterious Magikai.

His lips curl up at the edges in a smile, and the delicious feel of conniving ripples over me.

"You might be surprised. One thing I did learn from the Collectors is greed. The need to acquire. A more polluted version of what dragons do with their hoards. All powerful magicals are at risk. I'm betting the Magikai are no exception. Who knows what a few choice texts could get me?"

I laugh at that, grinning back up at him.

"You're going to buy your way into their good graces." A small pang of regret hits me. "But you'd have to give up some of your books."

"Yes, but you've shown me that would be a small price to pay. As much as I hate revisiting bad memories, I already did it once to save myself. I can do it again, if it helps others."

At that selfless proclamation, I decide to throw my cards on the table.

"Dragon, one might think you were trying to seduce me with all this flattery and talk of joining the ranks of the moral but mad, such as myself."

His head dips down, lips hovering just above mine.

"Is it working?" he whispers.

A Were can only take so much, people.

I throw my arms around his neck, hauling him against me as our lips crash together. From the moment his mouth meets mine, I'm driven by hunger. Nahum reaches into the water, hands gripping my thighs and lifting my legs up to wrap around him. He wades further into the water, carrying me.

I break away for air, bringing my fingers up to what are surely bruised lips.

"You're not messing around, dragon. But if I can express some surprise ... this all seems a bit ..."—I search for the right word—"wild, for an upstanding librarian of a male."

He rolls his eyes, but a smile is still on his lips.

"I'm *old*, not old-fashioned."

He brings his face back down, but I put a finger over his lips.

"How old?" I ask, more to see if he'll answer than anything else. Just another piece of innocuous information magicals often keep to themselves.

He screws up his face.

"Eight, nine hundred years? I'd have to do the math to be sure. It's not something I dwell on," he admits.

"An old man," I accuse, giving his lips a playful tap with my finger. He just laughs, biting the tip of one.

"And you?"

"A lady never tells," I state, winking before I add, "Four hundred ... ish." Joy clouds over me, suffocating. He's so happy by my admission of that simple answer. Because I'm opening up.

He sets me on the underwater shelf I was resting on before.

"One thing that does make me old-fashioned. Before anything happens, I just want to make sure that you're all right with this?" He gestures between us.

"You're asking for my consent?" I question, a bit shocked to realize that all the other males I've been with, including Damien, have accepted kissing as equivalent to consent for all other things.

I reach for him, hooking my legs back around him.

"An enthusiastic yes," I state. He growls, capturing my mouth in his again as he backs us into the wall. A shadow falls over us, and I look up to see his purple-marked wings wrapped around us.

"Sorry, I can—"

"Keep the wings," I state, breathless after the kiss.

He smirks, dipping his head to bite at my neck. He braces himself against the stone with his wings, using his arms to lift me.

"Those do present some fun possibilities," I tease. His eyes light up, and I'm certain mine are going black as I feel my fur under my skin.

"I aim to please," he growls.

His wings hold us in place as he brings us together, and I trace claws down his back.

The rock wall shakes behind us with our movements, ripples forming on the water as pebbles fall from the ceiling. I cling to the dragon as we rock against one another, water sloshing around us. Being with him feels right, and for a moment I'm tempted to pull away. Right means feelings, and feelings mean caring. And caring means you can have the things you care *about* taken away. But the dragon feels too damned good to stop.

I look up at him. Nahum's eyes have gone as black as my own, but the gold flecks remain. Glinting lights in a deep pool. I let myself fall in and get lost.

16

Boat Ride of Shame

Nahum and I enter the kitchen, clothes on but still damp. The others are all seated, snacking on a charcuterie someone's put together.

"And just what were you two up to?" Chrys asks, voice sing-song.

"As if you didn't know," I toss out at her. "And as if *I* didn't know, that *you* know. Remember witch, I can read you like a book."

At her side, Aggie goes scarlet, her cheeks almost as dark red as her hair.

"That's ... I mean ... we're all staying here—"

"Just be glad you don't have enhanced hearing," I quip. If I'd brought Todd on this trip I'd be in for a lot more of an earful, since he would've gotten one, with his bear-shifter hearing.

"What about you, vamp? Going to slut-shame me?" I toss over to Hugh.

"A vampire does not *slut-shame* their lord or lady. And as you well know, I'm accustomed to witnessing all sorts of behavior in the manor. No judgment from me."

"Never, I didn't mean ... you can do what you want, of course. I just didn't realize you two were—"

"Don't sweat it, witchling. I didn't take it personally," I reassure Aggie, much to her relief. Thank goodness. It's so much easier being bombarded by positive emotions than negative ones.

"Who knew old folks could be so active." Chrys quips.

"We're not elderly! This isn't some sort of magical nursing home." I fume.

"My grandma, what large teeth you have." She chuckles while Hugh puts a hand over his own face as his laugher joins hers. Even Aggie can't hold back a giggle.

There are some more well-deserved jabs from Chrys and Hugh, along with some sniggering pixies. I'd say we take it pretty well. Myself, because I snark right back. Nahum, because he ignores every comment, but I can feel he's not any more apologetic for our actions than I am.

After even Chrys has run out of jokes about 'getting wet' in the hot springs, we head to bed. Ready to start the journey back to Sac early in the morning. I lie in my alcove, staring at the cave ceiling. Eager to head back to Sacramento. To settle things. This island is no tropical destination, and not my usual vacation setting, by any means. And yet, I'm dealing with the same preemptive nostalgia I felt coming from the dragon earlier.

"Mind if I steal away some more of your evening?" The shifter in question ducks into the small space, no wings this time. They'd fill this room. I kick my legs over the edge of the bed and sit up, patting the spot next to me.

"Help yourself."

He sits, running a hand across the back of his neck. Conflicted. The sensation hits me like rain droplets, souring my own mood.

"Listen." I may as well give him the out now, before he gets any further. "You seem like a genuinely decent shifter, and heart-stoppingly attractive to boot. But you don't have to worry about me. I'm not the type of gal who gets overly attached. When we leave, you're welcome to go back to your books, or your Magikai sleuthing. You don't need to be concerned that I—"

A hand slaps over my lips.

"Hrmph," I start, reaching up to shove him off, but he interlocks his fingers with mine instead, purple eyes vibrant.

"Listen, before you continue your tirade? Please? Only once." He holds up a finger. I grumble as he drops his hand, shooting him a disgruntled glare. But I keep my mouth shut. I *suppose*, maybe, it could be just a tiny bit possible, I could stand to hear other people's perspectives more often. Not that I'm sold on the idea.

He smiles, the impact as dazzling as ever.

"Thank you. What I was *going* to say, is that I don't want to go back to my books. Well, not *only* my books. I am intrigued by you. I find you interesting."

You could do worse, Never.

"You're unique. And you should know I hold those compliments in the highest esteem. The same qualities I cherish in my most prized books. Not that you're something to collect and shelve." Well, that saves me butting in. "What I'm trying to say is, I am interested in you. But I haven't ventured off this island for more than a few weeks at a time since I escaped the Isle. And even then only to obtain books, gather supplies, and maintain some old connections with the magicals who search out texts for me. This whole idea of getting involved, with you *or* a cause—it's new. I don't know what I can offer. Dragons, we're almost always loners. But, if we were to be, that is to say, if our plans overlap?"

He's twisting his hands, looking down at his lap.

"My sweet, sensitive dragon. Am I to understand that you are here to ask me to be your in-town booty call when you happen to stop by Sac?"

He waves his palms.

"That's not what I meant at all, I—"

I collapse into laughter, dropping my head on his lap, which silences him effectively enough.

"Let me quote someone wise I know." I wink at him. "I'm old, not old-fashioned. I get it. I've been an enforcer for long enough to know how hard it is to maintain a relationship while following a mission." I mean, I also never bothered to try. "And I'd be more than happy to show you the sights if you come to town."

He breathes a sigh of relief, my intuition working in my favor for once, as I feel his tension slip away.

"In that case." He pushes off the bed, moving toward the archway. As he leans to go through, he places a hand on the rock and turns back.

"But if you need any help. With this Claw, and this *Damien*, you can reach out." He walks back over and hands me a card with glimmering purple ink. When I set it down on the bed, the writing disappears. His phone number.

"Nahum!" I call after him. "You know, I was thinking, if you're available, I could start showing you some of those sights now?"

He grins before joining me in the bed and ensuring I lose another night of sleep.

"At least it's not sunny!" Hugh's demeanor is cheerful as we load up the boat, books placed beneath the captain's awning with great care. After all, they're merely on loan. And I don't care what sweet nothings Nahum may whisper; no dragon is going to accept having their hoard damaged.

"Yeah, just great," Chrys mutters, staring out from the cave entrance at the grey drizzle.

"Thank you!" Aggie flashes a dazzling grin at the pixies, three of whom are flitting toward her with a pink, polka-dot umbrella. She pops it open, scooting next to Chrys and covering them both as they head for the boat.

"Let me know how the process goes!" Nahum shouts up to Hugh, who's organizing our supplies on the boat. Hugh shoots him a thumbs-up. He's been antsy since they figured things out yesterday. And they're still both refusing to tell me about the process quite yet. I'm giving Hugh until we land in Sac, and then I'm going to stop asking for answers and start demanding.

We're out of excuses, and the other three have the boat ready.

"It's been a pleasure hosting you," Nahum states. Someone's going to have to tell me what finishing school he and Hugh attended. So much formality.

I stand in front of him, offering him a hand.

"Like you said, if you're ever in town."

Nahum grabs my hand, giving it a few shakes. As I move to let go, his grip tightens, pulling me back toward him. His mouth captures mine, hungry and demanding. He dips me, a hand around my back and raindrops coating my hair as we kiss.

I suck in a breath as he pulls away.

"Wow. Not bad, dragon, not bad at all."

What was that I said about formality? Maybe I'm rubbing off on him after all.

I'd much rather head back into the hot springs, but instead I join the others as we push off. The boat ride is smooth, other than the miserable rain, which the witches keep at bay. As soon as we're within cell range, I take care of flights. We bring the boat into Scotland, all the better to stay away from the Claw. At some point, I'll have to return when I'm not simultaneously running from and running down a Claw member. Scotland's nice any time of year. Such a shame.

I get us a bed and breakfast near Aberdeen. Our flight doesn't leave until "whose idea was it to schedule things this early?" o'clock tomorrow, so we've got some time to kill.

All the frowns and shivering caused by a damp and dank boat are erased by early afternoon. Let it not be said that Never doesn't know how to be charitable. When she has money burning a hole in her pocket and is riding a dragon-high.

"Do you *truly* think this was all necessary?" Hugh asks, head poking out from behind a pile of boxes.

"Yes!" Chrys and Aggie quip in unison, then fall into a fit of giggles. They've both got a week's worth of outfits, complete with shoes, somewhere in those boxes. Not that I didn't snag some items for myself as well. As for Hugh? A set of very expensive inks with quill and parchment. And a trip to a local bookstore. The way he tore through the shop, pulling tomes off shelves, would fool anyone into thinking he hadn't seen a library in decades. Still, it's the most his mood has lifted since he found out whatever he did regarding our Were-turning procedure.

We enter the bed and breakfast with our piles of parcels. It's a secluded and quiet, renovated house. Breakfast and dinner served in a downstairs dining area that houses a bar. Twinkle lights and artistic photos of distilleries line the walls. The entrance has a sitting room with a roaring fire, and the owner's cat. It puffs up as we come in, and while it lets the witches pet it, it hisses when I walk by. I'll never admit it out loud, but I know Weres smell too close to dogs for their taste.

Someone taps me on the shoulder, and I turn to find the woman from the wife-and-husband duo who run the place. She's got windswept, chin-length hair, and an apron thrown over her clothes.

"Glad I caught you! This arrived earlier today; we were told it was time-sensitive and of a very urgent nature." I take the envelope from her with a murmured thanks.

"You all head on up to the rooms, I'll meet you at dinner." I throw the instructions at the others, waiting for the sound of footsteps on the stairs to fade and doors to shut. I know without opening the envelope that I won't like the contents.

"D" is scrawled on the outside.

I'm tempted to throw it in the fire, but instead I rip it open and stand by the flames while I read.

Stop running and face me. We have things to settle.
Come alone.
You won't like the consequences if you ignore my request.

There's a location and time scrawled on the bottom, and I'm lucky that years as an enforcer have honed my ability to see and store details. I scrunch the paper into a ball and *do* end up tossing it on the fire, where it smokes, edges curling in as they blacken. Good riddance.

17

White Flags & Witch Hunts

I keep a poker face on through dinner. When the others suggest scotch around the fireplace, I duck out with an excuse about needing to buy a few more odds and ends in town. Being at Damien's beck and call rankles, but I'm not going to risk the others for my pride. His note leads me to a nature area—sandy beaches along a river that empties into the North Sea. Mostly it's flat and open, but I approach from the trees, silent. As I move, I put my fur on. A lone figure stands on the sands, and my nose tells me no one else is nearby. I creep forward, breaking into a run as I exit the trees. I launch myself at Damien's back, but he spins at the last moment, dodging me.

"Uh-uh," he chastises me, waving a white piece of fabric.

"Cowardly move," I accuse. His eyes go dark, the hand clutched around the fabric growing claws.

"Hardly. A *smart* move, given how unreasonable you've insisted on being lately. You know the rules. A white-flag meeting. I didn't bring anyone, and I can smell you didn't, either. Conditions have been met. You can't harm me, or I have someone on my side ready to go tattle on you to the Magikai."

"Fat lot of good that would do, considering you're all criminals." I snap my fangs at him, but don't move any closer, leaving a good several feet of space between us.

"You'd think so, wouldn't you? But as far as the Magikai are concerned, I still work for them, and I'm keeping a potentially dangerous organization in line while maintaining a very precarious undercover position."

I pace, sand shifting under clawed feet. They're fools if they believe that. But I have no way to prove or disprove what he's said, thanks to my ability amounting to squat in his presence. I cast several glances at the offensive white flag. It would almost be worth it to shred the whole thing, along with Damien's face. But breaking a white-flag truce doesn't just put my own head on a block. It condemns anyone on the offending side.

"Fine. Have it your way, then." I fold furred arms across my chest, tail swishing against the sands. When he doesn't speak, I let the fur fall away, putting on my skin in a show of good faith. "Let's get this farce of a conversation over with. I have things to do. Mind telling me how you tracked us down so fast?"

"Easy. You went into the North Sea. I confess we lost you after that, but it was simple enough to keep eyes along all potential landing spots from here to Norway. You had to show yourselves eventually, and I determined we'd be ready when you did."

I flash him my teeth. "Impressive. Not sure how you managed it."

"The Claw has eyes everywhere. All sorts of resources. And those will only grow if they topple the Magikai." He folds the white material, stuffing it into a jeans pocket with a smirk.

"And just when do you plan on getting rid of them? If you're not careful, this little pretend role you've got going on with the Claw is going to become real."

"Would that be such a bad thing?" he demands.

I pause, turning on my heel to stare him down. The whites of his eyes are showing again, a feral edge to his stare.

"What? Are you serious? Don't tell me, after all this time trying to convince me we're on the same side, you're going to start spouting that Jeweled Claw nonsense."

I go right back to pacing as he glares.

"No, not the same thing. Ekaitz was violent and short-fused. I'm not suggesting we just let magicals wipe out the humans carte blanche. I'm only suggesting it *does* make sense, not having to hide from them. I mean, who's the weaker species here? Us or them?"

"I cannot believe what I'm hearing. You're delusional, Damien. I don't know what's gotten into you. I've found you insufferable since the moment you left me in those woods. After all these years, I can only think of two possible explanations. Either you're evil, or you're an idiot for falling for the Collectors' tricks. Now I guess I know it's both. Because you'd have to be both to want such a thing, and then to think it would work. Go pound sand, you deluded jerk."

He slams his fists on the ground. Pound sand indeed. His teeth show, and a growl ripples across the top of his muzzle.

"I'm suggesting this for us! Do you think I'm out to get anyone? I'm not. But consider things from my perspective. If I could have shown myself, finding you would have been a hell of a lot easier."

"Ah yes, you could have torn through towns as the big, bad wolf. Demanding they hand me over like a virgin sacrifice." I flutter my eyelashes at him, holding interlocked hands in front of myself. Then I twist my features into a scowl. "Grow up."

He snarls, spittle flying in flecks and a few landing on my cheek. I glare, wiping them with the back of my hand.

"You have no idea the effort I put in! And you were there, hiding among the enforcers the whole time. I mean, think of all I did for you! I spread rumors about Weres going extinct; encouraged all the remaining European packs not to settle in the USA. I spewed so many falsehoods over the decades that I've probably damned myself three times over. But I did it for you! I slowed the immigration of other Weres to a trickle, knowing you'd stick out all the more if you were one of the only ones. I had no idea the one circle you were throwing your identity about in was under the Magikai. If they hadn't kept me blocked out of all their other business, stuck infiltrating the Claw, I could have—"

"You. Insufferable. I mean. I can't!" I stomp my foot, take a deep breath, and blow out so hard my cheeks puff. If steam really could blow out people's ears like in those old cartoons, it would be funneling from mine. "All these years! I thought we were dying off. I have been packless, friendless, and alone. And now you're telling me that, not only did you know the truth, but you're the mastermind behind cutting me off? I should throttle you!"

I lunge forward, arms out and clawed fingers curling. Only the threat of the white flag stops me.

"It would have worked!" he insists. "And our numbers are dwindling, but they're much higher outside the USA thanks to me. If I'd have found you sooner, I could have explained. We wouldn't be in this mess, this endless agony where you refuse to come back to me. Refuse to take your place at my side."

"At your feet, you mean. That's what you'd like to see," I accuse, my anger burning hot like a real thing. All I need is another spark to light this whole thing on fire.

"It's the humans who belong below us. And other magicals. I know you don't want to hear this, but I've thought it out. Where Ekaitz went wrong is who he was recruiting: the fringes and dregs of the magical society. The ones who wanted to dip their muzzles into violence. That's not where I've been pulling my newest members. I'm trying to gather unique and powerful beings. Ones who could actually help us not just to mindlessly fight, but set up and rule an organized system. One where different species are utilized based on their worth and skill. A fair system. And one where I could have you."

Everything blurs. My head and the rest of me is trembling violently with contained fury. I keep my teeth clenched shut, afraid that if I open my mouth wide enough, a scream will escape. After a few breaths, I manage to speak.

"You sound just like the Collectors."

I lunge for him again, but my anger is making me sloppy. He latches onto my arm, just above my wrist. Holding me in a vise grip with his furred fingers, claws skating across my skin without breaking it.

"It's not the same thing. I love you," he insists, nuzzling the side of my face. I push down the urge to don my fur, well aware that if I do, I'll tear him open.

He changes to his skin to match me, and shoves his tongue into my mouth, aggressive and unyielding. Of all the problems Damien and I have had, our physical relationship wasn't one of them, but this makes me want to gag. He paws at me, even with human hands, grabbing and clutching as I shove against him. I manage to get a knee bent up between us, kicking him in the gut. Surely the white-flag rules allow for me to defend myself from harassment? I extricate myself as he wheezes, clutching his stomach. He looks up at me, eyes watering.

"Why do you have to keep letting what happened to you on that Isle get in the way of what we could have? I would never treat you like them."

My mouth tastes bitter.

You just did.

I'm ready to run. To hell with this truce. Then I smell it. The witches. Aggie comes sprinting across the sands. She smiles, relief crashing into me in a wave.

"Here she is!" she yells over her shoulder. Red eyes appear from in between the trees; Chrys and Hugh come running out after the witchling. Aggie's expression twists into a sneer, and I look down to see Damien's hand around my wrist, squeezing.

Aggie lifts her hands, and in a second I can foresee the results. Her stripping him, the Magikai taking us all out over some stupid and archaic white flag etiquette that only helps the villains.

"No!" I yell.

Before the magic even leaves her fingertips, Aggie's thrown backwards as something collides with her gut. She sits up from the sand, wheezing. Over Damien's shoulder, a line of Claw members emerge from the dark. I still can't scent any of them.

"So, you found your own witch to help hide your despicable crew," I observe, shaking loose from Damien's hold.

"Your witch broke the truce," Damien accuses, but he smiles.

That bastard, he was depending on me breaking it. He wants an excuse to get rid of the others and haul me away.

"She never touched you. Your witch broke it by firing back. But I'm generous. Let's call it a tie and get on with tearing each other apart." I offer.

The witch behind him raises her arms as more and more Claw members join them along the sands. I'm not great at mental math, but I know when I'm outnumbered. I turn toward the others. Chrys is hauling a gasping Aggie to her feet.

"When I move, run," I instruct, willing to bet that Damien won't kill me right off. But I doubt he'll have any such compunctions about my friends.

As I turn back toward Damien, I let my fur out. The familiar and fantastic ache of crunching bones shivers down my spine. Damien scowls, retreating back behind his witch, the coward. I sprint toward them. I'm mere feet away when a shimmering purple wall crackles into place in front of me and slams into the sand between our two groups. I skid to a stop.

Damien glares at me from the other side.

"I don't understand! I did what you wanted. I got the Claw to stop chasing after that other intuitive you're so keen on helping. I saved her." Damien yells at the barrier between us.

I round on him. He's not putting Ever in jeopardy as well. After he's gone, my next mission is making sure she isn't brainwashed by the Magikai.

"No. *We* saved her. Aggie, Todd, Lynx, and me. Along with Nadia herself. I found a new family, and you found a den of criminals."

"You're not the only one who can mature, you know!" Damien seethes, muscles flexed and claws snapping against one another.

"Yes, but it seems I'm the only who has!" I sass back at him. Two points to me for a snappy comeback. It always drives me crazy when I don't think of these things until later.

"Why is it so difficult for you to accept that I'm on your side? Why?" Damien demands, his voice taking on a pleading tone. I'm not so easily fooled. Not anymore.

"Gee, I dunno." I place a claw under my chin, tapping as I tilt my head. "Maybe because you've lied to me at every turn, and you're chasing me across the literal world? Maybe that!"

Okay, I may have gone from mature Were to sarcastic teen in one comment, but I'm right, aren't I?

He growls, stamping a paw and swiping his claws at the barrier. The purple magic sizzles as he lets out a howl.

"Oh yes, there's that maturity you were telling me about," I drawl.

"I'm not trying to hurt you, Never, I'm just trying to catch you."

"I see. And as fun as that sounds, I'm afraid I'll have to decline." I stick my tongue out at him, a gesture that's a bit more difficult when you've got a muzzle.

He lets out another growl, this one deep and reverberating. He pounds his furred fists against the barrier, setting off sparks with each contact.

"Stubborn! Insufferable! Foolish female!"

"That's me, darling." I bat my eyes at him.

"When this barrier comes down—"

"When it comes down, I am going to run at you with everything I have, given our truce is broken. We are going to finish this bloody and twisted thing between us once and for all. And Damien, darling, I don't plan to stop until you're finished breathing."

The Bone Reader may hold my debt, but I'm determined. I've waited nearly two hundred years, and I'm sick of being denied. Damien tries a few more times to call out to me, but I ignore it. There's nothing more to say. And yet, we manage to find words at every encounter, don't we? Bad relationships are like that, I suppose. Hashing and rehashing things that have already been said, all over the minute possibility of achieving a different outcome. But I already know the outcome for us.

"Never." I feel Aggie's apprehension as she tugs on my arm. "Don't you think we ought to go, now? While we've still got the barrier? We could get a head start on them."

I throw my head back, a barked laugh coming out.

"Please, witchling. We can take those numbers. There's four of us and maybe forty of them. I like those odds. Plus, we've got a stripper on our side. You'll have all those men naked and on the ground in no time flat." I attempt a wink, another thing that's tricky to do in fur.

"I don't think we have four of us. Never, look." I glance into the sand behind us. Hugh is in a crouch, red eyes blazing. He's holding what appears to be a near-unconscious Chrys, eyelids twitching.

When you're an intuitive, all emotions are sharpened, but sometimes we bury our own. At least that's been my experience. Not this time, though. Shame rolls over me, deep and piercing.

"Did the spell do that to her? How? This is her key," I state, grasping at an excuse to avoid my own guilt. Showing up here determined to defend them, and instead letting her sap her strength to keep us safe while I jaw on at my dumb ex half-mate.

Aggie shakes her head, her wine-red locks flicking out at the ends.

"It's like what she did with the ocean water. Before, she wove the water in with her key for defensive shields. That's tough, but an abundant element. This time, though? She combined her key with other magic. The power she has to work for. She hasn't had time on this trip to gather much to fuel her abilities. That means she pulled from whatever she's got stored up, and I'm betting she took too much. We need to get her somewhere safe to recuperate. Now."

I glance back and forth between Chrys, the witchling at my side who is exuding waves of concern, and the edge of the crackling, purple barrier. I can't read his emotions, of course, but I can just imagine how smug Damien's going to feel if I tuck tail and run. Again. I keep vowing to take him out, but what have I actually accomplished so far? A whole pile of nothing. Nada. Zip. Zero. It burns me to consider letting him go again.

"We need you, Never," Aggie insists, "but if you have to stay. I'll stay with you. We can cover Hugh while he takes Chrys to safety." The witchling plants her feet, turning toward the barrier with her palms raised, ready to start stripping.

I look down at her. Her lips are set in a firm line, and determination slaps me in the face. She'd really do it. She'd risk her friend's safety to stay and help me. Even though I can tell she thinks it's the wrong choice. Even though, given the numbers fanned out on Damien's side, we'd probably lose. I wouldn't be able to protect her *and* myself. Not if I'm focused on Damien. This witchling is something else. Not fearless, although some magicals are—they get an overinflated ego. Aggie, though? She's scared. She still doesn't always trust her powerful abilities. And she's choosing me anyway.

The whole reason I'm going after Damien is because he abandoned me when I needed him. Okay, okay, that *and* everything that happened after. I can't do that to my friends. I won't. I wrap a furred arm around Aggie's shoulder. She jumps, surprise obvious.

"Come on, witchling, it's about time we got out of here."

"Really?" She keeps her hands raised, looking back at the Claw members.

I nod. Aggie breaks out into a grin and goes running over to the others. When I reach them. I bend down to scoop Chrys up. Hugh hisses at me, elongated canines bared. I snap my head back.

"*Excuse me*? You did *not* just pull that move on me, vamp." I snap my teeth at him. "I'm only trying to help her. In my fur I can carry her the easiest. Now, let's get moving." Hugh's holding her head wrap, which has fallen loose at some point. Her white curls spring loose in every direction.

"My apologies, Lady Never. I don't know what came over me," Hugh states, worrying the headwrap in his hands. I roll my eyes. I think I've got a pretty good idea of what came over him, if he'd asked my opinion.

"Never!" Damien's pounding the barrier again. Idiot. He has to know that's not going to break it. For a Were who once told me he preferred my original name, he's used this one an awful lot. For once I manage to ignore him, willing myself not to look back.

"You need me!" More pompous, self-righteous crap. I'm not dignifying it with a response. At least that's what I tell myself as I bite my own tongue to avoid snapping back at him. "The Magikai aren't what you think! There's corruption, and it goes deeper than you know. You can't keep working for them! Everything I've done has been for the good of the magical community. For you! You have to believe that."

If I could read him, I'd be able to tell whether he was sincere. Then again, if he hadn't gotten me into this half-mated mess, I still *would* be able to read him. So whose fault is that? Not mine, thank you very much.

"They're dangerous, Never, even to someone like you. I don't want you to get hurt. Think of your friends. They're in jeopardy as well. I could help you."

I pause only a moment. He could be right. After all, I've already been suspicious of the Magikai. Hell's moon, I was suspicious of them right after I joined. In my experience, no secretive, all-powerful governing entity is without its share of bad apples.

I feel Aggie's hand on my arm again.

"Lady Never?" Hugh questions, fangs back to their typical pointed size.

I hear Aggie let out a sigh, and both she and Hugh have relief wafting from them as I continue walking.

"Hugh, do me a favor and book us a charter. I don't think we'll be waiting around for our original flight." He nods, whipping his cell from a pocket. I'm loath to pay for it, given I haven't taken a paying enforcer job since this whole business started, but after four hundred years and change, I've got money to burn.

Damien's yells fade into the background.

18

Sometimes You Wanna Go, Where You Can Pester Your Favorite Bartender

I plop my furry behind onto a barstool, a sigh escaping. Thanks to the time change, we left in the middle of the night and landed in Sacramento early this morning. The only thing Hugh will tell me about his turning is that we have to wait a few days for "the timing to be right." So here I am, at ten o'clock on a Tuesday, barging in on my favorite barkeep.

"Geez, Were, you look like hell. Better yet, you look like you've been all the way there and back."

"Thanks, Elios. You have such a way with compliments," I drawl.

The halo-haired bartender winks at me. I'd laugh if I weren't so exhausted. He's certainly the more humorous of the two of us today.

"Vodka neat. Just keep bringing them," I instruct.

Elios lets out a low whistle, ignoring my request as he leans against the bar and gives me an even deeper, scrutinizing once-over. I'd be offended if I couldn't feel the genuine concern that beats out all his other emotions. After a moment, he leans back again.

"No frou-frou cocktails? You sure you don't want me to throw in whipped cream and an umbrella just for the heck of it?" He grins, the expression false. I can feel that he's trying to draw me out.

I'm in no mood, but he does have a point.

"All right, you've won me over, barkeep. Fancy whipped cream drinks for everyone!" I shout, holding an arm in the air. From a booth in the corner I hear a groan.

"She's back all of two minutes and already ruining my Tuesday," Lynx grouches from where he sits, grinning at me.

Todd's on the other side of the booth, and maybe it's just the fact that I haven't seen him in a while, but boy is this bear tall. Even in human form. He pops Lynx in the back of the head.

"Free's free, feline," he chides, then turns toward me, holding a hand up by his mouth. "Thought you'd fallen off the face of the Earth, Were! You've been missing for weeks! Have a nice vacation?"

I didn't even hear the two enforcers slip in. Sometimes I forget they made a menacing pair well before teaming up with me. I swipe the frothy, whipped-cream topped beverage Elios sets on the bar without glancing back, instead focusing on Todd. I try to separate his emotions from the limited crowd around the rest of the bar. Trepidation.

I lift the glass toward him in a cheers-ing gesture.

"Sure was! I needed to get away from you lot for a while, and a secluded beach was just the spot. Not a single bear or cat in sight." I make a face as Lynx hisses. While the two of them bicker loudly I lean back against the bar, pretending to sip while speaking out the side of my mouth to Elios.

"Which one?" There's only one reason Todd would bother with all this cloak-and-dagger bull about a vacation. If it were the Claw, we'd be fighting. Got to be another enforcer or Magikai representative somewhere in the bar.

Elios leans down with his ever-present dirty dish towel, swiping at an imagined stain on the bar top.

"Leopard shifter in the corner. He's got two warlocks flanking him."

I keep the smile plastered on my face.

"You've got a filthy mind, barkeep, but I like your style," I say loudly as I plant a kiss right on Elios's nose. He jumps back, genuinely shocked. Good. If the Magikai's spies notice anything it's just a flirtatious Were.

I take a long draw of the drink. The whipped cream lands on my lips and I lick it off, smacking. For a moment, all thoughts of being spied on flee my mind.

"Elios, I could kiss you again. What *is* this heavenly concoction?"

"A strawberries and cream cocktail, with more vodka in it than your requested neat drink, you insatiable beast. And I'm just now realizing my mistake. Tell me you won't be ordering this agonizingly difficult to make beverage regularly."

I nod my head up and down several times, and Elios throws his head in his hands with a groan.

"I really should know better by now," he mutters.

"Yep, you really should," I state, unapologetic as I make my way over to the boys. I put a telltale swing into my hips, leaning even further into fun-and-flirtatious Were. Nothing to see here, Magikai spies, just a lady hyped up after a relaxing vacation, here to have a good time with her friends. When I agreed to train Ever, I asked the head representative of the Magikai for a delayed start date. I felt his suspicion when he agreed, and I'm willing to bet he's been digging into what I'm up to in the meantime.

I down no less than three of the lip-smackingly good strawberry and cream concoctions, Elios's grumblings increasing with each order. After what seems like an acceptable length of casual chit-chat, Todd recommends we head out.

"Maybe grab some food, what do you say?"

"I could be talked into a steak dinner for lunch, assuming you're buying," I respond, batting my eyelashes at the bear. I have to hand it to him; he's a good actor. He doesn't even flinch, let alone bust out laughing. Instead he hits me with a toothy smile, a dimple in one cheek.

Come to think of it, ladies, Todd's pretty swoon-worthy. Someone should get on that. But I digress.

"Always happy to treat a lady like yourself to dinner," he responds. Maybe not his best work, given how far from ladylike I am, but not everyone has my talent for fake flirting.

I scoot myself along the booth and drop the last empty cocktail glass back at the bar.

"I'm going to get that recipe out of you, barkeep. These are too good to only have when I'm here," I state loudly, leaning against the bartop and widening my eyes at Elios in a read-what-I'm-saying expression. I probably look like a loon, but he picks up on it.

"Secret recipe, but I suppose I could share it if it'll get you to stop hassling me," he says, almost shouting. He dips his head in close, pretending to whisper it in my ear. Truth be told, the drink is delicious. I *am* going to want this recipe. Although I'm probably going to be too lazy to make it and will insist on Elios doing it anyway.

"Call me if they follow us," I instruct, reaching across the bar to hug him and kissing each cheek.

"You're a saint, Elios!" I squeal, doing all I can to appear the dippy, delirious female.

He blushes and grumbles something along the lines of "insane Were" as I make my way out of the bar behind Todd and Lynx.

We head back to my house, which is still under Chrys's protective spell. She and the witchling chose to head on to Vegas with Hugh, with plans to return on whatever day his Were-turning paperwork indicated.

"You have anything to drink around here?" Lynx prowls the kitchen, opening my cabinets and leaving the doors ajar.

"Stand aside, kitty cat." I shove him with my hips, pulling out a glass canister. I pull the top off and smell, then frown. "Not as good as they would've been, after a few days, but still very drinkable," I pronounce as I begin grinding some local coffee beans.

"I meant the kind of drink you had at the bar," Lynx corrects, sliding under my arm.

"You have triplets at home. One would think you'd need all the caffeine you could get," I observe, my voice rising over the hum of the grinder.

"That's precisely why I don't need it. I'll be up at all hours, jittery. And I have to sneak sleep in between the three of them," he insists, pulling out a bottle of wine and uncorking it with a claw.

After I prepare coffee for Todd and myself, black for me and "just one sugar please" for the bear, we make our way to the living room. There's something unspeakably comforting about sinking into your own furniture after a trip away.

I fill the males in on everything while we sip. When it comes to the Isle, I feel their concern rising. This whole opening-up-to-people thing is *rough*. I can see why others avoid it. Still, as I share a bit of myself with the others, the weight of the Isle gets lighter and lighter. Maybe when this is all done, we can dig through their trauma and I can return the favor.

When it comes to Nahum, I *do* skim over certain details. I end with my confrontation with Damien on the beach and subsequent charter flight.

"And here I am," I gesture, arms spreading wide, "home sweet home. Soon enough, Hugh will divulge how to turn him. Once that's been done, the Bone Reader's been paid, even though I will technically have to take Hugh up there at some point. Even so, once he's a Were I'll be free to take care of Damien once and for all. The only issue is going to be how to draw him out. I'm afraid I may have hurt his ego a bit on the sands." I grin at the memory, hands wrapped around a warm, second cup of coffee. "Maybe I'll storm his compound in Oregon? That's where the Bone Reader said they're currently holed up. He should be back to the States any time now, fuming over his failure to tag and bag me like a hunted deer."

"I don't think we'll need to go as far as infiltrating some Oregon compound," Todd shares. "The Claw is here." He takes a sip of his coffee with a loud slurp.

"In Sacramento?"

Lynx nods, along with the bear.

"In my city?" They nod again.

I growl and kick a potted plant, which tips over, cracking the vase. Whoopsie.

"How did he even beat me back here? Of all the cheek. The audacity! To show up and threaten my home. This cannot stand!"

I'm pacing, coffee safe on a coaster. Who in all hells does Damien think he is? Showing up here and trying to oust me. The very nerve. I left my first home after my family was harmed. Then I found Damien. My second home would have been my life with him, which he ruined. Then I was trapped on the Isle. After that, I took the long way down to Sacramento. A city which at that point didn't even exist yet, in its present sense. It was pristine, inhabited by those who had more of a right to it than the settlers who showed up ever did.

I'm on a rabbit trail. A dangerous thing for a Were.

"He didn't beat you here, Never," Todd says, one hand reaching out to rest on my forearm. All solid-muscled reassurance. "The Claw agents showed up here soon after you left. They've been causing all kinds of trouble. It's been a full-time job for all the nearby enforcers, keeping their crimes under wraps. The Crown, however, followed you. Although I'm willing to bet this is where he'll return. He knows you're here."

"Maybe this is a good thing," Lynx urges. "This is our turf. We have a home team advantage here."

"What is this, a baseball game? Turf?" I demand, rounding him. He sighs.

"You really are insufferable. You know that, right? It's not a sport, and it's not a laughing matter. I don't take it lightly, either. After all, my mate and children live here too. Thanks for the matching triplet bassinets, by the way. I'm just as motivated to protect them as you are to protect your home."

He makes a good point.

"Send them to the Vegas vamps," I suggest. I sense his apprehension. "All right, so my coven's mansion isn't exactly a suburban mother's paradise, and typically not what I'd deem child-appropriate. Still, with Chrys's defensive spell and a crew of bloodthirsty vamps, it *is* secure. And Fiona did fine with them over the holidays," I insist.

"Fine. It actually isn't a bad idea," Lynx admits, giving in.

"Excellent!" Todd states, clapping his palms together.

"I don't suppose you have anyone you need to send off?" I question the bear.

Todd shakes his head.

"No, but the bears will want in on this. They don't involve themselves in the affairs of others very often. But you are already on the payroll, and I think they'll take a threat to their territory rather seriously."

I'd almost forgotten that I owe Todd's brother Rex, king of the bears for this region, use of my intuition. Just add it to my growing to-do list, I suppose.

"All right. So we've got me, you two, the witchlings, and a newly minted Were, if turning Hugh goes as planned. I'm not bringing in the vamps, since we're using them to guard the kittens. Who else can we pull in? Damien bringing hundreds of Claw members here is going to be hard for us to hold off alone."

Even as I'm saying it, I know what needs to be done. I just don't want to. I fight the urge to throw a toddler-worthy fit.

"Fine. *Fine*," I sigh, not that anyone is making demands. "I'll call the Magikai. Get them to send down some other enforcers. Least they can do, really, especially if they're already keeping tabs on me.

They can't afford to let the Claw win over Sacramento, any more than we can."

In theory, other enforcers should help, but they aren't all like the three of us. Near-rogue contract agents who aren't on the regular payroll, and not drinking the Kool-Aid. I'm sure whoever they send will be loyal to the representatives of the Magikai, and more than happy to report anything and everything they observe back to the nosy magicals.

"I hate to say it, but that's probably our best chance," Todd allows. "Maybe get Elios to loan out some of those bouncers of his. They were a help when we pretended to kidnap you and Ever."

I smile at the memory.

"Ah yes, one of my more brilliant plans. Yeah, sure, get them as well."

"Should we call the other Weres that you saw in Europe? Or the dragon?" Lynx asks.

I tap my chin. I'm tempted. Then I picture Damien and Nahum meeting on the battlefield. That's the *last* thing I need.

"No," I decide. "I'm not asking them to come all this way and leave their own homes vulnerable. They'll need to be prepared soon enough, if the Claw wins here."

"Then it's settled. The musketeers ride again!" Lynx announces, lifting his hand in the air like he's holding a sword. I roll my eyes at the feline.

It's not every day you host a battle royale in the middle of downtown. And I know just the way to do it. Once I've contacted the Magikai, all that will be left is for Damien to make his presence known.

19

Antagonistic & Anonymous

"You're asking quite a lot," Amun, head representative of the Magikai, says over the phone.

"Given what we're trying to accomplish here, I'd expect you to be a bit more generous," I respond, voice tight and clipped.

He doesn't snap, or growl, or yell. But it doesn't matter. Because his indignation slaps me in the face, even through the phone. Ah, the joys of long-distance intuition.

"From everything you've told us, and that we've been able to figure out, it seems we wouldn't be in this situation at all if it weren't for your poor track record with dating."

Ouch. Score one for Amun. Grumpy old lion. I take a deep breath, then another one.

This is a time for diplomacy, Never. Not a tantrum. You need his help.

I knew I should have napped before I called. More fool me.

"Be that as it may, if you could see your way clear to sparing some upper-level enforcers, it *would* go a long way toward getting the Jeweled Claw out of your mane once and for all."

I can feel that he's already made a decision, but he's also annoyed at me.

"Let's say I do send them. What's in it for me?"

"How about what I *just* said, feline!" Well, there's diplomacy out the window. "Look, you're pissed at me. I get that. I've never been under the Magikai's thumb, which gets under your skin. You roped my intuitive protégé into your loop, and I still got us an extension before that particular joy of an assignment starts. But this hasn't been a cake walk for me, either. As you so conveniently happen to be forgetting, my ex-mistake wasn't leading the Claw when they first showed themselves. A storm dragon was. And Damien's the one who killed him. Under your orders, I might add. At least that's what he told me. And if that's not true, then it seems *you lot* are the ones who can't keep your people in line. Not me. So I suggest you get it together and send us some reinforcements. Because if the humans of Sacramento witness this battle, your 'don't let the humans know' law is toast. Capiche?"

Man, it feels good to let off steam. I'm even able to smile as I feel the rising levels of rage coming through the phone. That doesn't mean I don't latch onto something else in the emotional mix. When I mentioned humans seeing things, he was worried, but with a strange thread of something else that *did* get buried under the anger. Interesting.

"We will send reinforcements, because it's clear that's the only way to contain this mess you've created. As soon as it's done and the Claw has been dealt with, I expect you to begin your work with the girl, whom I will deliver to you personally. No more delays, and no more excuses."

The phone slams down on his end. Is it possible they actually have a landline somewhere?

Looking forward to it, Amun. Something is fishy among the ranks of the Magikai, and you're giving me a perfect excuse to figure out what.

Originally I'd been insistent on training Ever my way. I'd planned to keep us as far away from Magikai headquarters as possible, as often as possible. Now, though? It seems I might have something to explore.

After my lovely "the Claw got here ahead of you" welcome-home party, and a snippy lion, I'm more than ready for that nap. I don't even look at the clock before I burrow under a blanket.

The sun isn't all the way up in the sky when I'm pulled from a deep but disturbed sleep. I shoot a glance over at my alarm clock—4 a.m. I groan as I twist the covers back over my head.

I dreamed of fighting Damien while the Isle burned in the background. It's no use. I shove the covers I just pulled up back off again. I'm sweating. As long as I'm awake, maybe I should grab a shower. I didn't bother when I got home, and now I'm regretting it.

Yeah, some cool water sounds like just the ticket. Then I can give this whole undisturbed sleep thing another go. I sit up, legs swinging over the edge of my bed, when my ears perk. Goosebumps arise on my arms. There's no sound or scent, and Chrys's defenses should hold, but it doesn't matter. Some sensation, primal and deep, tells me I have an uninvited guest.

I throw on an off-white, oversized t-shirt that trails down to my knees. Fur might be the smarter move, but on the off-chance it's some human burglar, I'll stick with my skin for now. I pad through the dark hall, past my kitchen and out the front door. As I step on the lawn I can see him, striding out from the lingering shadows as night fades away.

"You again," I snap at him. This particular visitor has darkened my doorstep once before. And I really do mean that. A magical being I can't place as any species I've ever encountered; he seems to control shadows. They spill from him, hanging in the air like fog, then fading away as he gets closer to me.

The male comes to a stop maybe a foot away, giving me a glance up and down. Whatever he sees doesn't spark any particular emotion. The very cheek! Here I've got my tousled hair and legs on display, and he doesn't even react. I flip my hair and put on a smirk.

"Did you get sent back on another errand, or are you just here to gawk at me?" I question.

The male has a flash of affrontedness before settling back to his cool and calm feelings. He's just a bit taller than me in my skin. As the shadow pulls inward, his features clear. Hair a deeper black than any shade I've seen before, eyes vibrant blue, in a striking contrast to his hair. When the shadows recede I notice the same thing I did last time he was here. His skin now is an ivory shade. But just before it settles on that color, it's a pale, icy blue.

I've not the faintest clue when he was born, turned, or made. That being said, his sharp cheekbones and the self-assured way he carries himself would help him very comfortably blend in with aristocrats of former ages. He's also got clothes: a well-tailored suit. Simple lines, expensive fabric. No telling whether it's a separate spell or if he's not something that loses the outfit when he shifts. On the slender slide, but athletic nonetheless. And dangerous. *That* detail is exactly the same as before.

Amused. Another similarity. He doesn't find me scary at all. Which pisses me off to no end.

"I'm here on behalf of the Bone Reader, yes. He wanted me to check in on your progress in regards to the new Were. Make sure you weren't tempted to double-cross him or delay. After all, you put off chasing after your ex for quite a few years. He's not willing to wait that long."

"He could damn well have told me that himself," I snap. "And I don't recall having a babysitter being part of my bargain with him. I would think that, given he's well aware his magic won't allow me to end Damien unless his side of the bargain is fulfilled, he'd trust I've been working on it."

He laughs, the sound echoic and disconcerting.

"Spice and sass. That's how he describes you. And he's not wrong. That being said, we would like a more detailed explanation of what progress has been made."

I frown at him, my nose twitching as I fight the urge to snarl.

"As a matter of fact, I just returned from the very trip that provided me the answer on how to turn a new Were. I've even found a willing candidate."

"So you have them?" The hold over his emotions breaks, eagerness spilling from him as he leans forward and looks behind me, as if I might be hiding the Were on the lawn.

I roll my eyes, putting a hand to my temple.

"He's not here! Moon's sake, someone's in a hurry. You can tell your employer that he's going to need to wait just a bit longer if he wants his Were. But soon. Is the Bone Reader still going to consider my end of the bargain fulfilled if the transition fails?"

Hugh volunteering himself was a relief. If something happens to him, I'd be even less willing to trick anyone else into attempting the process. This might be my one shot. And if that's not good enough for the Bone Reader, I may never be able to kill Damien.

"He'll consider the debt paid in full, so long as a genuine attempt was made in good faith," my unwanted visitor intones, staring down his nose at me.

"Well that's ... reasonable," I stutter. There's one burden lifted. "I wouldn't have thought the Bone Reader so considerate."

The visitor cocks his head, shining blue eyes locked on me. I get the feeling they can see more than just my physical features. Not intuition, exactly. But like calls to like, and it's as if my magic can tell he's got something else up his sleeve.

"You really wouldn't have expected this of him? Even though it should be clear that he holds you in high esteem?"

"A favorable opinion doesn't make him less of a businessman." And that's what he is. "He hasn't stayed successful for this long by letting people get out of payments."

The male nods, tapping his chin.

"True, but whether he considers something a payment or not falls within his purview. Now that we've got that squared away, there's also a piece of information I've been tasked with sharing. I don't suppose you could see your way to inviting me in?"

This gives me pause. He's already standing on the lawn, meaning that whatever he happens to be, he's fully capable of blowing straight through Chrysanthemum's defensive spell. That being said, maybe it doesn't let him get all the way into the house. Why else not just let himself in, lounge in my living room? There are a few magical species left who have odd magical constraints. Needing to be invited over the threshold is one of those. It's most commonly attached to vampires, although there are some additional details that make that statement not exactly true. Rakshasas are another, but this male doesn't smell or look like one. There's always the chance that he's in disguise, although I didn't feel any such deceit. Perhaps I can gather a little additional information.

I don't say anything, but I turn and stride back toward the house. When we get to the door, I don't open it. I just take a step to the side.

"Well, are you going in or not?" I ask, waiting.

"You *are* a clever one, aren't you?" His eyes gleam as he reaches for the doorknob. He twists it and pushes the door open, then lifts one leg high in the air, wobbling just a bit. He winks as he plants a foot on my entryway hardwood. "I do not need to be invited in because of any magical limitation. I just consider it the polite way to do things."

"And popping up on my lawn in the middle of the night falls under that umbrella?" I grumble at his back.

I step in, the small space of my entryway all of a sudden feeling claustrophobic as I stand chest to chest with the visitor. It's not that sensation of proximity awakening lust. That moment when you find yourself close to someone, and in that second before you kiss, there's this peak of tension and anticipation that tingles your whole body.

Yeah, that.

Well, this ain't it.

It's as if the visitor takes up more space than he should. His whole presence is at once ominous and overwhelming; maybe even awe-inspiring. But not exactly frightening. Too much. That's what it is. See, even an intuitive can struggle to name her feelings at times. This skill should come with an emotional dictionary.

I sidle out from our face-off and back my way into the kitchen, keeping an eye on him. I don't trust him enough to turn my back on him, and I damned sure don't want to insult him yet. Or *again* might be the more apt word.

"You're welcome to plant it in the living room if you like." I gesture toward the open space, sun just beginning to stream through the windows that make up the wall across from my kitchen counter. He nods and moves toward the area, head turning every which way as he takes in the interior of my home. He does a loop of the living room, seeming to consider all his options with care before perching at the edge of a couch cushion, back ramrod straight. Like a bird ready to take flight at a moment's notice.

"Coffee?" I ask, already scooping beans into a grinder for myself. After this early wake-up I am going to need *all* the caffeine.

"Oh, I really shouldn't," he begins, "then again, what could it hurt? Yes please, if you're already making some. Don't put yourself out on my account." This male is an anomaly, manners and clean-cut features housing something dangerous that lurks beneath the surface. I just can't seem to get my guard to drop around him, not that it would be wise to try.

"No trouble at all," I quip as I press the button on the grinder. "Pour-over or French press?" I ask when it stops.

"Whatever you're making for yourself." At least he's a guest who is thus far easy to please. When I had the girls here, I had to keep all sorts of snacks and goodies in the cupboards for the teens. I feel a physical pang in my chest. It's only been a few days, but I already miss Aggie. Even Chrys. And I've been missing Ever since she left for Colombia.

Soon enough, I tell myself.

I prepare two mugs of pour-over and bring the steaming coffee into the living room. I hand him a cerulean ceramic mug. He grabs it, and as he brings the cup to his lips I realize I've given him a mug that near-perfectly matches the shade of his eyes.

I take my own cup and sit with knees bent and feet tucked up under me on my plush, cream papasan chair. The witchling and Ever love this thing. Who knows what this magical being would make of those two.

He sips, and sips, and watches, and sips again. I drink some of my coffee, then tap the mug with my fingertips. After another moment, I decide I'm tired of waiting.

"You know, you could say something. That's what some of us call conversation," I snipe, holding my claws in so they don't damage one of my favorite mugs.

He just smiles, close-lipped, and then gives a slow blink.

"I was simply waiting for you to initiate the topic. It's only polite, as the guest."

I smack my mug down on the nearest end table and sit back in the chair, arms crossed.

"You're the one who wanted in. And while I don't mean to be an ungracious host,"—yes, I do—"you could get on with whatever you came to say. Some of us do have other things on our agenda, you realize."

Here he goes again, finding me humorous. Not offended, not cajoled in any way. The knowledge eats at me. His response makes me feel more like a toddler mid-tantrum than a grown-ass Were who ought to be able to scare off one pesky magical entity.

"I like you, Never," he states. At least he's starting with one of my favorite things. Compliments. "You amuse me. You're very intriguing."

"The Bone Reader feels similarly; hence why he's bothered to send someone after me," I guess.

"That he does. That he does," my visitor muses, nodding a few times with his eyes half closed.

I snap my fingers.

"Hey! Over here! The Were you're supposed to be talking to. Look, I'm not going to say I'd normally be more gracious a host than this, because I wouldn't. I don't know you. I don't trust you. That being said, I wasn't lying about having things to do. Rather important things, as a matter of fact."

"Ah, yes. As soon as you've cleared your end of the bargain with the Bone Reader you'll be free to pursue your vendetta against your ex half-mate." I growl at him. He holds one palm up in a conciliatory gesture, the other hand still wrapped firmly around his coffee mug's handle. "I meant no offense. It's just information from the Bone Reader. Although I would ask, are you sure you *want* to go after him, given your connection?"

His blue eyes glint, and I see stark white teeth and canines that come to an elegant point as he raises a lip and lifts the mug to his mouth once more.

"I have to," I confess, "which you already know if you're so well-informed. I made a magically binding vow after that lying cheat abandoned me to the Collectors and the Isle a couple centuries ago. If he's not dead by Samhain this year, I will be."

"You chose Halloween as your due date? How very spooky of you. Why?"

"It's the day I escaped the Isle." The words roll out before I so much as consider trying to hold them in. What would be the point? He knows enough of the situation already. This particular detail isn't one I'm hiding. Although it does cause a familiar image to flare in my mind. Flames, and me walking down a beach with my fur on. Bloodstained, furious, and desperate to escape the Isle and never look back.

"Is that why you're called *Never*?" he asks, and I realize I've said the last bit aloud. "Never look back and all that."

"My name isn't for you to know. Perhaps I chose it because I n*ever* answer stupid questions like that," I snark. "Why are you digging into my personal life?"

"I'm trying to help. You're already well aware that the Bone Reader has a number of skills. The obvious one, of interpreting skeletal information, of course. But aside from that. Over a considerable number of years, he's acquired a vast array of products, enchantments, spells, abilities. Some of his own and others brought as payment. So I'll ask again, do you really want this Damien dead? Because it's very possible the Bone Reader could get you out of it."

"He what?" I demand, leaping from the chair. "You could have led with that!" My claws come out, and I'm very glad not to have shredded my favorite piece of furniture.

For his part, Visitor, as I'm dubbing him until I get him a better name, stays seated. He sips his coffee, no outward or emotional stress. Just that moon-damned amusement at my expense.

"For a price, obviously. And I wasn't going to lead with it until I knew where we sat on the Were issue. But now that particular payment is almost out of the way, I've come to put this offer on the table instead."

"Why wouldn't he have simply offered me this deal in the first place? He knew I was after Damien!"

Visitor inclines his head.

"So he did. Do you mind providing a refill? The coffee is quite good."

I shake my head.

"Answer my questions first."

"Very well. He gave you the deal on hunting down Damien because he knew how much you wanted it. He knew you'd bargain for it without concern for the price, and he's been quite curious about whether new Weres can be created for some time. You've got your interest in names; he's got a vested interest in whether dwindling magical species might have a chance to make a comeback. Now that you've done it, or at least shown the process still exists, he's showing you some grace. By all means, keep hunting Damien if you want; I'm only providing another option. I can tell you the cost of getting you out of your contract would be less than that of another new Were. Just let me know what you want." He holds his empty mug out toward me, a grin on his face. I swipe it from him and march to the kitchen.

I take my time with the second round of coffee, to give myself time to think. I make myself another as well, though for once I'm not sure I need a single milligram more of caffeine. My mind's buzzing enough as it is. Even so, the warm cup in my hands is comforting as I carry it back to the living room.

"No. I don't want out of my original deal. I made a vow to myself. I intend to see it through. I need to." I pass him his mug.

He neither approves nor judges. Just resigns himself to the idea, as if I've made a decision no larger than choosing whether to put cream in my coffee. Perhaps, in his eyes, I haven't. After all, what does this random magical care about my morals and choices?

I'm well aware I probably look like the universe's largest procrastinator. You may be thinking, "Come on, Never, if you're supposed to be this big, bad Were, how come you haven't taken Damien out by now? Having second thoughts? Get on with it already!" And if you're not, don't worry. I've thought it plenty enough times for us.

It was different, though, when it was just my own fate on the line. I could afford to waffle a bit. But our last encounter in Scotland gave him a chance to admit it with his own words. The magical world, the safety of humans? Yes, I do care. But on a more personal note, my family. Who knows where his stupid hierarchical system would class a fatherly feline enforcer, a stripping witchling, or a vamp-turned-Were.

After a round of silence punctuated by a few more short attempts at conversation regarding inane topics such as the weather in Sac, and how the Bone Reader is faring, my guest gets up to leave.

"Thank you for the coffee," Visitor says, setting the empty cup on my kitchen counter.

He walks toward the front door, pausing as he reaches for the handle.

"Given your choice, I feel inclined to provide you with one other snippet. I think, all things considered, it wouldn't go against the Bone Reader's original deal with you. After all, he did promise to give you the information he gathered on Damien."

"Ah yes, like the fact that he was in Oregon. Which proved incredibly unhelpful, given that he didn't in fact stay there, and instead chased me halfway across the globe." I fold my arms, huffing out my nose.

"This may prove more useful. Damien's going a bit mad, I'm afraid. Unraveling rather quickly. I don't think you'll find him the same Were he was, even at your last encounter."

"Why?" I ask. I hate that I can't help the small splinter of concern. I'm planning to kill the guy, so it doesn't make any sense to worry over him. But I know Visitor's right. I saw it myself. Something is *wrong* with Damien. Something more than before.

"That detail is certainly *not* part of the bargain. But I'll give you this. He's bringing the Claw down here. And the rest of his reinforcements should arrive within days. On the evening of the full moon, if my calculations are quite correct. You've denied Damien what he's asked for, and in exchange he plans to deny you of the home you've built for yourself."

My claws rip out, muzzle growing and fur cascading down my back. Double damn. I almost made it through this meeting without shredding a good shirt.

"He can try," I snarl. "But he will *never* take what's mine. Never."

Visitor smiles, his skin tinged with blue at his neck. Shadows spill out of him.

"I don't doubt it. A fitting name indeed."

The shadows swallow him, and as they evaporate, the space where he stood is empty. Not even a scent of who was here.

20

Pizza Party or Pity Party

"And what's this bit mean?" I demand, staring at the indecipherable text Hugh has just handed me. He and the girls hit my house about an hour ago, after ensuring the vamps hadn't run my Vegas mansion into the ground.

"Says here the originating Were, or the one turning someone else, must attempt the turning in their home territory. And Lynx's mate and children got settled into the mansion just fine, if you were asking," Hugh responds.

I wave a hand.

"I trust you to handle things," I murmur, hit with surprise as the words ring true.

I go back to the document. Lucky Nahum and Hugh were able to make some sense of it, because staring at it is only giving me a headache.

"I did wonder, you don't think it could be referencing your original pack?" Hugh tilts his head as he awaits my response, eyes closer to raspberry red than crimson. He needs a drink, sooner rather than later. As if on cue, Chrys walks into the living room holding a stainless steel water bottle. She hands it over to the vampire, who takes a long sip. He sighs, licking a crimson drop from one fang. Relief wafts off of him toward me.

I scowl.

"Not one drop on that chair, vampire. Blood is more difficult to clean than popcorn crumbs."

"What'd I miss?" Chrys asks as she flops onto the couch. She's got on a loose, off-the-shoulder sweater, and blows a stray curl out of her eyes.

"We're trying to decide where Never's home is, based on how the Were-turning process works," Hugh informs her.

"The answer to that is simple. We stay in Sacramento," I state.

Hugh leans forward, tallying arguments on his fingers.

"But you've got a house here, another in Tahoe. You have the coven in Las Vegas. Then there's your pack's original territory, which is spread across Norway, Denmark, and even northern Germany. You said it yourself, you're still technically a Were princess. And, while I hate to bring it up, you also spent years on the Isle, so—"

"Doesn't matter. I've made a lot of mistakes in my centuries of life, but I'm right in this. Sacramento is my home. It's where I met my real family. It's the place I want to keep safe. It counts." I feel calm settle deep into my bones, and I know it's more than just my own certainty. The magic on that parchment is already at work, and like a living entity, I think it can sense me.

Hugh pauses for a moment but moves on.

"All right. Then we come to the next bit. Turning only works when done in the week leading up to a full moon. You get one seven-day window per month. Well, not technically; I suppose there's actually two full moons a month in some cases, but even so—"

"So it's like a period. Except instead of prepping tampons and aspirin, you're prepping to Were-out for the first time," Aggie quips.

Hugh's face pales more than normal, as Chrys guffaws.

"Aggie, you are priceless!" The other witch states. "Truly you are."

Aggie blushes.

"Well, it is," she murmurs.

"You're not wrong, witchling. If I know anything about magic, I'm willing to bet this turning process will also be uncomfortable." I turn my gaze back toward Hugh, who's perusing the parchment in between sips from his water bottle.

"Never is right," the vampire says. "Even as the volunteer for this, I've got to admit it looks rather excruciating. The recipient of the Were gene must, of course, be in the Were's territory with them. They've essentially got to be mauled by the Were, and then fed wolfsbane. Suggestions on how to improve the chances of someone living through the process include aiming for a blood moon or harvest moon, something more than just a regular full moon. Also, the more injuries, the better your chance of success. All very gruesome."

He grimaces, lip curling up over one red-stained fang. I punch an arm in the air.

"Three cheers for the worst-case scenario!" I yell. After all, I did warn him it would likely be something unfortunate. That's just how magic tends to work. Big prize, big cost. "Any other tidbits we should know, other than how we can adapt it for your vampy self?"

"The individual who becomes a Were must be a willing participant in the whole ordeal. So at least we got that part right from the get-go," Hugh states.

"No wonder there aren't many made Weres. Who in their right mind is going to submit to that kind of process just to become some furry monster? No offense, Never, you know I think you're great, but this whole plan sucks," Chrys grumps, frowning down at her sweater.

I swallow the snarl that's made it halfway up my throat. I'd take it a lot more personally if it weren't for the affection brimming from her when she stares over toward Hugh. People often forget you can't keep secrets around me. Still, though. *Monster?* Ouch.

"I'll let it slide this time, witch. Although I feel pressed to mention that Weres are gorgeous, yes furred, beings of immense immortal beauty." I toss my head back, shaking out my hair as I imagine my fur.

She just giggles, along with the witchling and Hugh.

"If you say so."

A thought makes its way into my mind.

Nahum thought you were beautiful.

I feel my traitorous heart skip a beat as I recall the dragon's smoldering purple gaze. Stupid internal organ. Stupid feelings. I've got to be absolutely addled to be drooling over a tome-guarding dragon with baggage. Baggage from the Isle, which I'm also carrying, I might add. I can't afford to get caught up in any romantic entanglements when I'm on a multi-century mission to eliminate the last relationship I took seriously. After all, Damien finds me beautiful as well. Doesn't mean he isn't dangerous.

"Never, Earth to Never!" Chrys yells, waving a hand in front of my face as Hugh clears his throat.

Oops.

"Don't mind me, I was just thinking about all the knowledge we got from that trip. That cave had some very interesting books."

"Books. Right." Chrys laughs. "Because it seemed to me like you were more interested in—"

"I know why the individual being turned has to be a willing participant," I interject. It's another answer that, as I speak it, I can feel is right. "Love. Trust. That's the only thing that would make someone submit to this process. I mean, yes, it's certainly possible someone just finds Weres wildly sexy, and who would blame them? Or they're just coveting the strength that comes along with it. But to let someone bring you to the brink of death and give you poison just to be turned? You'd need a strong motivator."

Hugh is frowning down at the parchment as though it's offended him somehow. For just a moment, his fists tighten on its edges. As the page begins to crinkle, I shoot out of the chair and snatch the translation from the vampire's hands, smoothing the edges.

"If you're not careful, you're going to land yourself in an endless nightmare of ruined books, vamp," I tease. "We have to return the book and its translations to the dragon, and I'm willing to bet he wants it unshredded."

"It won't work," Hugh states, sulking. He's all disappointment and bitterness. Like soot and ashes left on a cold hearth. "Lady Never, I am loyal to you. I respect you. But I don't, I can't. I mean—"

"You're not in love with me. It's fine, Hugh. I'm not going to decap you for it." When he lets out a sigh of relief I remember their last vampire lord. And his harem. I could see how what I said wasn't exactly a given.

"It's not that you aren't a very attractive female. You are. It's just—"

"Say no more," I cut him off before he gives himself away, "you can't handle the sheer level of magnificence that is *moi*. It's not your fault. Few can. And of course you find me attractive. I'm rather dashing." I wink, flashing my blue eyes at him.

"Um, Never. Isn't *dashing* a description for boys?" Aggie asks, voice quiet.

"I know what I'm about, witchling! *Dashing* I say!" I grab my shirt as if it's got lapels, striking a pose. "But I don't think that particular detail will be an issue. I'd guess love just has to be a motivator. A love that outweighs what you have to go through. Whether that's a love for the Were turning you, or someone else, or for power, or just loving the idea of changing your current form."

This comment gets the discussion back on track, after a few "awww"s and such from Aggie. Chrys volunteers the stash of wolfsbane that we'll need. Her family full of poisonous-keyed relatives comes in handy, especially since the parchment specifies it must be freshly harvested wolfsbane. The mauling part will be easy enough, although for once I'm not keen on the idea. Perhaps it's something to do with the fact that I embrace violence when the target deserves it. Try as I might, it's awfully hard to find something about Hugh annoying enough to make me want to slice him up. Still, I shall persevere.

"And when would you like this event to go down, Hugh my friend?" I enquire.

"I was thinking, tomorrow," he murmurs, twisting his water bottle around and around in his pale hands.

I blink.

"Come again? So soon?"

Once you turn Hugh, the last potential obstacle to facing Damien is gone, and you can finally, finally be free of it all.

At least that's what I tell myself. I'm beginning to realize that maybe Damien's not the only baggage I've been lugging around.

Chrys nods, along with the vamp's pronouncement.

"That works. I can have one of my cousins drive up with the wolfsbane tonight." She pulls out her phone, thumbs flying, and puts it back in her pocket in under a minute. "Arrangements done," she confirms.

I lunge for the remote as Hugh clears his throat. When I look over, he's got his hand raised up.

"What is this, a schoolroom? Speak, vampire!"

"Just one more thing. And I hesitate to bring it up, but, have you considered the potential implications of your being an intuitive?"

"That if I turn you, you might become one as well?" Of course I have; it's one of the first things I thought of. "While I admit I'm not thrilled about having you here to give me a taste of my own medicine all the time, it might be helpful to have another intuitive around *to keep this lot in line.*" I yell the last bit toward the door, where I can smell Lynx and Todd have just made their entrance.

"And if I can pose a last question to *you*, historian, did you and Nahum figure out what, if any, special arrangements need to be made, given your bloodsucking state?"

He tugs at the neckline of his shirt.

"It, uh, didn't come up. We couldn't find a single text in any language referencing whether an entity that isn't human even *can* be turned. But I thought ... you need to do this anyway, and I'm committed. Why not try?" He glances over toward Chrys.

For the life of me, I can't figure the two of them out. Other than her cheating ex being a vampire, I can't see why his species would matter. But even I know when to leave my nose out of things. Sometimes. Every now and then. In this one situation only, and I'll probably butt in sooner or later.

"If you're willing to roll the dice, so am I," I state.

Todd and Lynx join us, crowding onto the couches and carrying sodas. Still hard to believe that in under a year I've gone from movie nights for one to this crowd. Todd throws an arm over the couch, and I rest against it.

We're maybe thirty minutes into the first film, some action thing full of explosions that Todd chose, when the doorbell rings. Someone using the correct method for gaining entrance into my house—imagine that.

Todd stands up to walk toward the door.

"If that's not our pizza, you can tell whoever it is to go pound sand!" I yell from where I'm sprawled on the couch. Chrys giggles. Aggie does as well, but she hides it behind her hand.

"I can do that," Todd yells back from the doorway, "but I don't think a representative of the Magikai is going to take kindly to being told to get the heck off your porch when he's come all this way."

I kick my legs up and throw myself off the couch. As I hold a finger up to my lips, the girls go quiet. I still haven't told the Magikai about Aggie's particular key, although it may well have made it back to them through other means. And I haven't mentioned Chrys at all, or our small Were issue. Which will only *be* an issue if Hugh's first shift goes terribly, horribly wrong.

I make my way to the door, keeping my skin on. I'm mentally preparing to spout a greeting that's snappy but still falls within the confines of reasonably respectful when I see the effort is pointless.

"It's you," I say instead.

Representative Unkai inclines his head. As a raiju, he has a lot harder time hiding himself from humans than the rest of us. I believe what I've said before is weasel, wolf, sea serpent. I stand by that. He's got blue fur, or at least that's what it looks like. But when he flies, it flows around him like the fins of a fish. Wolf-shaped head, sea-serpent-esque horns. And a long body, like an Eastern dragon.

"How'd you manage to make it here without being spotted?" I question, stepping aside to let him in.

I'm not exactly friends with any of the Magikai's representatives. But if I had to pick, Unkai is the best of the options for who they could have sent. He starts weaving his long form through the doorway, his head reaching my kitchen before the end of his tail has cleared the entryway.

"I used cloud cover," he offers.

Duh, Never.

Unkai is the only raiju I've ever seen in person. He lives in the sky, making his home in the clouds. I imagine his biggest concern is not being spotted by a passing airplane.

"So, Amun sent you to keep an eye on me?" I question, offering the representative a cup of coffee. He scrunches up his nose, shaking his massive head.

"He sent me to make sure this entire affair is handled correctly," he says.

"Unkai," I respond, sipping the coffee I just offered him, "you know I can read you. Come on out and say it. You're being polite to the point of inaccuracy."

He sighs, shaking a shaggy head.

"Fine. I was trying to spare your feelings. Amun's furious at you. The way he sees it, you've been toeing the line with the Magikai since we recruited you. He's been willing to overlook it, given your impressive track record of hunting down rogue magicals; having no qualms with eliminating people."

"*Bad* people," I correct.

He dips his furred chin.

"Bad people. But dead nonetheless. Now, though. You've pushed too much, too quickly. Trying to keep the other intuitive Were away from us, refusing to train her without special concessions for time, and this business with Damien and the Claw. During this battle, if you don't do what the Magikai expects and eliminate the Claw and your half-mate, you'll be next on the chopping block."

Well, I did ask for honesty.

"And does he realize that would be a lot easier to do if he would send the army of enforcers I asked him for? I'm good, but I'd appreciate a little backup, for once."

I don't manage to rattle him; in fact, I can sense his agreement running deep, under all the bureaucratic nonsense that's piled over his true emotions.

"That's why I'm here. We have enforcers. Plenty of them, but Amun doesn't want them under your control. I've got them camping outside city limits at various spots. They're ready at my signal to descend on this city. We've got skilled fighters and plenty of warlocks and witches to block and conceal the areas with the fighting from prying human eyes. All we need now is you."

"Me?" I point toward my chest. "I thought Amun wanted me far away from all this mess."

"Just away from meddling with his own enforcers. I'm sure it will come as no surprise to you that he'd like you at the front of this fray. Handling the Crown yourself, given you're so intent on engaging with him anyway. He wants you to offer Damien a white-flag meeting. Use it to settle the when and where of this whole battle. Then we can salvage some level of decorum in how this all goes down."

I snort, letting him know just what I think of the idea of doing this with decorum. There is no respectable way to shed blood. But I need to take out Damien myself anyway, so in spite of my annoyance at the Magikai, I've got very little reason to argue.

"Fine." I hold out a hand for him to shake with his own furred one. "But I take out the Crown. And none of the individuals in my group get blamed or persecuted by the Magikai for anything that happens. *You* supply whatever magic is needed to conceal us, and if we get seen, then *you* are responsible. Not us."

He holds his furred paw inches from my hand for several moments, still in the air. I stare him down as I feel him roll through consideration, conflict, and acceptance.

"Deal," he states as we shake. "Now then, if that's all, I really must be getting back."

I step in front of the doorway.

"One more thing. I'll be the one to show up, but I want you all to reach out to the Claw with this white-flag invitation. This needs to be legitimate. Tell him to meet me the day after tomorrow." I name a local coffee shop. One that's smack dab in the center of downtown, where Damien will be less inclined to Were out.

Unkai agrees and excuses himself, front paws off the ground before he's left my porch as he soars into the clouds.

"Hugh," I say as I return to the couch, "I hope you meant what you said about being ready."

"As good as any time," he responds. "You can turn me tomorrow night, and by the full moon, in three days, we'll know whether it's worked or not."

Worry hits me from the others, the bulk of it coming from Chrys.

We're really going to do this.

21

Designated Bear Driver

"How do you want to do this, vampire?" I ask, staring hard at Hugh.

He taps his chin, in what I am fast learning is a signature move when he's deep in thought. And he's *always* busy musing over something.

"Drunk. If I can pick."

"Now *that* is a fantastic idea. Although you do realize the amount of alcohol you'd have to consume to get a vampire hammered is astronomical?" And I don't envy him the hangover. Hard to get us drunk, and be rewarded with a headache that would kill a human ten times over.

"I'm aware. But given that I'm going to allow myself to be mauled for the slight chance that I might become a magical who can stand sunny trips to the library, I think it's understandable. I don't suppose you could recommend a fine establishment that could cater to someone with a rather sensitive palate? I can't say I was ever loaded with cash as a human, but quite a few of the museum donors were rather generous. Our gift baskets tended to include very fine wines and liquors from around the world. Never? I don't think I like that devilish grin you've got on your face."

I steeple my fingers under my chin, widening my smile even further. One hand snaps out, my fingers wrapping around Hugh's wrist and tugging him along after me.

"I know just the place, my friend. To the bar!"

Hugh groans, placing his head in his hands once we've arrived at the Lusty Lute and I've planted him on one of the barstools. Elios cocks an eyebrow.

"Something wrong with him? Other than the fact that he's glued at the hip to my favorite unhinged Were? The one I should never have given my cell number to, since she's dragged me into my own bar well before opening?"

"Nothing a delicious cocktail can't fix, my good sir!" I quip as I sit my butt on a barstool alongside the woebegone vamp.

"Never, when I said I wanted a drink, I was rather thinking something more ..."—he shifts his eyes left and right and lowers his voice to a whisper—"classy than this establishment. You know?"

"I heard that!" Elios gripes from farther down the bar. I tap an ear. Just because he's cursed doesn't mean his hearing's gone out as well. As far as I know, it's mainly his appearance that's affected. Albeit in a big way. The satyr makes his way back over to us. "I'll have you know I carry a respectable selection of liquors of all kinds. You know, for you snootier lot." He snorts at us.

"My beloved Elios. I *knew* you secretly appreciated my love of complicated cocktails." I beckon him closer with a hand. I lean so close the hairs on the side of his balding head sway as I whisper into his ear. *This* is how to avoid being overheard by shifters.

"We've got a rather important and painful magical procedure coming up. Poor vamp's trying to go full-on Were. Hasn't been done before, as far as we can tell. And he's decided the best way to handle it is to get rip-roaringly drunk. You can help us with that, can't you?"

Elios pulls back, scrunching up his mouth as he stares at Hugh.

"Vampire, I'd advise against meddling with ancient magics. You might find you don't end up liking what you become. That being said, to each their own. You sure that, whatever you're about to go through, it's what you want?"

"Most definitely," Hugh states, sitting up straight and staring Elios down. The barkeep goes still, then inclines his head.

"All right, then. If you're sure. Now, I know I'm bringing the insane one a board of vibrantly colored cocktails. But for you, I'm thinking a nice-tasting board of overpriced scotch?" He tilts his head.

Hugh nods.

"The smokier the better, and overpriced is no object. Lady Never's picking up the tab." Hugh shoots me a smile as I scoff, but I can feel worry and apprehension seeping out of him. Not that I blame him. My claws are nothing to snort at. And I'm not going to be able to hold back if I want this to be successful.

"One ridiculously expensive round of scotches coming up. And did I get your order right, Never?"

"If you could make any of the cocktails smoke, spark or spit fire, I'd be much obliged," I counter, knowing he'll take it as a challenge.

Not five minutes later, we're sitting in front of a bar-full of beverages. Scotch on scotch on scotch for the vamp. Three cocktails planted in front of myself. As expected, one has a hazy fog hovering over it. Elios lights the second on fire, the top of the beverage igniting in blue flame that burns off. The third looks like someone lit a sparkler inside the liquid, with small mini explosions popping, one after another. I lean in close, but not near enough to get a spark in my eye. I speak to Elios over the rim of the drink.

"This one's new. What do you call it?"

"Magical Pop Rocks. See if that doesn't cure you of making these ridiculous requests," he says tersely, then grins before he moves off to the booths to take the order of a group of wolf shifters who have wandered in.

I take a sip—and jump back as I realize how aptly named the drink is. Small pops explode on my tongue. I chug down half of it in a go, then lick my lips.

"Elios, you madman! Fruity, sweet, and sour all at once? A literal explosion on your tongue? This is a dangerous beverage, my friend!" I yell across the bar. He cringes as the wolves laugh. "I'll have two more!"

A muttered statement about "unhinged," "insufferable," or some such reaches my ears. Next to me, Hugh gets to work. We've been in the bar a while, drinking in companionable silence, when a shadow falls over me.

"Why am I not surprised?"

I turn to see Todd behind me, arms crossed and a scowl on his face as he surveys the bar, chock-full of empty glasses. I've lost track of time, but I can see the sun blazing as the door closes.

"Todd, my ursine-inclined friend!" I hop off the stool and wrap my arms around him, squeezing. He grunts. "It's not what it looks like. And for once, I really mean that. The vast majority of these are for the vamp."

I sweep an arm out to where Hugh sits sipping what is his seventeenth double scotch, if I haven't lost count. His lead lolls in between swallows. He lifts a hand and waves at the bear.

"He smells like a drunk tank," Todd complains, nostrils flaring. "You could probably burn him from the inside out with an unlit match at this rate."

"Too true. But we're not going to burn him. I'm going to slice him up worse than a grater shredding cheese." I grin up at the bear.

"Well, that's ... graphic." Lynx steps out from behind his friend, a grimace plastered on his face.

"This from the male who cleans out his triplets' diapers on a daily basis," I quip, nudging Todd with my elbow. He just rolls his eyes and shakes his head.

"We'd better get going. You asked for open space, where you'd be undisturbed, right? Well, I convinced Rex to give you access to a portion of the woods free from any of the other bears," Todd states, walking around the back of us and shoving Hugh toward the door of the bar.

"Mighty generous of your brother bear." I squint up at Todd as we step outside and the sun hits my eyes. I shoot a stare over to Lynx, who is slathering vampscreen on Hugh. "Any chance this lovely gift is going to cost me something?"

"Nothing you don't already owe my brother."

"What was that?"

Todd lets out a long-suffering sigh. I know, because I can tell just how put-upon he feels.

"All I meant is, you promised him some intuiting, and he's ready to start collecting."

A formal meeting with Todd's stuffy, self-important twin is somewhere near the bottom of my "things I'll be in the mood to do after savagely attacking a friend" list, but he's right. I do owe the bear king. Fair is fair. And I need to be in good standing with them if they're going to help us against the Claw.

"All right," I allow, begrudging this turn of events.

We pile into Todd's truck, Hugh and Lynx sliding into the backseat.

"Ugh, he smells like a college party dorm the morning after." Lynx shoves at the vampire as Hugh teeters and leans against him.

"'S an oddly spebific, sepific, specific—"

"Specific," I offer the vamp. He snaps his fingers, grinning with his fangs out.

"Yes! That's the one! Oddly pacific smell to mention. And I resent that. I always maintain the highest level of hygienousness." He hiccups.

It takes us over an hour to make it to a reasonably secluded portion of the bears' territory. The downside of living in a large metropolitan area.

"We're lucky it was this quick. They've been doing more and more construction. Expanding subdivisions," Todd grumbles.

If we're not careful, we'll get crowded out. Integrate or get exterminated. Like an endangered species. But that's a problem for another time; today's issues are big enough. Todd pulls the truck off the main road and into the trees. He comes to a stop, and Lynx helps a very unsteady Hugh out of the back. As I exit the vehicle I see a figure step out from behind the trees. My claws flash out on instinct, but I shake them away when I see who it is.

"Welcome back, Never. I was beginning to think you might be reneging on your end of our deal," Rex calls out as a greeting. He's maybe an inch shorter than his brother, although the twins share the same deep brown skin and muscled form. Todd's eyes are a lighter shade, Rex's a darker brown.

A lot of their difference comes down to their attitudes. Rex's undercurrent of resentment rankles me. Nothing overt or overwhelming; just enough emotion for me to feel. Like the ticking of a clock in the background that won't stop. It's maddeningly continuous. I wonder if he's even aware of it at this point, or if he's acclimated to it.

"More than happy to see to my end of our little bargain," I state, offering the bear king my hand to shake.

"Surely, though, you don't intend to invoke your right to my intuitive skills just now? We are in the middle of something."

I bat my eyelashes, leaning in toward the king and looking up at him with my best attempt at doe eyes. Not that predators are generally good at imitating prey. He clears his throat.

"No. But immediately after. Todd and our healer can see to the vampire. We've cleared out a cave for him where he can stay until the full moon comes. You, however, can make your way back to me."

"And do you live in a cave as well?" I press, not certain whether or not the comment will push his buttons. It doesn't.

"We have a large one where we host the whole sleuth. But it's rarely used. We tend to enjoy our independence and our privacy. Be that as it may, I am more than pleased to host someone as infamous as yourself." Rex reaches toward my hand again, and I let him take it. He wraps his large fingers around my wrist, turning my hand palm-up and setting a key in it.

"My cabin. I'll expect you later tonight."

"Now listen here. If this is some sort of booty call, I can assure you the only call being made will be yours to emergency services, after I wipe the floor with your presumptuous ass."

The words tumble out of my mouth ... just before I realize that he doesn't have even the slightest bit of lust or lasciviousness wafting off of him. He truly is all business.

He sputters.

"I didn't mean. I wouldn't—"

I hold up a hand.

"Never mind. My bad, bear. Truce?"

He blows out a breath.

"Why do I feel that aligning with you is going to be more exhausting than it's worth?"

"Now he's got the idea!" Todd exclaims, slapping a hand on his brother's back. They really do know how to treat a gal, huh? I'd be offended if I weren't so thrilled at the idea of being hard to handle.

"Not to rush this moment, but I do believe I'm sobering up," Hugh states. He's still leaning against Lynx, but his speech is a lot steadier. We'd better get on with this. Moon's damned vampire metabolism.

"Follow me," Rex directs, turning to stride farther into the woods. We tramp after him for another few miles, easily covered by the five of us in a matter of minutes. We come to a reasonably open space, deep in the woods.

"You shouldn't be bothered here. Even so, I'd have my brother and Lynx keep an eye out, just in case the vampire's screams draw in any curious hikers or non-magical predators," Rex suggests.

"And you?" Todd questions.

"I'll be waiting for Never," he says. He drops to the ground as he begins to shift, and in a matter of moments a dark brown bear lumbers away from us.

Lynx gives me a salute before shifting as well, springing into the woods. He's got the best eyes of any magical I know, so at least we've got that going for us.

"And you? Are you going to leave us as well?" I ask Todd, finding my throat suddenly dry. He shakes his head as it grows shaggy, and I find myself staring up at a massive bear. If we do happen to see any hikers, they're likely to keel over of sheer fright. No actual bear is this large.

Unlike his twin, Todd has no issues about speaking in his furred form.

"I'll stay here and circle the perimeter of the clearing. That way I can step in quickly if ..."

"I lose control and accidentally murder the vamp?" He's not the only one who's thinking about it. We shifters may look human part of the time, but deep down we're anything but. I care about Hugh, but Weres do not tend to be mindlessly vicious. If I'm hesitant, I risk the process failing. If I'm too violent, he could die.

So, no pressure.

22

Turning

"Anything you need to say before we begin?" I ask, standing in front of Hugh.

He's an emotional mess, so many feelings vying for attention that it's enough to make me dizzy.

He shakes his head. "Let's just get on with this." Resignation and hope battle it out for the top spot.

I lunge forward, swiping out at him but retracting my claws at the last moment. It's still enough to throw him off balance as I make contact with his arm. He stumbles sideways with a grunt, then stares down at himself. No blood.

"You keep throwing punches like that, and we're going to be here all night."

I start to swallow down my annoyance but realize I can use it as fuel instead. I swipe out and slap him, claws dragging across his face. They leave a nasty line of scratches, but he just grins, wiping a hand across his cheek.

"That's more like it."

I kick out, connecting with his chest. Hugh flies back, landing on the ground with another grunt, but he just gets up and sprints back toward me, all vampire quickness. The process picks up speed. Now that we're going, I just want to get to the end of it. Hugh lashes out at me only once, hissing and slashing my forearm. I can't stop the snarl that erupts, but I don't take the blow personally. The rest of the time he just grits his teeth. I'm thankful at this moment that I'm only feeling his emotions and not his physical pain. I don't know how Nahum does it. Lucky for me, Hugh stays focused on his purpose for doing this. His determination and hope keep my senses clear.

The dark overhead deepens as we continue. I poke fun at the bloodsuckers, but they're tough to put down when you aren't willing to rip their heads off. The moon looms over us, high in the night sky, by the time Hugh starts to teeter. He's a tough little leech, I'll give him that.

"Never. I'm ready," he states, huffing even though he doesn't actually need air. He's bent over with his hands on his knees, but he straightens up. He locks eyes with me, one of his own appearing to be swollen shut. He's right. This has to end. I spin and level a kick right at his head. As it connects, he's thrown back. He stumbles once, and then he's down.

I move to step over him, make sure he's all right. Todd beats me to it, speedier in his bulky bear form than one might think. He stands in front of Hugh like a guardian, baring teeth at me. I raise my arms.

"It's all right, bear. I'm not going to hurt him." I know it's an ironic statement; sue me. Todd dips his muzzle and lets me close. Hugh's still alive, but unconscious. Which would be the best-case scenario but for one thing: he's still got to take the poison. I reach up toward my neck. In addition to the vial that the Bone Reader gave me, I added a pouch to hold the crushed wolfsbane from Chrys.

I shed my fur and put my skin back on, kneeling in the grass by Hugh. I tap him lightly on the cheek several times.

"Hey, vamp! You've got one more thing to do, and then you're welcome to sleep off this whole experience until the full moon is here."

After a moment he groans, and I take my opportunity. I grab his chin and pour the powdered wolfsbane into his mouth. His throat catches, and I press his jaw shut so he can't cough out the poison. He swallows once, then again.

"Is it gone?" I ask.

The sound he makes isn't exactly a yes, but I feel the faintest glimmer of affirmation. I let go of his face, and he slips back into unconsciousness. I look up at Todd.

"Do you know where the cave is that your brother set up for him?" Todd nods. "I don't suppose you'd deign to carry him on your back?" Todd will be much quicker as a bear, and I breathe a sigh of relief when he nods again. I know he could speak, but this moment feels heavy enough. I don't mind being left alone with my own words.

"I'll go back to your truck and take that to your brother's house," I tell him. Todd lifts a lip, showing a row of fangs. I get his gist. "I won't scratch your car, you grumpy thing," I assure him before lifting Hugh onto his shoulders. The bear takes off northeast, into the trees. I trudge back to the truck.

It's got to be late by the time I make it to the king's cabin in the woods. Doesn't seem to make a difference. I won't be needing the key; he's still sitting in a rocking chair out front. His brown eyes flash against Todd's headlights and I click them off as I stop the truck.

Bears are a bit of an oddity in the magical world. Not because they're predatory shifters; those are a dime a dozen. But, unlike many magical species, bears don't tend to covet wealth in the same way. The cabin in front of me is undoubtedly something made with his own hands, possibly with help from the other bears. It's sturdy but simple. The whole thing can't sleep more than two or three people.

"Nice place," I comment, tossing him his key.

He tilts his head as he catches it.

"You know, given I'm not intuitive, I can't tell if you're being sincere or not."

"Oh, I am. Just because I like the finer things available in the city doesn't mean I can't appreciate a remote getaway. One thing I *am* familiar with is the fine art of being alone."

After all, I practiced it long enough. I just went about it a different way. The bears keep physical distance between themselves and others. At least this group. I may have planted myself smack dab in the middle of what has become a bustling and crowded city, but it wasn't that way when I first arrived. I still keep a cabin in Tahoe, in the more remote area of the woods, if that even is such a thing, instead of nearer the shopping and tourists. Aside from that, though, I kept myself isolated just by refusing to let anyone in. Until the past year, when the witchling and Ever came tumbling into my life.

I follow him into the cabin, and my suspicions are confirmed. Wood accents. Simple appliances. Old-fashioned stove in the corner of the living space. Without asking for permission, I drop backwards onto a wood-framed couch. The cushions, thankfully, are plush and comfortable.

Rex snorts but doesn't comment on my poor manners. Good. I think I'd be too tired to care if he did. I push my luck, kicking my bare feet up on his coffee table as I lean back into the pillows, arms behind my head. Now I've got his attention.

"I'm going to assume you're already well aware of how annoying I find it that you're dirtying up my furniture with your dusty paws," Rex states, his words clipped.

"You got that right, bear king. Don't get me wrong, I appreciate the use of your forest and your help with the Claw back when they were hunting down my intuitive friend, but I've got to admit it does rankle me, being at someone's beck and call." Even so, I drop my feet back onto the carpet. No need to poke the bear, right?

"I'd remind you that you agreed to this deal, but it would be a waste of breath. You're many things, Never, but not unintelligent. In light of that, let's get straight to it."

I drop my arms and lean forward, resting my elbows on my knees as I glance around the room and sniff.

"Speaking of which, why are we the only two here? I expected that you'd have bears lined up for me to read. Or at the very least, a secret prisoner you needed me to have a go at."

I've hit on something. I can feel the confirmation.

"There is someone we're keeping here that I'd like your opinion on, but before we get to that, I'd like you to read me. My brother's given me the rundown on how your ability works, at least as far as he understands it. You're aware of the emotions of others, even when they're trying to keep them hidden from those around them."

"Correct, but he may have failed to pick up on one key limitation. If you're hiding a feeling from others, I'll get to the bottom of it well enough, but if you're lying to yourself ..." I shrug. "That's another matter. I've come into contact, for instance, with a number of sadistic and evil individuals. I'm sure it makes sense that as an enforcer it's a bit of an occupational hazard. Some of them are well aware that what they're doing is wrong. Some feel regret. But many don't. So, for instance, if I'm interrogating some shifter accused of kidnapping, I have to be very careful to ask the right questions. If I ask him if he took the individual, I can sniff out the truth well enough. But if I ask if he's done anything wrong, I might get a different answer. Because he might not see his actions as wrong, if he thinks he has a right to them."

Todd considers this for a moment, pacing around his small dining and kitchen area before coming to a stop behind a tiled countertop. I can, of course, feel the waves of emotion that come from him as he thinks over my response. Instead of commenting on them he turns his back on me to pull a small appliance out of an oak cabinet. He plugs it in before turning around. Now, if I was at odds with Rex, I'd take him turning his back on me as a massive insult. An indication he thinks I'm so weak that I'm not a threat. In this instance, though, in his own home, where we're working together, it's a show of trust. That I won't go for his back.

"Care for a cup of tea?" He tosses the question over his shoulder.

"I'm normally more of a coffee and cocktails gal myself, but sure, what do you have?"

He pulls out a glass cylinder with loose-leaf tea and starts preparing some cups. He takes his time pouring the water and waiting for the kettle to be ready. I smell floral and sharp scents.

"Rose mint, caffeine-free," he informs me as he passes over a mug. Mine is cream, with a brown handle and interior. On the front of the mug is an image of a standing bear hugging the state of California. His depicts a large black bear shadow next to a smaller cub, the words *Papa Bear* written in curly script.

"A bit on the nose, don't you think?" I toast him with my mug.

"A bit. But I enjoy them. It started as a joke when Todd gave me my first one years ago, and since then the others have supplied me with a full collection."

Color me surprised. He finds it endearing and humorous. A softer side of this stoic king. And a tinge of nostalgic melancholy. I take a long, slow sip. The rose flavor sits at the edges of my palate, not overpowering the sharp mint. Overall a very pleasant drink. I might even have to get some for myself. I set the mug down, even utilizing a cork coaster on the king's coffee table.

"All right, then, Rex. Now that we've established the limited, but still impressive, uses of my abilities, what do you need?"

"I need to know how I feel about my brother." He holds up a hand as I start to object. "I don't think you'll have any trouble. It's not that I'm lying to myself, but I don't think my mind's made up either way. There's just too many feelings to untangle. I can't do it myself. Open shows of emotion aren't exactly my forte."

Vulnerability. Not something I get the chance to feel often in my world. Magicals, even ones you'd consider friends, are always on guard. It's just how we are.

"Okay, let's get this done." I slap my hands together. Best to strike while the iron's hot. If he closes up emotionally, I won't be able to hold up my end of the deal. "Focus on your brother, in relation to some questions I'm going to ask you."

"You're not going to ask me *why* I want this information?"

I wave a hand.

"I'm curious, but I'd rather dig for the information. I think that'll work best. Now then, I want you to think of your brother in relation to your crown. You're twins, right? Surely there was some discussion as to who was going to rule this sleuth of bears. Think back to any questions you heard in that regard, any tense moments with Todd, or others."

He's quiet, but his emotions are telling as he goes back through his memories. The tension I asked him to look at is definitely there. He's likely got plenty of material to pull from. I wade through the rushing river of his emotions, trying to pull out the most frequent themes. Distress. Loyalty.

"All right, we're getting somewhere. Take all those memories, and through that lens, think of how your relationship with your brother is now. How do those things, and whatever happened, impact the two of you as you relate to each other's lives?"

One clear sensation smacks me in the nose. I swear, sometimes I really do want to go stumbling with the strength of the sensations that come rolling at me.

"Altschmerz. And by the feel of it, you've been carrying that around for a *long* time."

Rex blinks at me, and confusion falls over him like a waterfall.

"Look." I level a stare at him. "As long as I'm here, I may as well be accurate. I keep my intuition simple, for the most part. But you wanted the real, real. You, my good bear, are tired. Bone weary, deep down, from some issue that has gnawed and chewed at you for years. And as far as I can tell, it's impacting your day-to-day life. Clearly, it has to do with Todd. Now, only you know what that's about. Some brotherly spat, perhaps? Over your kingdom, over a female, over who got to go first at tic-tac-toe when you were toddlers, for all I can tell. But whatever the instigating event is, I'm sure you know it. Solve it.

For good. Only that will make the sensation go away. Then you can shed the altschmerz like an unwanted coat in summer."

He lets out a sigh so deep that it turns into a growl halfway through.

"Unhappy? Would you like to fill out a customer satisfaction survey?" I drawl, looking down at my nails. Spoiler alert, they're unpainted. No point, with what my claws get up to. And that's *one* expense I'm not paying for.

"Why do I get the idea that I wouldn't want to hear what you'd do with such a survey?"

I shoot Rex a wink.

"Now we're getting to know one another. You're right. It'd end up as kindling in that stove." I hook a thumb toward the clunky old thing that smells of ash and smoke.

"It seems solving my problem isn't going to be simple," he laments, staring at the ashes like they mean something more to him than they do to me.

"Most things worth having aren't simple," I remind him. Moon knows I've had to learn that lesson over, and over, and over again. I can be a bit stubborn when it involves coming to terms with realities I don't like. Just a bit.

"So, about that individual you'd like me to see," I venture after an awkward silence.

He shakes his head, then slurps up the last of his tea.

"It can wait. At least a little longer. You must be tired." I can tell when someone wants to be alone. Which is fine with me. I rise from the couch and shoot the bear a wave before making my way to Todd's truck.

It's all I can do to keep my eyes open on the drive home, and I only manage it by stewing over Hugh recovering in a cave somewhere in the forest. Either I'll see him at the full moon, a fellow Were, or I'll be burying him afterwards.

23

Out of the Frying Pan

The warm aroma of fresh coffee grounds hits my nose as I enter the shop. I suck in a deep breath, savoring the tantalizing echo of taste. Scanning the tables and chairs, I see Damien hasn't arrived for our little war meeting. Just as well. On little sleep and no caffeine, I'm liable to slap him the moment he shows his face.

I make my way up to the counter and order a seasonal lavender latte from a beanie-wearing barista. Spring menu. I'd say they're being just a skosh over-optimistic, given that it's still drizzling outside and hasn't hit a temperature over fifty degrees, but I'm not one to argue with a tasty cup of caffeine.

Once it's ready I manage to find a spot in the corner that isn't taken yet. Perhaps because it has a front-row view to someone peeing in the alley outside. Thank goodness the thick glass blocks my sensitive sense of smell. Not exactly what I want to be sniffing while sipping on my coffee. I'd like to kick my boots up on the table and relax, but I doubt that would go over with the baristas. Unlike Elios, they're keeping their bar top spotless. Instead, I angle my chair away from the outdoor restroom and take a calming sip of lavender goodness.

While I enjoy the floral latte, I entertain myself by imagining the satisfaction I'd get from throwing the scalding beverage into Damien's face. It's one of those things I've seen in the movies and always wanted to try. Alas, it would also mean wasting a perfectly good cup of coffee, and that I will not do.

And, it might be considered a breach of the truce to toss it all over him, no matter how deserved.

My muscles tense as the entrance bell to the cafe chimes, body reacting before the scent even hits me. Damien is here. Plenty of the patrons look him over with appreciation as he makes his way to the counter. He's a handsome devil, and I mean that in every sense of the word. Not that I blame them; they don't know him like I do. Although everyone does give him a wide berth. The two individuals in line step back, choosing to peruse the menu again rather than hold up Damien's order. Humans sometimes react to on-edge shifters like this, with no realization of why they're frightened. Damien's scowling up at the menu as if it's offended him. He manages a toothy smile at the barista as he orders a drip coffee, but the stormy expression returns as he's handed the cup and makes his way over to me.

"You're wearing a white shirt. How fitting." I lift my cup to him, smirking.

He keeps the scowl in place as he looks down. If I were a Were of weaker will, I'd be stuck drooling over the way the fitted shirt hugs his muscles. Like I did a few months ago.

"We're both supposed to bring something white to this truce. As a sign of good faith. Which I see you've ignored."

I gasp, eyes widening as I look down at my own ensemble. Fitted jeans, black leather jacket, a grey shirt beneath.

"Would you look at that? Must have slipped my mind. Oh well." I throw one leg over the other, bouncing a foot up and down as I sip my latte from its very white compostable cup. This counts. They're really on to something with this lavender idea. I wonder if Elios could make me a similar concoction, perhaps with vodka. Moon knows I'll need it after this meeting.

"Well?" Damien all but snarls at me. I cock an eyebrow up at him.

"Well, what?"

He slams the coffee cup down on the table, brown liquid spilling from underneath the lid as he squeezes it.

"*You're* the one who requested this meeting. I'd hoped you had something worthwhile to say. Or was this just a way to waste my time? I won't be deterred, Never. I've made up my mind. You haven't given me any other choice."

"Choice? Oh, I'm sorry, I think you must misunderstand that particular term. You see, a choice is when someone decides to do something of their own free will. You know, like *not* overthrow a city of humans and reveal the magical world just because their ex doesn't want to be around them anymore. Like not trying to force said ex into a relationship she has no interest in. That's what we call a temper tantrum, Damien darling, and I rather thought you'd outgrown those by now."

He does snarl this time, the sound drawing a few curious stares. I smile and sip until the nosy patrons turn around to their own conversations again.

"You made your choice years ago, when you promised to be my mate. You're the one backing out of the deal," Damien accuses. "I may not have set out to enact the Claw's policies, but I have no qualms with them, either. And if that's what it takes to get you back by my side, where you belong, so be it. I'm done being railroaded by you."

I'm so mad I can't respond. I set my cup down on the table, well aware that if I grab it now I'll shred it. I squeeze my fists, shaking as I work to hold myself back from revealing a Were to every human in this cafe. Damien smirks as he stares me down, and while I can't read him, I'm certain he's just smug as can be over having gotten a rise out of me. After a few deep breaths I lean back into my chair, one hand reaching up to fiddle with the vial given to me by the Bone Reader. I've been wearing it around my neck on a silver chain since I received it. He said it's for Damien, and that I'll know when to use it. Tempted as I am, this isn't the time.

"You called this truce. This is your last chance. Come back to me." Damien reaches across the table as he stares at me with bedroom eyes, but I keep my fists to myself.

"Never," I manage through clenched teeth. My name's coming in handy all over the place these days.

The edge of his lip curls up, and I can see his canines lengthening. He leans forward, whispered words full of menace.

"Then I will bring this city to its knees. I will destroy everything about it that you love. I will track down your new *family*," he spits the word, "and hold them ransom for your cooperation, if that's what it takes. If I have to, I'll take down the Magikai myself."

On that last point we might just agree. Not that I tell him. I'm still making up my mind on that front, as is a lady's prerogative.

"And you *will* be brought to heel. Make no mistake," he finishes, seething.

Heel. Like a common dog? The very idea. He showed up with *all* the audacity today.

"If you'll excuse me," I say, pushing my chair back and walking to the counter. I snag a coffee cup off the bar as someone reaches for it. "My apologies, but this really is necessary," I tell an open-mouthed patron as I steal their beverage and throw a bill down on the counter in its place.

I walk back to our table.

"Damien, dear, let me show you just what I think of your threats." I pop the lid off the coffee cup and fling the whole lot of it in his face. The movies didn't do it justice. This is *so* satisfying. He sputters, arms flinging hot coffee droplets across the cafe.

"I'll see you on the battlefield. Scott's Park, at sunset tomorrow, if you have the guts to back up your threats. That's where I'll be," I tell him as I plunk the coffee cup into a recycling bin.

He's clenching the table so hard that I see indentions on its surface.

"Bad breakup," I explain to the surrounding tables, who aren't even trying to hide the fact that they're staring as I walk away. I'm sure Damien's watching, so I put an extra swing in my hips. I only hope he can read my meaning.

Kiss my ass, jerk.

In my defense, I'm tired and worried about Hugh. Damien's threatening my home and my friends. The Magikai representatives are all over my tail for no good reason. I could have told them it was a terrible idea to send me for this white-flag talk. But what my employers want, they get. At least when they're providing us the numbers to hopefully save Sac.

I stew over things as I make my way back home. Most shifters have two souls; Weres have one. But I'm still divided. The Never I've lived with for centuries would have kicked and screamed, but then she might well have given in to Damien. But a second voice has awoken in these past few months. And it's reminding me now that to do so would forfeit my friends. The ones who are depending on me. And the one who insists I have a right to my own life. The thought hasn't fully sunk in when I smell a rat. Damien's following me.

I run through alleys and streets, taking a roundabout way back to my place. When I hit the park nearest my home I glance around, but it's empty. I leap onto a park bench, vaulting onto a lamppost. I shimmy up and drop on a second-floor deck, then swing up to some sleeping Sacramento resident's roof. I spot Damien below, sniffing the air, and I drop flat on my belly, crawling toward the back of the house.

It takes me three blocks to be satisfied I've lost him. I'm not playing fair, but neither is he.

"Honey, I'm home!" I yell to the others as I throw open my front door. I flop down on my couch and fill them in.

"You did what?" Todd demands as I relay my rather spectacular coffee throw.

"He goaded me!" I argue back. "And you should have seen his face! Worth it."

Todd sighs, squeezing between his eyes as he shakes his head. Behind him, Lynx is grinning like a madman, not that the feline's going to contradict his partner out loud.

"I think it's great. If you ask me, you should have slapped him. With claws," Chrys states, handing a hot cocoa to Aggie.

The witchling takes a sip.

"I agree. It's not fair you have to act all nice and respectful, after what he and the Claw have done to us. They chase us across the world and the Magikai can't do anything, but the minute he shows up here you have to listen to them? It sucks!" She's got her knees tucked under her on my papasan chair. She frowns, and a crease forms on her forehead as she purses her lips.

"Tell it, witchling," I respond, raising a glass toward her.

I frown as I realize I'm waiting for Hugh to chime in with his two cents. Todd's brother hasn't called, so I assume he's alive.

"Does this count as a broken truce, though?" Todd presses, one hand still on his temple, as if I've given him a headache. Not fooling me, bear boy. There's concern, but also approval.

I shrug.

"Does it matter if I did? What is he going to do? Threaten to destroy the city, kill all my friends, usurp the Magikai's leadership, and drag me off against my will? Oh wait!" I slap my head. "That's right! We're already in that exact situation."

"Do you really think he'll show up to the park, though? If he's trying to get back at you, why would he do what you ask? He could just as easily stage some spectacle in the city center and expose us all," Lynx reasons, flicking claws in and out.

I set my drink down on the table. Water, for anyone asking. I know, we're all surprised. She can hydrate.

"He will show, and I will tell you why. Because that Were is at the end of his rope." I know it, and even without being able to read Damien I am as sure of that fact as my own heartbeat. "He's tipped his hand to the Magikai, and that makes this his last chance to get to me. And I assure you all I have no intention of letting that happen."

I kick my legs up and stride out of the room, all contained rage. They let me go, but I'm touched by the compassion that follows my intuition down the hall. I shut myself in my gym. I keep my skin on, to make the task harder, working up a sweat as I pound a punching bag. I hit and hit until it goes flying off the chain and into a wall, and a cloud of the stuffing rips out.

24

Into the Fire

I'm surprised when I wake up to the sound of bacon sizzling, the smell wafting into my room. The sun is up, and when I roll to my side the clock tells me it's ten a.m. I can't recall the last time I slept in like this.

"What do you want in your omelet?" Todd asks, one hand flipping eggs in a skillet as I walk into the kitchen. He's got an apron on, but moon knows where he found it. Next to him, Lynx jumps back as bacon grease hits his hand.

"And they can cook? Be still my heart." I fake a swoon. "What are my choices?"

Todd gestures toward a series of bowls on my counter. Chopped peppers, diced tomatoes, onion, spinach, and a whole array of other potential toppings. I lick my lips.

"Mushroom, cheese, and green olive, please."

"That sounds terrible!" Lynx states, true disgust rolling off him as he sticks out his tongue.

"She says *please*. Color me shocked," Todd teases as he pulls the toppings I requested and gets to work.

"Where are the girls?" I ask, looking around and giving the air a good sniff. I have the answer on my nose before Todd responds.

"The gym for Aggie. Practicing, she says. And Chrys left before sunrise to fuel up. Sacrifice some squirrels or whatever dark witches do." He flips my omelet and slides it on a plate once it's cooked through.

I pick up a fork and take a bite.

"Delicious!" I wave the fork at him. "If you should ever find that hunting down bad guys loses its appeal, you'd make a decent chef."

Todd's lips tilt up in a half smile, but I can feel how much the compliment means to him. Come to think of it, I've never actually asked the two about what got them involved in becoming enforcers. I know why I do it, and I know the Magikai have plenty of their in-house trained enforcers. Todd and Lynx are contract-based, though, like me. What made them choose this lifestyle, of all things?

"Any word on Hugh?" Chrys asks as she walks through the front door, which slams shut behind her. She's sweaty, skin glistening and curls pulled back off her forehead. She's got on workout clothes and fingerless gloves.

"Never! Can you help me practice a couple of moves? It's not the same working with your punching bags!" Aggie yells as she walks down the hall from my gym. She's in a magenta sports bra with blue leggings. I guess I'm the only one still in pajamas.

Seems my enforcer question will have to wait for another time.

After wolfing down my omelet—yes, *wolf*, har-de-har, no shifter jokes at my expense, please—I join Aggie in the gym. Chrys comes as well, and she listens to my suggestions, but I can tell her mind's wandering. To a certain vamp sleeping off a Were attack in a certain cave, I imagine. If we make it through this fight, checking on him will be the first thing I do afterwards.

By lunch, the girls are wrung out. They both hit the showers, huffing and exhausted, but the preparation has had the reverse effect on me. I'm wired. Itching for more movement, my limbs refusing to stay still.

Aggie and Chrys emerge smelling like floral and fruity body wash, both sporting comfortable pajama pants. I'll just swap them places. I head into my room and toss my sleep shorts into a hamper before grabbing a pair of black athletic leggings and a stone-blue sports bra of my own. I pull my hair back and don some sneakers.

"Back before the action starts!" I assure the others as I sprint out the door.

It might come as no surprise at all that, while I do get in a several-mile run around downtown, I end up at Elios's place soon enough.

"You smell like a wet dog," the bartender accuses as I slump down on a barstool, blowing a sweaty strand of loose hair away from my forehead.

"Yes, and *you* reek of judgmental bull, you old goat," I snap, but blow him a kiss to soften the blow.

He just rolls his eyes before pulling a glass from underneath the bar and wiping it out. Today's towel is almost white, a stark improvement on his norm.

"Whiling away your afternoon over a drink?" Elios questions, turning behind him to grab a bottle of vodka. I hold up a palm.

"No, thank you."

He whistles.

"Politeness *and* turning down one of my cocktails? This fight must really be eating at you," the barkeep observes, tone flippant but worry hitting my intuition.

I've no plans to give up Elios's tempting concoctions, but nothing sounds palatable at the moment. I'd rather fight the Claw on an empty stomach than risk yacking on the battlefield. Not exactly an intimidating move.

"For some reason, I find the idea of having my city torn apart over one male's pigheadedness a less than appealing proposition," I inform Elios.

He stares at me across the bar, eyes flicking to his left as he whispers.

"And the idea of the Magikai rolling in to defeat them, steal your victory, and soundly put you in your place even less so, I'd imagine."

Let it not be said that Elios is unobservant. Despite his questionable cleanliness, the satyr has picked up on even more information than I've let slip.

"That could be," I allow. "I assume the zoo of shifters in the corner are here on our benevolent government's behalf?"

He gives a swift dip of his chin, hiding the movement as he leans under the bar and grabs another glass to pretend he's cleaning. I scent them out as best I can without turning around. A good dozen shifters over in the corner, of all varieties. A spare warlock, a couple witches, and even a vampire. Not unique on their own, but a considerable show of force as a unit.

Against my earlier decision I do accept a glass from Elios, though it's just water. I sip and let my ears go furred, poking through my hair. Sitting in a partial shift requires concentration, and I split my focus between that and what the Magikai gremlins are discussing.

"Reckless. Completely out of control. You know we're only here because she killed the last leader of the Claw."

"A dragon," another agrees. "Stabbed their Crown right in the heart and then just let the rest of them get away!"

Damien killed the dragon. Damien ran off with the rest of the Claw. And I didn't let them; I was stripped by Aggie and carried naked and wounded back into my own mansion.

I bite into my tongue until I taste copper, the only way I can keep myself from snapping at these thoughtless Magikai minions.

"Well, *I* heard she's running with some vampire gang. What kind of shifter does that? Do you think she's sleeping with them all?"

"That would explain why she's spending so much time at a coven in Vegas. We *do* have the best entertainment. Maybe she got more hooked on that than the city's gambling." The group's vamp is speaking. I'd like to throttle him, but I'm conserving my energy and focusing my anger on more important targets.

You're all in for one hell of a surprise when I show up to headquarters with another intuitive in tow.

If I make it past tonight, that is. And what are they griping for, anyway? Shouldn't they want the Claw gone?

"She must be competent, though, to have been an enforcer this long. And not even with training from the Magikai themselves." Moon bless whichever shifter just piped up. One of the others scoffs.

"Hardly. Just a disposable mercenary they send out for odd jobs. More than likely it's just luck that she hasn't been killed yet, but I can't imagine they'll let her get away with this mess. Bringing a fight this big to such a large city? They can't let that stand."

I start to growl, then chug the rest of my water to drown out the noise.

Say that to my face and I'll bite yours off.

These magicals wouldn't know an independent thought if it bit them in their moon-blessed hindparts. I'd feel sorry for them if I weren't so furious. The injustice of it all. I didn't ask the Claw to show up here. And what do they think would have happened otherwise? If it wasn't Damien seeking me, it would have been the former leader overthrowing some other spot to oust magicals and declare war against the Magikai. I'm the lesser evil.

But I doubt Amun or the other representatives have spun the story that way. Dangerous and out of control Were makes a much better motivating tool to the others. They can't risk having some rogue enforcer without any of their training or backing showing them up. It's bad for business. So help me, they are going to regret forcing my hand into training Ever at their headquarters.

I vow here and now to make it through this fight, just to shove their noses in that particular mistake. One promise I'll be happy to keep.

The door to the bar slams into the wall as someone shoves it open. I turn to see Rex striding in, flanked by a few of his bear guards. He runs a hand over close-cropped hair as his brown eyes find me across the bar.

"Never! Tell me you're not drinking away the afternoon while the Magikai's enforcers are crowding up your lawn!"

I sigh, rolling my eyes.

Thanks a lot, bear.

Oh well, what's done is done. I hop off the stool, shooting the enforcers in the corner a toothy grin.

"Sorry, bear, I didn't realize they'd crowd my space quite so early. Must have only sent their A-team to my place. Moon knows it's only the lowest, most bottom-of-the-barrel enforcers who would be left out of the loop. All crowded up in the bar, gossiping like an old lady's sewing circle, for instance."

A chair squeaks as one of the shifters stands, fangs and whiskers sprouting as he raises a fist. The warlock grabs him and eases him back into his seat.

"Smart kitty," I croon, and he snarls, leaping up again.

"Not in my bar!" Elios yells, perhaps sensing the mess a fight would cause.

"You want to take this outside?" the feline asks me as fur grows over his sneer.

"That depends; are you prepared to be buried next to Elios's trash bins? If so, lead the way, cat." I sweep my arm toward the door. The shifter yowls, leaping toward me as I lift hands that grow claws.

He's arm-barred before he gets close.

"Now that's settled,"—Rex wipes his hands together while the winded shifter tries to suck in air—"let's get going. After all, we can't start the meeting without our fearless leader." The cat hisses as his friends pull him back. I turn over my shoulder and blow him a kiss as Rex sweeps us from the bar.

"You've got a couple of screws loose and a concerning desire for violence, but you're fearless nonetheless," Rex mutters toward me as we exit.

"I could have taken him," I pout back.

He just shakes his head.

"That's not the point. Did it ever occur to you that there are times when diplomacy is better than destruction?"

"Never," I sass. When he frowns at me, I blow out a breath. "All right. Of course I have. I'm more than capable of plastering on the fake political smile, but those idiots are lucky I'm not wiping their blood off my boots."

He snorts out a laugh.

"You're in sneakers. And that may be, but it's not the point. I'm of the opinion you could take most of them. All of them, if they weren't attacking as a unit. But like it or not, they are the backup we have, and we're in the situation we're in. Perhaps a compromise? Hold off on throttling our allies until we've taken care of the Claw. One enemy at a time, hmm?"

I tap a finger under my chin.

"Done." He chuckles, yanking me closer and rubbing a fist in the top of my hair as I shove him off. "You know, Rex, you're not half bad when you drop the stoic exterior. Maybe I'm not the only one who needs to show more than one coping mechanism to the world?"

He freezes, and I feel defensiveness wash over him as I realize I've pushed too far. Me and my mouth. But then, it melts, giving way to sincerity.

"Maybe," he allows.

We've reached my neighborhood, and may the moon strike me down for a liar if there aren't a good couple hundred shifters dotting the block, some in full fur. Witches are walking the perimeter with glowing hands, throwing up what I hope are concealing spells.

"What in hell's moon are these magicals doing trampling my lawn?" I demand as we push our way through the crowd. Rex is bigger, but I'm stronger than I look. I make my way to my own porch to see a cringing Unkai next to some shifter I've never seen before. Wolf, by the smell of him.

"I told you she wouldn't like it," Unkai tells the male.

He just snorts, looking down his nose at me. He's just as tall as Todd, with tanned skin and freckles across his nose that would look boyish on most individuals. His jaw is square and prominent, and the sheer amount of chiseled muscle on him is almost laughable. Self-importance oozes off him.

"It's really not up to her. The head representative put me in charge here."

"Never, meet the leader of the enforcers," Unkai states, gesturing between us.

"Charmed, I'm sure," I all but growl at him. He just smirks.

"Aren't you going to ask for my name? I hear it's a quirk of yours."

I put on an airy laugh.

"I hardly think it will matter. I'll be shocked to my shoes if you make it through this battle, but best of luck."

He's not as easy to goad as his underlings in the bar. He gives me a tight smile, but I can feel the rage surging beneath. Rex might be right about respect, but I've had enough of males barging into my space and telling me what to do.

"Diplomacy," Rex mutters in my ear. I plaster a simpering smile on my face as I stare up at the enforcer.

"I'm sure an intelligent male such as yourself has the whole battle strategy planned out already, but if I could make one small suggestion?" I throw him a pout.

"Let's hear it," he barks, not taking me any more seriously than before but giving me a once-over. Sometimes I *really* don't need intuition to read males. He licks his lip as he leers at me, and that tears it.

"You all take care of keeping the humans safe and then get out of my way while I take out the Crown." I snap my teeth in front of the enforcer's face, unsurprised that I've got a muzzle halfway grown out. I pull it back, flashing a human smile. "Please," I add.

"Fine, that's what we were planning to do anyway." The enforcer shrugs, shoving past me and going down to the grass to mill around with his fellow brainwashed Magikai minions.

"And what *is* your name, anyway?" I call after him, unable to help myself.

"Brutus," he shouts back, a sneer on his face that just dares me to comment.

"He's kidding, right? He has to be kidding?" I look across the lawn at the other enforcers. "Dull? That's the meaning we're going with? *Et tu Brute*? No? Just me then, huh?"

Rex hooks a hand around my elbow, tugging me past Unkai and through my own front door.

"Do you *always* have to be so salty with other people?" he asks, exasperation raining down from him.

"Funny, I would've described her as *sour*, myself." Todd grins, poking his head into the entryway.

"And here I consider myself sweet. You two sure know how to charm a gal." I stick my tongue out at the bears as I walk down the hall toward my room, pulling off athletic clothes covered in dried sweat on the way.

After a quick shower I return to find two witches perched on my bed. My Were senses rebel against the idea. Dens are very personal. But given the circumstances ...

"Ready for this?" I ask them both, plopping down between them in a towel. No use putting on fresh clothes just to shred them with fur when we leave.

I'm surprised to find more uncertainty coming to me from Chrys's side. I tilt my head, raising an eyebrow at her.

"No taste for blood?" I ask her.

"I don't have the experience with anything of this magnitude. It'll be a test of my abilities," she responds, to the point.

Aggie flexes her fingers.

"I'm ready." And she means it. I'll say this for my naive witchling; she's tough when it counts.

"Time to head to the park!" Todd yells from the entryway. "Magikai have it all blocked off from any snooping human eyes. And their enforcers are patrolling the adjoining streets and alleys for Claw troublemakers."

I hear my front door squeak open and the lumbering sounds of two bears and a feline filing out.

I hop off the bed and turn toward the witches.

"Well, ladies, looks like it's time to go. Better hurry, before we miss out on all the fun."

I offer them each a hand and pull them up, squeezing Chrys's.

"He'll be all right. He's tough," I state, before turning around and letting my fur roll over me.

Here we go.

25

Not Just For Show

The lawn has cleared out by the time we make it outside; just a few stragglers hanging around at the edges of the block. I can only assume that's intentional, given the way their heads swivel, monitoring my house from every angle. A waste of time, if anyone had asked me. Damien knows good and well that I won't be at home hiding from a fight.

That's not the Never he knows and pretends he loves.

The park is close by human standards, let alone the distance a hyped-up Were can cover. The bears are being rather accommodating. Aggie on Rex's shoulders and Chrys on Todd's as they lumber behind me. Lynx is serving as point as we make our way to the battleground, and we're still a good mile out when he hisses an alarm.

"They're here. Just like you thought they would be, Never. Dozens of them, but not hundreds. Wreaking havoc across the city, no doubt." His eyes stay focused on the park in the distance. I can barely make it out on the horizon.

"Damien promised to bring this city to its knees. I suppose it's nice to know he can keep his word occasionally." I laugh it off, but the statement tastes bitter. He'll follow through on destroying what I love, but not on anything he could have done to prevent this. As I feel moisture in my eyes, I blink tears away with a snarl.

Not today. I can cry over him when he's dead. Right now I need every ounce of anger I can get. In my mind I go over all the reasons he deserves this. It's his fault the city is under threat. His fault the Magikai are here, poking into my life. His fault that they think I'm some crazed Were who killed a dragon but couldn't bring down the rest of the Claw. His fault I had to go back to the Isle, and got chased across Europe, and made a deal with the Magikai to go to their headquarters to train Ever. All his fault. The only good thing that's come out of this is Nahum, and who can say whether that will go anywhere.

When we make it to the park, the Claw who are present are spread out in a uniform pattern, across from a line of enforcers. The Magikai-approved kind who get gold stars, not the cast-off contractors like Todd, Lynx, and myself. Glittering armbands the color of gems glint from the Claw's sleeves. But there's someone important missing.

"Where is the Crown?" I demand, ducking under an enforcer's arm as he tries to bar me from passing.

You'll have to do more than that.

I draw myself up to my full height, baring fangs at the Claw members. I can set aside my pride enough to accept the Magikai's help in order to protect the city, but make no mistake, this is *my* fight.

"Damien!" I yell when none of his group responds to my question regarding his whereabouts. "Show yourself, you moon-damned coward!"

A few of the Claw suck in their breath at the insult.

"The Crown doesn't answer to you," a shifter near the front states with a sneer. I sniff. Tiger? Guess we'll see soon enough. "He will show himself at the opportune moment, and join us to celebrate victory over the Magikai and this ridiculous protection of humans."

I shrug furred shoulders, as if it doesn't matter much to me.

"In that case, I vote we get on with it," I state as I hear enforcers shifting behind me. Snarls and growls erupt on both sides.

The possible tiger-shifter takes another step forward, still in his skin.

"Prepare to be defe—"

My jaws snap shut on his throat before he can finish the sentence.

Guess we won't be finding out if you're a tiger after all, I think as the noise reaches a fever pitch around me. Guess we've begun.

The others are locked into fighting across the park. Jets of colored light fly past me from both sides; witches hard at work. I wrap furred fingers around a vampire's arm as he sprints by me toward the line of enforcers, and then take him down.

The whole thing dissolves into a melee of fur, fangs, lights, and blood. A roar sounds to my right, and I look to see Rex and a few of his bear guards swiping at various Claw shifters. Chrys is pulling her magic-on-magic shield stunt. She's holding a vibrant glowing wall in front of them, lowering and lifting it as needed so the bears can land blows but the Claw can't get through.

Past them, Aggie is taking down Claw members one at a time, while Todd savages anyone who gets near the witchling. She sucks a vamp dry, leaving a whimpering, sunburned mess. Then she downs a wolf shifter and some reptilian magical. I swipe and kick as I make my way through the crowd, scanning all the while for any glint of Damien's fur.

I spot a similar shade of grey, but it's just a wolf shifter. I sniff, and place Brutus, the leader of the enforcers. He's got a group of other shifters at his back, and they're running after several arm-band-wearing Claw members. To the edges of the park and an adjoining street. Focusing, I can feel how satisfied the Claw are with the scenario. With a growl, I abandon my hunt for Damien, just for the moment, and go after them.

As I round a corner, I see our fearless but idiotic enforcer leader sprinting into a massive storm drain that was installed for reasons unknown. It's not as if we have enough rainfall here.

"Stop! It's a trap!" I yell, but if he hears me, he ignores me. They've entered the tunnel and I'm almost caught up when a deluge of water comes rushing out, head enforcer and the rest of them trapped within the flow.

The water stays in a perfect cylindrical shape, and the enforcers within claw and kick but can't make it past whatever invisible barrier is in place. The Claw have somehow circled their way back behind us and are picking off waterlogged enforcers as they flow past. I don't know whether Damien recruited another dragon that can control water, or some sort of elementally-keyed witch.

I'm going to regret this, I lament, thinking of the wet dog smell, as I lean forward and plunge my top half into the water. I reach and sweep my arms out, hooking one leg behind me onto a tree root to keep from falling in. A pair of hands hits my right forearm, and I manage to close my claws around a couple other limbs. I throw myself backwards, ankle taking a painful twist against the weight. I've managed to yank out three enforcers: two witches and Mr. "I'm in charge here" head enforcer Brutus himself.

He's sputtering and coughing as his fur falls away, and I'm left with a waterlogged human male instead of a large grey wolf.

"Happy now?" I snap as I scramble out from under him. Confusion slaps at me.

"I don't understand! I'm trained for all scenarios. How did they trick us?"

"For exactly that reason. Training. I'm willing to bet you've not seen one jot of actual action like this. Maybe now my self-taught, street-fighting, always-be-suspicious-of-everyone methods aren't looking so unprofessional after all, hmm?" He has the grace to look sheepish, a small blush on his freckled cheeks as embarrassment coats him, not that he admits it aloud.

I pull myself up, readying to jump back into the water, which still has a good dozen enforcers trapped, a few of them already unconscious under the water. Then the cylinder explodes in a shower of purple light as Chrys's defensive wall slams into it.

The witch strides up behind me, lips set in a thin line and jaw tense as she concentrates. Enforcers drop to the ground, as bears and a few shifters I recognize as Elios's bouncers thunder past the witch to defend the waterlogged magicals from being picked off by the Claw.

Across the drainage ditch from us, another figure stands. *So Damien does have another witch, then.* She's got thick, black, flowing hair that's whipping around her face as she pulls a wall of water in front of her. The wave lifts to impossible heights, enough to drown us all. The light of the full moon dims as the water blocks it.

"Chrys," I murmur out the side of my mouth. I may be the first to compliment myself, but I'm also the first to admit when I've got nothing. And I can't do anything against a tidal wave.

"Working on it," she says through gritted teeth. The purple wall in front of us has disappeared, and some of the enforcers start shouting as their panic rains down on me. I don't move. I trust the witch.

"Just. One. More. Second." She's breathing fast, muscles tensed all the way up her arms and sweat breaking out on her brow.

In front of us, I can just make out the blurry figure of the opposing witch as she drops her arms. The water lurches toward us.

"Sink or swim, witch!" I yell over the thunderous sound of a crashing wave. Everything in me tells me to duck, or run. Instead, I fling myself forward as I see Chrys start to waver. I throw myself down behind her, forcing her back upright. Droplets of water spatter my fur; screams erupt as our 'hardened enforcers' run.

The water stops. I chance a look around Chrys, and see within the wave are small glints of purple light. She's using it. Weaving the water into her own shield, like she did in the North Sea. But it's costing her. I can feel the exhaustion building. I twist and stand behind her, hauling her back against me and throwing my furred arms out under her own so hers can rest on mine.

"You can do it!" I encourage.

Chrys screams, the sound building as she pushes against the wave, and then it begins to move the other direction. She sucks in a shallow breath, and one more scream erupts as the water shoots back at the opposing witch, cascading over her. The water-wielding witch topples, falling under her own wave, and Chrys collapses against me, eyes rolling.

"I'll be damned," Brutus exclaims behind us. The head enforcer stayed; that's something at least. Shock hits my intuition from his direction. Did he really not think anyone but his own crew had any useful skills? Judgy, judgy.

Chrys has managed to knock out the majority of Claw that were with the other witch, but a few stragglers remain. A couple of vamps and a massive, shaggy bear with a torn ear make their way toward us. I give Chrys a small slap on the cheek.

"Time to wake up, witch!" She doesn't stir. I hoist her into my arms, prepared to run and fight at once if I need to.

I snarl as the trio gets close. One vamp blurs as he speeds up and runs at us. I slash out, landing a glancing blow as I try to balance Chrys with my other arm. The second vamp's already in motion, and while I twist us away, he manages to slash her cheek, one thin line of red blooming on her face. I lower her to the ground in front of me, determined to protect her.

"I've got your back," a voice mutters behind me. At least the head enforcer isn't completely useless.

The bear lumbers toward us, opening his mouth in a roar as spit goes flying. He's big. Bigger even than Todd. The vamps crisscross and attack, and Brutus manages to hold them at bay. The bear stands on his hind legs, and I ready myself for his paws to come down on us.

Something slams into the bear from the side, and the shifter goes rolling. A russet blur circles and hits the bear again, slicing at its muzzle. A Were, frenzied and snarling.

It worked. It's Hugh.

The vamp turned Were is far too fast for the bear, clawing, climbing and leaping over the large predator and slashing claw marks into the ursine shifter as he goes. His eyes glint a saturated green for a moment before turning a deep and disconcerting red.

Green. So that's what they looked like before he became a vamp.

At my feet, Chrys groans, clutching at her head without opening her eyes. Brutus has one vamp down, but his face is bloodied. He should have put his fur back on. The second bloodsucker tries to leap over my shoulder to the witch, but I grab him by the head with a clawed hand. I start to pull, but then he's wrenched away from me as Hugh slams into him. He mauls the vampire before I can blink. As the head enforcer edges toward us, Hugh snarls at him, swiping out with his claws.

"Is he supposed to be on our side?" Brutus questions.

"In theory," I respond. I've never turned a Were before, but I can feel Hugh's protectiveness and his rage. He's not stable. Who knows what he'll do? I edge forward, furred palms facing out.

"Hugh, I don't know how this thing works, but I turned you. I'm supposed to be responsible for making sure you don't go on a killing spree. Chrys is fine." I gesture down to the unconscious witch, who groans again. "Well, she *will* be fine. We're on your side."

He gets closer, red gaze all animal, no glint of humanity. He sniffs at me, a low growl at the back of his throat as he leans toward the enforcer behind me.

"Show him your neck," I command the enforcer.

He snorts, indignant.

"Like hell I will."

"This is no time for a measuring contest. This Were is freshly turned and feral. But he's on our side. You're a male, and you're threatening the witch. Show him your neck."

Brutus huffs, but he does what I ask, lifting his still-human chin high.

Hugh's eyes glint green as he leans closer, fangs dripping. He snaps his jaw, teeth closing on the air an inch from the enforcer's throat. Shouts sound behind us, and I turn to see a cluster of other enforcers running our way.

I brace myself for a brawl, but Hugh scoops up the witch and bolts. One thing I *am* confident about is that he won't hurt Chrys.

"Nothing to see here, folks, let's move it along. Back to the real action!" I shoo the oncoming enforcers.

No shock to me that I'm ignored as they surround Brutus and haul the shifter up. He's got a swollen eye and a bloody cheek. I'm about to give him snark about being bested by a singular vampire.

"I'll give her this. She can fight," he acknowledges as his comrades help him limp away from me.

"Maybe she really *did* take out a vamp lord and a dragon single-handedly," one of the shifters with him mutters.

I'm still being ignored, but at least this time the comments are complimentary.

I turn my nose back to the air as I catch my first scent of Damien.

26

Damien Darling

After what feels like forever but is more like seven shifters, three vamps, and a pesky warlock that had a lightning-related key, I get a glimpse of him. Damien's tail flicks behind one of the park's many trees, and I sprint after him. As I round the tree where he disappeared, I'm knocked flat by a blow to the chest. A ginger touch against my side tells me I've more than likely cracked a couple of ribs. Above me, and I do mean *way* above, a bulbous and wrinkled face leers. Something slimy hits me in the cheek, and I realize I've been drooled on.

I gag and just manage to roll out of the way as the tree limb my adversary is wielding slams into the ground next to me. Either he's slow or he's only supposed to maim me.

"A troll!" I yell into the dying light, certain Damien's baiting me. "Where did you manage to find one?" They've stuck to the most isolated portions of mountain peaks for years, living off goats and the stray hiker here and there. I dodge as the tree limb flashes overhead, leaves swishing.

I can keep away from it. Trolls are bumbling and slow, but pack a punch. My problem is that Damien's scent is growing fainter. Curse the Were. I snap my teeth in the air, and an idea hits me. It may work, but I'm going to owe my poor taste buds a serious apology. I duck under another swing and dart between the troll's legs, nipping first at one massive fleshy ankle and then another. The troll bellows, limb smashing into nearby tree trunks as he rains down blows with abandon. Still, he stays up.

Maybe if I climb him? I sink my claws into a leg, shimmying up as he swats at me like I'm a fly. I'm hopping up his back, one clawed leap at a time, when he lands a lucky hit and I'm flung against the nearest tree trunk. I hit hard and slide to the ground, trying to shake away the dizziness. Everything is blurry.

"—ver!" I make out what might be the last part of my name. I collapse to my side—calling it a tuck and roll would be a vicious lie—as the tree above me shatters. The troll roars, leaves around it shaking, just as something slams into its back.

The troll staggers, stumbling in front of me. Then, it changes. The muscles go all floppy, and the troll's limbs start to look a bit like a deflated balloon. Its head is still huge, and the creature starts weaving. After a few failed attempts at retaining balance, the troll's head slams into a tree and it slumps down, unconscious and tongue lolling.

I struggle to push myself up, vision beginning to clear.

"That has to be the work of my favorite witchling!" I shout. Sure enough, Aggie walks through the trees, blushing but proud as she soaks in the compliment. "Nice work, witch. Would never have guessed that's what happens when you strip a troll."

"Shifters get naked, but trolls go limp. They must not find me attractive," she quips.

I whistle.

"Very nice, witch. You may well be corruptible yet. My bad habits are rubbing off on you."

She just rolls her eyes. I'm so proud. Another Never classic. I wave her off toward Todd as he lumbers over.

"Go back to the group. Help out those useless Magikai enforcers. Moon knows they could use it. I'll handle this."

Aggie chews her lips, but she lets Todd nudge her back toward the park with his nose. Her reluctance sits in the air as she goes. I sniff, managing to pick up Damien's scent easily enough under the troll stench. In spite of my lingering dizziness and aching ribs, I push myself into a run again. I'm out of the park and into an area that's already been cleared, either by the Magikai or the Claw. No human scents hit my nose, at least no current ones. There's the old smell of excrement and garbage coming from some industrial bins. Damien's scent leads under an overpass, by some boarded-up warehouses, and all the way to a dirty alley.

I stop to catch my breath as the alley comes into view, well aware that this can't be anything but a trap. It doesn't matter. I have to go in. All these years. I still have until Halloween to get the Were, and it's only February. But for better or worse, I've hit my limit. There won't be any future conflicts. One way or another, I'm seeing this through tonight.

As I get closer, forms step out from the shadows. It's well and truly night above us, the full moon casting an ominous glow over everything. I count ten Claw members lining the alley, five on each side. At the end, a chain-link fence to his back, stands Damien.

"A gauntlet of magicals to fight off? Just for me? Damien, you shouldn't have," I say.

"It seemed only fair to make you chase me. Clearly, it's not working the other way around," Damien responds. His voice is flat; no humor and no anger. Not that I could feel either.

"Can I assume that when I enter that alley, they're going to attack?"

"Unless you're ready to admit where you belong. By my side. Renew your promise to me, and I'll call them off." He pauses a beat, and perhaps he's not a complete idiot, because he must catch my refusal. "I'm not playing around, Never. These are the best and deadliest of the Claw. They won't hesitate to hurt you. For your sake, give in now."

My lip pulls up as I flash my fangs.

"Why? Because if I don't they're going to drag me to you, bloody and screaming? I didn't think that's how you liked your females, Damien. Learn something new all the time, I suppose."

He growls, the sound echoing off the alley walls.

"It's not like that! But yes, if that's what has to be done to put you in your place, then that's what I'll do."

No sense wasting any more time. And it's the only way to find out what I'm up against. As I run, I let every single terrible thing that's happened to me fill me. Let it take root deep within and then rise. Scream therapy isn't quite the same in fur, but what comes out isn't quite a howl, either. It's something more grating. More desperate. I let my feelings go, all my built-up anguish and hurt echoing across the alley. I feel the fear, the anger, the disgust from the group in front of me. But I don't care what they think.

The first two individuals, a warlock on the left and a snowy white feline shifter on the right, cringe when I get close. I barrel into the warlock first, and am thrown back just as fast as I make contact. I feel burning and stinging anywhere his skin has touched. I look down to see fur falling away, leaving some very unattractive bald patches. They'll grow back. I change my tactics, listening behind me and lunging out of the way at the last moment as the feline comes up from behind. She attempts to stop but still collides with the warlock. The kitty cat yowls as her fur falls and the smell of burnt hair fills the alley. Before she can get herself together, I step on her tail and rake claws across her. Street fights aren't the time to play fair, kids. It's about survival.

I haul off and kick her back into the warlock, both of them slamming into the alley wall. She yowls again, then whimpers and limps away, a few steps before falling. Her fur stays on, so she's alive, but she's out of this fight. Holding my breath as I anticipate the pain, I roundhouse the warlock. The paw pads on my foot scream in agony as I make contact, but the warlock's head slams into the brick and he slides to the ground.

The next two sets go quicker but cost me just as much. A pair of wolf shifters who must have had some professional combat training, followed by a bear and feline duo. They don't hold a candle to Todd and Lynx.

"Six down. Four to go. Unless you'd like to Were-up and face me yourself?" I ask, my breath coming in shallow huffs after I finish the third duo. Damien just crosses his arms over his chest and sneers.

He wants it to go like this. Wants me to be winded and weak by the time I reach him. And I can't see how to avoid it if I don't just tuck my tail and run. My ribs have started knitting themselves up after the troll, but my side still aches. I've got fresh, red skin with no fur where the warlock hit me. The wolves have left me with all kinds of sore spots on my arms and legs, and the bear got in a decent enough swipe to my face. I'm pretty sure a bone under my eye has cracked. But I keep going. Pretty soon I'm done with opponents seven and eight.

"Not getting away this time. This ends today," I whisper through gritted teeth as I step over a feathered shifter and a drake. "You *wish* you were as cool as a dragon," I snap at the drake's unconscious form. Fun fact. Dragons and drakes are similar to Weres and wolf shifters. Two souls vs. one.

The last two individuals between my ex half-mate and me are in fighting stances, ready. One is a Were. Moon knows how Damien conned one of our kind into this ludicrous organization. I don't know him. He's got black fur along his back, and soft white on his belly. The second individual is a tall, lithe grey elf. He's brandishing a whip embedded with barbs.

I look up toward Damien, who's sitting atop a closed dumpster.

"Entertained?" I snap up at him.

"I did my homework," he responds, eyes glinting.

Something sour makes its way up the back of my throat, but I swallow it down. He knows. Maybe not all of it, but enough. What happened to me after he left me to the Collectors. And instead of apologizing, instead of explaining, he's using it against me. My legs are shaking, threatening to give out. I'm sore, bruised, and broken. And so tired. Maybe I can still get away.

I'm eyeballing the items in the alley, judging whether I can jump over a dumpster and leap onto a nearby roof. Maybe run the rooftops until I'm back to the park. I'm tensing my legs to jump when the elf speaks.

"She's going to run!" he warns.

I could. But what would that solve? Yes, the Isle haunts me. But it doesn't have the hold it used to. I'm not the same Were I was when I lived there. I rescued another intuitive Were from a similar fate. Let friends back into my life. Faced the Isle. Damien's trying to make me feel like I did back then. Scared, and alone. But I'm not. In fact, I know someone else with Isle experience. Nahum. And he believes in me. He was inspired by me. To get involved. I don't want to be the Were that goes quietly into chains, or the one who tucks tail. I want to be *that* Were. The one my friends care about. The one Nahum believes in, who makes him want to try.

I shift my stance and throw myself not toward the trash cans, but at the elf. I hear a snap as he cracks the whip behind me, but he misses. I barrel into him, and I let all my anger loose. In the background I can hear the cracks and thuds as the whip is snapped repeatedly, sometimes making contact and sometimes missing. But it echoes as if from far away. I feel liquid trailing on my fur, and I know I've been hit, but I can't bring myself to care. There's a haze over my vision, and it doesn't recede until the cracking and snapping cease.

I wrench the whip from the elf's limp fingers, growling up at Damien as I throw it from my grasp. I won't need it. I turn toward the black and white Were, knowing I must look a bloody mess.

"Only one to go," I snarl at him, lifting a single furred finger.

He runs.

I snort after him. Good riddance.

"Ten for ten." I snap at Damien.

"That was disappointing. Still, I think I accomplished what I hoped. You've not managed to take me out yet. Not even when you were at your best. What chance do you think you stand now, injured and alone?"

Damien hops off his dumpster and walks the few steps toward me. He sniffs, lip curling back over his front fangs.

"You stink. When this is over, we'll need to get you cleaned up. This is no way for the Crown's mate to look."

"What happened to you?" I yell at him, livid for perhaps the five thousandth time that I can't use intuition with him. "I'm willing to believe you've always been a red flag with legs, but you're not the same Were I knew."

A growl builds and he snaps his teeth just in front of my muzzle.

"*You* happened to me. You and your ridiculous grudge. Running off after you escaped the Collectors instead of coming back to me. Hiding from me for decades. Then you show up here when we were chasing that other intuitive. You wanted her safe from the Claw. And I gave it to you. I overthrew the last Crown for you. You have no idea what that cost me. No idea what I paid for it. And *still* you refuse me."

This may come as a surprise to us all, but I keep my trap shut. We're getting somewhere.

"This is your fault," he snaps, and then he backhands me. I stagger back, slamming into the brick wall of the alley. I work my jaw open and closed to confirm it isn't broken, stunned.

Remember that thing I just said about getting somewhere? Scratch that. He's going down.

27

Fate Sucks

He doesn't say anything else when I throw myself on his back, clawing down his sides. He just grunts and reaches over his shoulder, tugging me off. We scuffle in the damp alley, echoes sounding whenever we slam into a trash bin. Small clouds of dust billowing when we crush bits of loose brick.

And for all of it, we're evenly matched. Not that I'll ever admit this to Damien. After all, he's in pristine condition. If he hadn't sent me through a gauntlet of gore, I'd be kicking his furry behind; bet on it. A metallic rattle sounds as I'm thrown into the chain-link fence, and I see my opportunity. I turn and begin to climb. If I can get the high ground, I can throw myself off and go for his head.

I'm yanked off the fencing by my neck before I've reached the top. My back slams into the ground, and Damien's nose is shoved in my face, wet fangs glistening in the moonlight. I kick and twist, prying at him, but I can't shake his grip on my throat. He just pushes me further down, and I gasp and choke as stars flash across the edges of my vision.

Even with his paw pressed against my neck, his claws digging in as they wrap around it, I have a difficult time believing what's happening.

As I think back through it, Damien's never actually hurt me before tonight. Physically, I mean. We all know I've ranted and rambled on and on about the emotional damage. That aside, inflicting wounds has been something he's been content to farm out to his lackeys, until now.

"Finally. Snapped. Did. You?" I wheeze, each word an effort. Light blinks at the edges of my vision as darkness closes in.

"Why couldn't you just do what I asked?" Damien whines, as if this is my fault even as he squeezes.

Damien, darling, are those tears? For moi?

I'd pause to think about that, if I had any time or breath to spare.

As it stands, I manage to slide one furry arm out from underneath myself. I move it up my side slowly, just managing to wedge it between the two of us as I reach toward my neck. Damien's grip loosens just a bit.

"I don't want to hurt you, Never."

No? Could've fooled me.

"But you're being so difficult. Why can't I make you understand?"

I *never* really understood him, and he never really understood me. Therein lies our issue. I've managed to hook one claw around the delicate silver chain at my neck. I slice through it and just manage to catch the gift from the Bone Reader as it slides down my chest. I wrap my claws around it and swing.

The vial smashes against Damien's face. The moment it breaks, I can breathe. A good deal of that may be because he lets go of my throat. But another piece is because I have finally, finally done what I set out to do. If the vial works. The Bone Reader said I'd know when it was time, and about to be choked out by Damien seems like that time.

For the span of maybe a second, we both freeze. The contents of the vial break loose. I'd always thought it was filled with a blue liquid. It is, and it isn't.

Hesitantly I reach out and tap one suspended drop with my paw. Sure enough, it comes away wet and cold. But the droplets don't fall. They float, swirling and expanding. The liquid forms a ribbon as it grows, then twists into a spiral around us that resembles a tornado. I stand and turn a circle, watching the magic water. One end of it stretches upwards, toward the sky. The other rushes downwards, cleaving a hole into the earth. The rest runs around us like a river.

We're stuck in the middle, and where we are the water splits, creating a small island that holds the two of us. Damien and I are trapped together, glowing blue rapids roiling around either side of us. I'm a split second from dipping a paw into the stuff when I hear whispers. I twist my head left and right, trying to catch who's speaking. But no one is here but Damien, and he's silent. He turns in a circle.

"Who's there?" he demands, fangs snapping at the voices and catching nothing but air.

The whispering grows louder, and then ... cackling. Three distinctive, crone-like laughs bouncing and bobbing over one another. I'm distracted by the grating sound until I hear something else. Damien. I spin back toward him as he yells.

"Never!" He reaches for me as he slams into the ground, his chest hitting the dirty ground of the alley. A glowing blue ribbon that twists itself out of the spiraling river has wrapped itself around him like a rope. The water is dragging him down. I have no idea where the river leads, but I know deep down to my bones that I have no desire to follow it.

"Never, please!" Damien reaches for me as he's pulled further into the rushing liquid. His features fall back to human, but he holds out a clawed hand as he's pulled into the rushing blue. It's dragging him under, through the ground and wherever it leads.

I have to squeeze my hands together to prevent myself from latching onto him. He was willing to kidnap me. He would have squeezed the life out of me instead of letting me live free of him. And still it tears me apart, standing here and doing nothing to help him. How must he be feeling?

And then it hits me. Square in the snout. *I know*. Desperation. Fear. Coming from Damien.

My eyes go wide. I haven't been able to even guess at the male's emotions since I bound myself to him in our 'almost mates' ceremony. I shouldn't be able to feel anything from him. Unless. Unless that bond is severed.

I stare at him, only his head and one reaching arm still above the crashing rapids.

"I can't." I don't even know if he hears my response. I drop my head for a moment, not wanting to look him in the eye as death drags him away. And that has to be what's happening.

Then again, it's been two hundred years. I owe him, or at least myself, this much. I lift my face, feeling the soreness around my throat where he grabbed me.

"I won't," I say, doubling down. He did this to himself. And now he has to bear the consequences. The vengeance of a scorned Were.

The whispering and cackling voices grow louder, and three shapes swoop over Damien and the river. Formless, ghost-like beings, grey like smoke in the air. I have no idea what they could be. I've never seen a magical thing that could turn itself to smoke. I think the shapes are going to descend on him, but then they swoop toward me.

"Thank you for the deliverance of this new candidate. And for your own contribution," they intone as one.

I don't have time to puzzle out the words before one of the forms dives toward my face. A hand darts forward from the spectral thing. Impossibly long, bony, with decayed fingers. It has several inch-long talons for nails. And then I feel it. A searing pain. One side of my face feels like it's on fire as half my field of vision goes dark.

I scream, the sound of it echoing and thrown back against me as the three forms cackle and circle.

I drop to a knee, clutching at my face. I feel and scent blood, but I'm a little afraid to look. Even so, I'm pretty sure I know what's happened. My face burns so intensely that it tips all the way over into a sensation like ice pelting me.

"The fates thank you for your generous donation," one of the whispered voices grates out. And then, they're gone. No more whispers, and no more Damien.

I rock back and forth, hands covering my face as the sounds of the rushing river that the Bone Reader's vial held fade away as well.

Just before the rapids slip away, I hear another sound. An earth-splitting roar, and from somewhere an emotion slams into my intuition. Overpowering, so much so that I fall backward. Agony. I stare overhead, expecting to see dragon wings, but there's nothing but the moon.

As the roar subsides, I risk a glance in front of me. The river is gone. As are the flitting grey ghosts, or shadows, or whatever they were. Sound comes rushing back in from the outside world.

The soft breeze, the cool air of the night, and the yelling of my friends.

"Never! Never!" I hear Aggie's voice, and the sound of her steps as she runs toward me. I stay kneeling, but I look up toward her. She gasps as she gets close.

"Oh no." She puts both hands over her mouth, and I feel the horror buffeting off her. That can't be good. "Todd! Lynx! Never needs help!"

Against my rather loud protests, I'm tossed on Todd's furry back like a pair of saddlebags. He runs us back through the park. Lynx keeps pace, and soon enough Aggie catches up, riding on Rex.

Todd growls as I try to fling myself off. He skids to a halt.

"Stay there. You're hurt."

"I'm furious!" I retort. "And I need to get back to the fight."

I fling myself off the bear, dizzy and stumbling from a splitting headache. Aggie hops off Rex and loops my arm over her shoulder, supporting me.

"There isn't a fight, Never. I don't know if the Crown is connected to the rest of the Claw somehow, or if the enforcers just really are good at their jobs. But it's over. We won."

I let her guide me back toward the bear. He lumbers through the park, and there are witches and warlocks shuffling around, glimmering hands serving as a clean-up crew. Broken playground equipment, toppled trees, and all manner of debris are being cleared away.

"This is anticlimactic," I say as we exit the park.

"You wanted something more than facing down Damien and single-handedly toppling the Claw's leadership?" Todd asks, head turning toward me as he carries me toward my home.

"Some thanks might have been nice," I grouse, trying to ignore the searing pain in my head. It's not working.

Aggie laughs beside us.

"I may be new to this game, but I don't think you're going to get that from the Magikai."

"You'll be lucky if they aren't waiting on your lawn to sweep you off to their headquarters," Todd quips.

I yank on his fur.

"Wait. Stop." He growls, and I bend toward his head. "Right. Sorry. But you've got a point."

I'm not backing down from those magical bullies, but I'm not ready to face them yet.

"I need a favor. Take me to the airport."

Epilogue
Why Is It Always You

I step out of baggage claim and directly into the frigid, bellowing winds. I'm bundled up head to toe, since I'm not wearing my fur at the moment. I pull some very durable, expensive sunglasses I purchased before the trip over my face. Have to be especially careful now.

After my battle with Damien, the reality of my situation was quickly apparent. Typically with magicals, as their injuries knit together there's a very specific sensation. That is, on top of the sheer and blinding pain. It's a tingling, dancing feeling. Then warmth, spreading through your veins and along your nerves. A much more precise version of what humans feel when they shake a foot back to life after it's fallen asleep. It's how we know we're healing. It didn't happen this time. I reach up toward the left side of my face, where a patch sits over an empty socket.

I guess I'm a bit vainer than I realized. I hated all the looks coming at me from the humans on the plane. Kind of hard to miss a tall, silver-haired woman striding down the rows of seating with a scarred cheek and ridiculous, pirate-style eye patch. It's not their looks that bother me, it's the pity and morbid curiosity oozing from the lot of them.

I take my time, shedding unneeded layers and stuffing them into a duffel as I walk further into the snowy wilderness. The trek takes hours, and I'm sweating by the time I pull off my scarf and then drop the duffel into the icy snow. It crunches as the weight of the bag presses against the white ground cover. This isn't soft and fluffy snowman snow; it's the kind of ice that clings and pelts.

I throw my arms out to the side under the winter sun, letting the change roll over me. One tear makes its way down my cheek, getting lost in fur that grows over it. I'm getting close. I'm not even sure why I'm here. Haven't I learned my lesson about tangling with the Bone Reader?

As I stride into the cave, I don't pause to shake off the ice clinging to my fur, and I don't wait for him to call out to me.

"Bone Reader!" I yell the only title I have for him, icicles above me shaking and vibrating as my voice echoes toward the back of the cavern.

"No need to yell," he chides me, several voices flowing over one another as he makes an appearance at last.

He stops in front of me, looking me up and down with eyes that keep changing color as I try to place them in my mind.

"I see you were successful in your quest to kill the Were."

"Oh really? You *see*, do you? And do you mind telling me, is that *all* you see, or do I need to point out the obvious?" I snarl, jabbing a finger toward my face.

"Ah, that," he says, voices calm. "The price of war, I'm afraid. And, if I may say so, the lowest price you could have hoped to pay, messing with the Fates."

"Messing with *fate*, you mean."

He chuckles. The effect is always disconcerting. High, nasally giggle, low booming laughter all at once.

"Oh no, dear. I know what I meant. The. Fates. Where did you think you sent Damien to? Surely the magical smoking forms were a clue?" He reads what must be my vacant expression. "No? I'm a bit disappointed. Then again, you are overcoming an injury. Pain may have addled you a bit. Perfectly understandable. Very well, I'll clarify. The vial I gave you was bargained to me by the Fates. You see, they've been after a new ruler for the Underworld for some time now, and I figured—"

"Underworld? What?" I screech.

He blinks at me, shock rolling off him at the interruption.

"Well, yes. The Underworld. Damien's now been tasked as its new ruler."

"All right, woah, hold it!" I stick my hands up. "Setting aside my giant pile of questions related to this predicament, why would the Underworld need that? Allowing that it's a real place, which is news to me, doesn't it have one? If it's real, surely the attached god would be as well? Hmm?"

"Ah, finally a question worthy of your intellect. Gods, some of them, were and are real. But they get bored flitting around, interacting with Earth and its inhabitants for all eternity. Several have disappeared over the years. Although whether they've found a way to die, or they've simply moved on to planes or planets we cannot hope to see, remains a mystery to most magicals. I do love a good bit of mystery. Have I ever told you—"

"Hey. Focus. Underworld."

"Oh yes, right. Well, that particular deity left his post ages ago. While it doesn't pose too large a problem for humans, it does for the Fates, who were stuck looking after the magical inhabitants trapped down there. They needed a ruler. One who could be imbued with the power of a god."

I want to clarify before I go into a full rage.

"So you, in all your infinite wisdom, sent them my ex?"

He nods.

"My ex. Damien. The one I vowed to kill. The one I wanted dead. The one who, if he still exists, and with the powers of a god, no less, may very well hunt me and all those I love down."

A chuckle. Several different chuckles.

"Oh, I don't think that will be a problem. I bet you'd be surprised by how much death has mellowed him out."

"I bet I wouldn't," I grumble to myself.

"He made his own deal, you know. Not with me." The Bone Reader holds up his palms. They're smooth and elegant, calloused and rough. "When he got the weapon to kill his predecessor in the Claw, the dragon who was hunting you down. Traded away his time."

"His ... time?" Consider me perplexed.

The Bone Reader nods, his features flashing and changing.

"When a shifter or magical's mate dies, you may be aware, they are at risk of mate madness. If they don't die themselves, of course."

"Of course," I acknowledge. "I've had to hunt a few down." Some of my least favorite enforcer jobs. They can't help it, but they're still dangerous.

"You may not have been dead, but you were out of Damien's reach. Half-mated, but still connected. Avoiding him and ducking him for years. He was on the slow and slippery slope to madness anyway, but for the ability to kill the dragon and protect you, he agreed to hasten the process. Surely you noticed the changes in him after he became the Crown?"

"That's. No. Yes. I mean, well, that's completely irrelevant! He wouldn't." I stumble over my words. I'm going to scream. I'm going to cry. I'm going to attack the Bone Reader. I'm going to find a way to the Underworld and slap Damien across his stupid face. I'm going to apologize. I don't know what I'm going to do.

"I can see you need some time to absorb all this. So, enough about him. Let's talk about you."

I growl low in my throat, then sigh as I sense violence coming from the Bone Reader. He's tolerant of me, but he's also an extremely powerful being, whose origins I can't even fathom. And if he's on a first-name basis with gods and the Fates? I'll humor him. For now. Moon knows I can't face what he's just exposed about Damien.

"All right, back to me. I'm missing an eye. In case you didn't know. Dare I ask what use it's been put to? Ground to smithereens, perhaps?"

The thought makes me ill, but I need to know.

"Nothing like that. It's being used to help the Fates see. An eye is only good for so long, you know. Every millennium or so, they have to get a new one. It must be from a magical, and always a unique one. You fit the bill."

"Lucky me," I grouse, folding my arms across my chest.

"Yes, actually. Lucky you. You fulfilled your vow against Damien, so your life is your own again. You lost your eye, but you kept your family. That is what you consider those other magicals you cavort about with, right? And, if I may be allowed another cryptic prediction, you'll someday be waist-deep in magic so profound that the loss of a singular eye won't seem nearly as heavy a blow as it does now."

I lift a hand to my eyepatch. Maybe he's right. But I'm not going to admit it.

"I could make you a new one, you know. A vibrant, shining, magical eye. Easy enough for someone with my abilities. I wouldn't even break a sweat."

Now it's my turn to laugh.

"Really? You're *that* powerful? You're not even questioning whether a feat like that is past your limits?"

"Please, Were. Limits are for lesser beings," he scoffs, voices rolling over one another.

Honest. He's being completely truthful. Which is what terrifies me. Still, it's a tempting offer.

"How much?"

He shakes his head.

"Consider it an apology; a gesture between friends. I knew the Fates would take something. I was duplicitous in our bargain. Unintentionally, of course. But to show you that I'm an honest dealer, I'll fashion you a new one. Blue, like your current eye, if you like. Or white. Shining like a star, if you wish. I can make you look however you want."

I think on it for a moment. I don't doubt him. The Bone Reader makes himself look like everyone and no one at once. It stands to reason he could fashion me an eye easily enough. Maybe even one to match the original. I could go back to looking exactly how I did before. My emotions rebel against the idea. I'm *not* the same as before.

I had something *worth* making a sacrifice for. And I have my principles. It hurt more than I want to admit, to get rid of Damien. But I did it, and I stand by it. If my eye is the cost ... so be it.

"No eye," I state. "But I wouldn't say no to a magical eyepatch. Something that will stay on my face without this silly string." I yank the black eyepatch off, the elastic around it ruining my hair.

"Very well." The Bone Reader holds a hand up and snaps his fingers. Fingers that, for just a flash of a second, look skeletal. Shining white bones. I blink, and they're back to their typical shifting shades. I feel something cool settle against my skin.

"Have a look," he offers, gesturing toward the cauldron where he reads bones. I lean over it. Last time I was here it was colorful. Today, it's clear and reflective. Perhaps the goblet changes like its master.

I laugh at what he's done.

"Silver!" It won't harm me, but old legends die hard. Why humans thought silver bullets hurt us, I don't know. But I appreciate his attempt at humor. "Very nice." It's shining, polished, and has a symbol carved into the metal, so shallow that I have to squint to see it.

"Any use asking what this means?"

"The metal itself is protective. That eye is now more impenetrable than the rest of you, by far. The symbol is a special touch from me. A calling card, if you will."

I can read well enough that he's set on being cryptic. I leave it alone.

"All right, Bone Reader, I've got one last question to ask. I don't have any bones, but I'm going to go ahead and presume that with your vast magical knowledge you might be able to answer this anyway."

"Very possible. But are you willing to pay the price?" He grins, tapping a finger on his eye. His maddening, shifting features make it impossible to determine what color the eye even is.

"I'd rather hoped you'd make it cheap, all things considered."

He laughs. Sharp staccatos, deep rumbles.

"Perhaps," Is the only answer I get. I forge ahead anyway.

"When Damien was pulled down to the Underworld, if that's what it is. I could feel his fear. So my vow really is fulfilled? I'm safe, and this is done? He and I are no longer mates in any sense of the word?"

"That is correct."

There's one item checked off. A sigh of relief escapes.

"So answer me this. Something else snapped at that moment. Maybe it was just the blinding pain—a little eye humor there—but I don't think so."

"Is there a question in there?"

"I don't know, is there an answer?" I snap. This whole ordeal has put me on edge, and I'm growing sassier toward the Bone Reader than one perhaps should with an ancient and powerful species one cannot identify. "That is to say, I'm not connected to the Underworld, am I? I'm not about to get dragged down there as Damien's bride?"

"Goodness, no. A deal's a deal. That vial separated you completely. Any connection to him, past *or* future, is broken."

Well, that's that, then.

"Never?" I ready myself for what this sliver of information is going to cost. "I do feel inclined to warn you that when you get back to your house, you're going to find one very upset dragon crashing on your couch."

"I'm, what? Nahum? What in moon's sake for? I didn't do anything to him!"

I mean, a particular cave scene makes its way into my mind, but he had *nothing* to complain about there. Certainly nothing that warrants breaking into my home, if he's even capable of getting past Chrys's spells. Aw, hell's bells. The witch. She'd probably just let him in.

"Would you like that last question answered? It might cost you."

I sigh.

"May as well. I have a feeling if I don't get the information now, I'll just be back up here asking about it at some point."

He nods, several different chins bobbing.

"Too true. And all I ask is a ride. You solved Damien, so your Halloween is free. I need you to pick me up somewhere."

"Your price is to use me as a personal taxi? Where from and where to?"

He waves a hand.

"Not important. I'll get you the information later. But are we agreed?"

"Fine. Yes. Now, out with it. Why is a nightmare dragon incensed enough to leave his secret island and fly halfway around the globe just to break into my house?"

"I would think that might be obvious, my dear. It's because you're his mate."

Acknowledgements & Notes

As always, I would like to thank all the amazing people who helped me take this book from an idea to a reality: my supportive family and husband, my wonderful editor Doreen, the amazing cover designers at Deranged Doctor Designs, and all the beta readers who dedicated their time.

Thank you to all the readers who are joining Never on her adventures! If you read and enjoyed this book I would love for you to leave a review wherever you find your new reads. These are very helpful to authors so other people can find and enjoy the book!

If you'd like to hear updates on Never or other projects please join me at:

Nightlochpublishers.com

Instagram: @reameswrites

Never's adventures continue on Halloween 2023 with "Never Ever", available for preorder now!

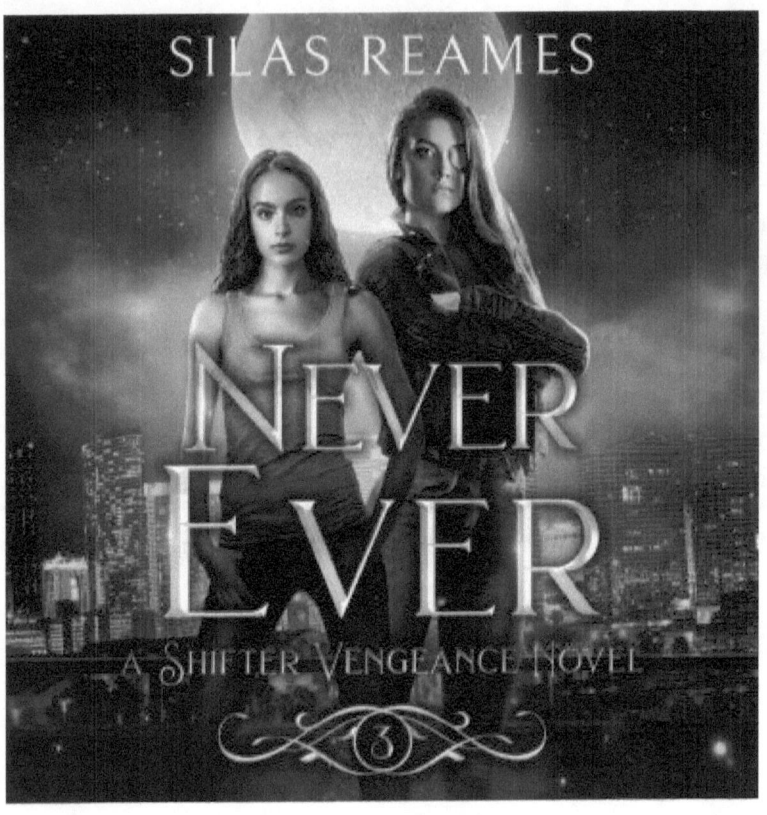

About the Author

Silas has long been a lover of all things reading. If you lose track of her in a bookstore, you're responsible for the pile of new reads she'll carry out.

When not writing or reading while drinking what might well be considered too much caffeine, she can often be found swimming or spending time with her husband and dogs.

Read more at nightlochpublishers.com/silas-reames.